WAR-TORN

THE WARRING REALM, BOOK 2

AARON D. SCHNEIDER

Edited by
ELLIOT & LISA EASTIN

INTELLECTUALLY PROMISCUOUS PRESS

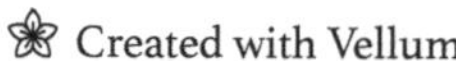 Created with Vellum

ALSO BY AARON D. SCHNEIDER

The Warring Realm Series

War-Born

War-Torn

War-Sworn (Winter 2018)

Sign up at www.aarondschneider.com to be notified about new releases.

I dedicate this book to my children, who remind me daily that I am but a man yet constantly encourage me to be more. Thank you, my babies.

Listen to the general every goddamn word
    How many ways can you polish up a turd.

— • Tom Waits, "Hell Broke Luce"

". . . and my existence, while grotesque and incomprehensible to you, saves lives . . ."

— • Colonel Nathan R. Jessup, A Few Good Men

"Oh, dear, what comfort can I find?"
    None this tide,
    Nor any tide,

— • Rudyard Kipling, "My Boy Jack"

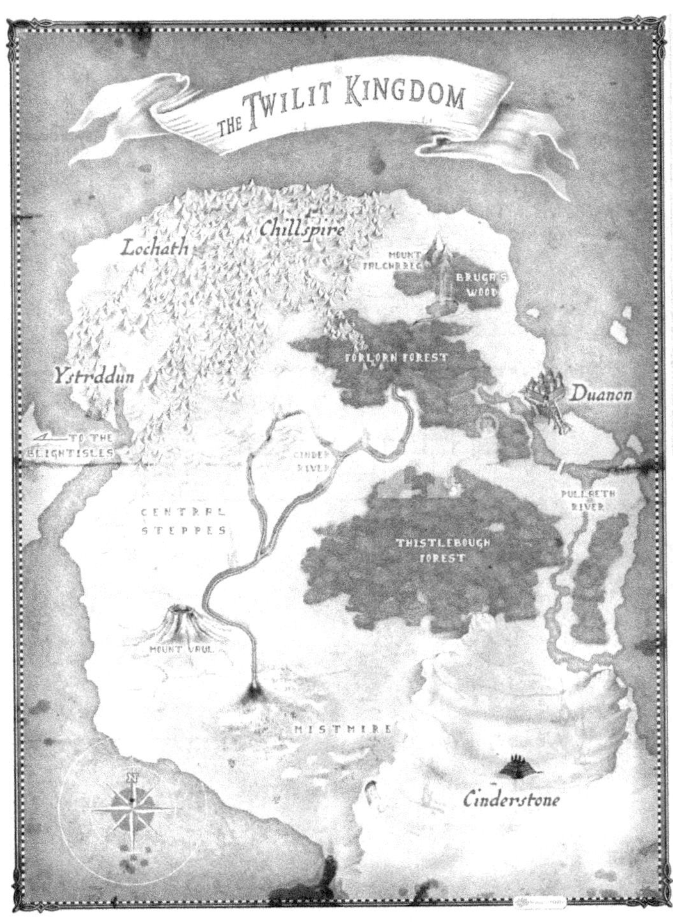

THE TWILIT KINGDOM
Chillspire
Lochath
MOUNT FALCHREG
BRUGR'S WOOD
Ystrddun
FORLORN FOREST
Duanon
TO THE BLIGHTISLES
CINDER RIVER
CENTRAL STEPPES
PULLRETH RIVER
THISTLEBOUGH FOREST
MOUNT VAUL
MISTMIRE
N
Cinderstone

PROLOGUE

Nibbin Bloodcrawl's legs pumped furiously as he raced up the steep steps. Occasionally he threw out a scrawny arm to help haul his pudgy body upward. His piss-yellow eyes spied a faint sliver of light between the boards of the trap-door ahead.

With so many steps to go and those things after him, the Goblin felt like he was in a waking nightmare; the monster was closing in, and no matter how fast he ran, escape seemed impossible.

He had built the stairs behind his study bookcase for just this kind of emergency, but at that time he was young and fit. He failed to account for how he would use them as age made him slow and fat. As a young, ambitious under-boss, he congratulated himself for his savvy at hiring a pair of Bogguns to create a path from his basement hideout under Duanon's walls to the streets within the city.

The more vocal of the craftsmen voiced a concern at the beginning of the project. "That be a fair few stairs to climb." He squinted over the plans. "Are you certain you wouldn't prefer a pulley lift or somethin' similar?"

"You think I can't climb a few stairs?" Nibbin growled. He had always been proud, and as fit and dangerous as any Goblin he'd ever met.

"What if'n your hurt?" the craftsman persisted, despite glares from his partner.

"Then I climbs them a little slower," he snarled, deciding in that moment to kill them both once the project was done. He considered killing them following the job regardless, to ensure the secrecy of the escape route, but the obnoxious questioning of his athleticism fully convinced him. He took great delight in whispering the offending question "What if'n your hurt?" in the Boggun's ear over and over as he throttled him. His partner was a little luckier, expiring earlier and quicker with a knife through his eye.

Nibbin used the craftsmen's last handiwork to haul their bodies to the street. Despite being in his prime, he admitted that hauling two corpses did make it a bit of a climb. The sound of his panting breath made him angrier, and he used it to spur him onward up the stairs. He carried the bodies to the battlements of Duanon's walls where he pitched them into the river.

Smiling to himself, he pocketed the key to his secret passageway and skulked off to amuse himself further that night. That had been nearly fifteen years ago, and it was the only time the stair had been used.

Since then, Nibbin spent more and more time in his study, plotting jobs and tallying the profits of his schemes and machinations. Little by little, day by day, his muscle-knotted arms grew thinner and slacker, and his sinewy stomach grew softer and wider. By the time the whole busi-ness with Grimple Guthook went sour, he had grown to be an uncommonly fat Goblin. He never quite understood that it was the reputation of his murderous Finger teams—not his own physical abilities—that afforded him respect and deference by all but the most successful underbosses.

In point of fact, Grimple's disrespect had been a contributing factor in why he was now clambering up his secret stair, wheezing and groaning, his steps slowing a little more with each flight. He always disliked the Guthooks, but when one of the matriarch's Hardnails, a loyal and dangerous member of a Finger team, reached out to him to work together he assumed it was because Grimple was losing her grip on her Fingers. She had been foolish to run off to fight alongside the human, taking some of her best teams to die for Queen and country. It only stood to reason that one of her own would try to wrest control from her. So naturally he agreed, if for no other reason than to displace a dangerous, experienced rival like Grimple Guthook with an indebted Hardnail ill-prepared for the burden of leadership.

When it became clear the Hardnail was playing him for a fool, renegotiating for information Nibbin's crew had craftily stolen, Nibbin was obliged to have his boys use the Hardnail as a target for knife-throwing competition. He supposed he could use the guard rotations and floor plans of the palace to plan the assassination of Grimple next time she was in Duanon just as easily as the Hardnail. He considered himself doubly lucky. He had disposed of an enemy agent and was poised to kill Grimple and take over her operations soon enough.

But then the Fiendspawn had come, creeping from between the cracks in the stone to extinguish life and light in a one putrid rush.

His Finger teams were gearing up for a smash and grab on a stock of weapons coming in from Chillspire and bound for the muster fields outside of Duanon while he and his Hardnails were busy going over what a particular buyer wanted. The air filled with the smell of old rat left to putrefy on the snare, and only finely honed survival instincts saw Nibbin ducking down and rapidly waddling toward his study while his boys died messily.

So here he was, leaning against the steps, dragging in one hitching breath after another. He tried to muster the strength to crawl a few more steps toward the light. If he could just reach the door he would be in the street, and it was not yet sundown. Rumor said that the get of the darkling serving the Queen could not abide the light of day.

No one else knew about the secret stair, but it would not take the unholy little monsters any time at all to ferret out his smell and come crawling up the stairs after him. He fought the urge to hold his breath and listen for them. If they found the stair before he reached the top, he was as good as dead anyway.

With a stifled groan he kept going, his belly scraping painfully against the steps as he climbed. His limbs shook in exhausted protest, and his lungs seemed incapable of dragging in enough air. He wondered if the exertion of climbing the stair, and not the Fiendspawn, would be the death of him.

Nibbin snarled defiantly at the thought, a bit of his old ferocity livening the saggy shell that was his body. He scaled the stairs faster, legs and arms working in unison to haul himself up the steps one after the other.

He nearly made it, too. He claimed all but the last two steps and reached out to the trapdoor when something blacker than the shadow of the lightless stairwell sunk barbed hooks into his calf.

Nibbin couldn't stifle his scream. He felt himself being dragged back down the stair, his body scraping and slapping down the steps. His fingers scratched and scrambled to find purchase in the stony surface of the steps, but the pull of the shadowy thing gripping his leg was merciless, and the Bogguns' stonework was smooth.

Eventually, the thing attached to his leg tugged forcefully and the side of Nibbin's head bashed against a stone step, staggering him. Another pull of his stunned person and his jaw smacked on the step hard enough to crack teeth and send bolts of pain radiating over his jaw and into his neck and skull.

Nearly halfway down the stair, Nibbin was no longer in any shape to fight anything, even gravity, and he tumbled the rest of the way down. He fell heavily into the concealing bookshelf, knocking it over.

Having broken a score of bones on the expressway down his no-longer-secret stair, Nibbin was nearly insensate with pain. He noted with dismay that several of his limbs no longer operated as they should. He sprawled across the toppled bookshelf, his breath coming in pitiful, wet wheezes.His focus faded in and out as dark things with long, cilia-plumed bodies coiled around him.

With the hand not broken in the fall, he batted at them, but one bent its head down to his shoulder and he felt, distantly, something sharp digging into his flesh. His arm fell limp with an agonized shudder. Something still gripped his legs in a barbed embrace, and as he lay there struggling for breath it ground its hook-like anchors deeper.

Nibbin whimpered and then heard a soft, hungry whisper at his ear. "What did you steal, and why?"

He wanted to beg for mercy—to promise them anything they wanted—but all he managed was a groan.

The sharp things in his shoulder and leg twisted viciously, and he choked on a scream that rose to his mouth sticky and thick, tasting of copper.

"What did you steal, and why?" the voice repeated.

"I-Infermashon…" he gasped, his tongue thick and slow in the gooey, jagged mess that was his mouth. "Planth… khill Griimpuhl…"

"What information? Where is it?" the voice asked, more insistently than before.

It became progressively harder for Nibbin to focus. What little he could feel of his body beyond the overlapping waves of pain was invaded by a numbing cold.

"Pleath…" he moaned weakly as the sharp things dug even deeper. But he was drifting beyond their reach. Blind panic dragged a few more words out of him, uttered in some mad hope that maybe, if he pleased the voice, it would save him from what came next.

"Study dethk… uh… top draaaa…"

And then Nibbin Bloodcrawl was dead.

"Did you find it in the desk then?" Queen Meabh sat upon her white throne, the audience chamber cleared of all but herself and the burnished, living statue that was Lord Nadder.

"I am afraid not, my Queen," the Tuatha reported, his face an impassive mask. "The Fiendspawn delivered every document that was in the desk, the study, and the entire safehouse, but not a page of it seemed to pertain to anything but typical petty crimes."

"Was every member of the underboss's FInger teams accounted for?"

"Yes, well, that is an area of some complexity, your Majesty," Lord Nadder felt the icy glare of the Queen sharpening on him with every word. "The Finger teams were accounted for, but there was another Goblin present of whom we were not aware. When first the Fiendspawn entered, they assumed he was dead, in large part due to the number of bladed instruments jutting from his body. He was fastened to the wall and painted with target rings, through which many of the blades were stuck. Again, even the lifescenting Fiendspawn believed him a corpse, but after the interrogation of the underboss, it was discovered that he was gone."

Queen Meabh of the Twilit Kingdom stared down at her retainer for some time, her face inscrutable but for the icy fire which burned within her blue eyes.

"So currently, We are aware that surveillance was performed and information gathered relating to our palace in Duanon, but what we do *not* know is what that information is. And the only intent of which We are aware is that it was to be used against Grimple Guthook. Are We correct in Our evaluation?"

"Yes, your Majesty," Lord Nadder replied cautiously.

"And we have no means to verify any of this, as none survived your investigation?"

"That is correct, your Majesty."

Further silence weighted the audience chamber until the typically unflappable Lord Nadder began to twitch and squirm under Meabh's merciless stare. At last, the Queen let her burning eyes slowly close, and she flicked her wrist in a dismissive gesture. "Go," she said, her eyes shut as though the sight of him was an offense. "See if you can salvage something from this wasted opportunity, barring that, locate your vanishing corpse."

Lord Nadder cut a quick bow and turned on his heels, thankful to have escaped the Queen's immediate vengeance but knowing that Queen Meabh would not forget or forgive his failure. He would need to discover, or fabricate, something spectacular to find himself in her good graces once more.

The corpse of Krint Guthook, Grimple Guthook's ambitious nephew and former Hardnail, trudged along with the unhurried but untiring pace of the animate dead, drawn along the most direct route to another safehouse under the walls of Duanon. Passersby might mistake it for another drunken Goblin wandering the Warrens—those disreputable streets on the base of the wall. With head slung low and arms dangling limply at its sides, it looked like a case of one too many drinks at the dockside taverns. But it would be early for such inebriation, even by Goblin standards. If they took a moment longer to consider how steady its stride was despite its swaying upper body, they might surmise that something else was afoot. If they came close enough to see the knife hilts jutting from his chest, things would really get interesting. As it was, not a soul saw Krint's corpse that afternoon. Lord Nadder's desire for discretion ensured the watches and wall guards remained busy elsewhere.

Krint stepped to a stone in the wall and waited until a section of the wall gave a shuddering klank then slid backward with the sound of stone on stone. A portal just large enough for a Goblin to walk through opened in the base of the wall, and a pair of hands reached from the shadowy interior and drew the corpse roughly inside. The faintest glow of narrowed golden eyes shone in the dark, and the stone slid back into place.

Krint's corpse was trundled down a lightless corridor before coming to an iron grate held in place by a heavy chain and padlock. The hands which had nabbed the ambulatory corpse drew out a key, unlocked the padlock, shuffled the corpse past the threshold, then relocked the grate. Another pair of hands took over the job of shepherding Krint's body before the padlock snapped closed.

The corpse, after no few twists and turns in the dark, emerged into a chamber lit by mismatched candles in various stages of melting and running down the walls below their alcoves. The second pair of hands belonged to a small, wiry Goblin female missing the last inch of her long nose, its nubbed end capped in blackened bronze. She looked at the other two figures lurking in the candle-lit room—one, a Goblin male so covered in crisscrossing scars that he looked like he might have scales, and the other, another Goblin female with several studs in her ears and nose.

"Here it is," the one with the truncated snout announced in a pinched, perpetually congested voice.

"Good work, Natt." The male stepped forward and took the arm of the corpse. Krint didn't seem to mind or notice. "Got it from here."

Natt bowed and darted back into the darkness of the corridor.

The male turned to the corpse and, without ceremony, yanked the blade-punctured shirt open, fabric ripping around the knives lodged in the flesh. A bronze disk with verdigris layers obscuring its engraved designs hung on a leather thong resting against the unbreathing chest. A thin leather slipcase wedged between the front of the Goblin's trousers and its stomach. The scarred one tugged the slipcase out and yanked the pendant free with a snap. Krint's body collapsed to the floor.

"Everything there?" the female asked, fiddling with a black-jeweled stud in her nose.

"Looks like." The male perused the contents of the slipcase and gave the corpse a perfunctory kick. "What we gonna do with this fool?"

"Lord Nadder's estate in Duanon. The special chambers below the manse, after he's been stripped and scrubbed. Can't waste an opportunity."

The scarred Goblin gave his compatriot a quizzical look as the her piercings glittered in the guttering light.

"Bit on the nose, don't you think?" He stared at the Goblin corpse. Krint had been a good Finger team leader, but he had gotten too full of himself. Poor bastard never even had a clue that Ma Grimple was counting on his betrayal, much less that the bauble she'd given him before she hit the campaign trail was originally from a particular swamp witch.

"Not 'bout sendin' a message, but trippin' him up," the female explained. "He finds the dead body he's looking for in his basement, he's got two choices. Tell the Queen he's got the body in his basement, with no new information about where it come from, or try to hide the thing and run the risk of bein' caught in the deception. Either way, we got nothin' to lose and everythin' to gain."

"Unless o' course we get caught puttin' him there," the male said gravely.

The two stared at each other for a heartbeat . . . then laughed, their wicked snickers echoing through the candle-lit room and the black corridors.

1

HOLLOWED

I awoke with a scream, hands sweeping out in wide, panicked swings at empty air. I tried to lunge at my phantom oppressors but tangled in the bedsheets from the waist down, I crashed on the lip of the bed and continued to slide. Hitting with a dull thud, I found myself sliding downward and off the bed entirely.

Rather than fight it, I let gravity have its way with me, then I was on the cold stone floor in a mess of sheets soaked in icy sweat.

The impact on the hard floor should have hurt, or at the very least, I should have recoiled in protest when bare skin made contact with the icy stones. But none of that happened. I was aware of the force of my body hitting the floor; I felt the pressure apply itself across my arm, shoulder, and back before dissipating. I felt the temperature of the floor and noted it was markedly colder than my bed, but that was it. Statistical information. My senses gave me a status update as impassively as those scrolling numbers on the news let you know how the stock market is doing. There was no real feeling—no actual sensation tied up with emotion and identity—just points of data observed. Location changed. Kinetic energy absorbed. Ambient temperature decreased. Report received and understood.

As I lay there on the floor of my chamber, the stream of data updating with every breath, I considered killing myself. This was not the first time I had considered it in recent days, but I still fought the tears which threatened to spill from my eyes. My breath hitching, I raised an unsteady hand and ran my fingers across my chest.

Across the plains of magically repaired skin stretching over muscle, my fingers travelled toward the shallow valley where my sternum sat. I found the recent interruption in the topography. Smooth and hard, a single teardrop-shaped stone an inch wide at its widest and no more than two and a half inches long nestled in my flesh and bone, skin grown snug around its edges. My fingers slid seamlessly from flesh to stone and then to flesh again, this invasive prosthetic now sitting secure and comfortable as if it had always been there.

"Gormstone," I hissed between clenched teeth as I fought back more tears and sniffed.

This was the reason for my suicidal ponderings, and I wept because I knew that no matter what I wanted—life or death—it wouldn't change anything. Not so long as the Gormstone sat in my chest, cradled by my unwilling flesh and bone. As long as it was part of me, my will was bound to serve Meabh, Queen of the Twilit Kingdom, with all the skill and strength I could muster. My mind was free to hate her, hating her now as much as I had loved her before, but I could not bring myself to work against her, even in a single, defiant act of self-destruction. I was prisoner to another's will, entrapped and empowered by the magic stone that made me into a living, breathing automaton.

In the days since the Gormstone was implanted, the

Queen had explained that part of the process of implanting the stone always killed the recipient, but then the magical artifact brought him back to life. Using my life essence, or maybe what could be called my soul, it would enhance my body. It would continue to cannibalize my essence, making me stronger, faster, tougher, and more dedicated to the Queen's will. She said with time, I would be free from all the distractions and connections which drove my mind and body away from serving her. I would become the perfect instrument of her will.

While I still could, I cried and mourned the little pieces of my humanity that were being stolen from me, even as I prepared for another day of training. Despite only three hours of sleep, my body dutifully reported that it was ready to perform at optimal levels. Report received and understood.

I rose and washed myself with the towel and basin which sat on a small table opposite my bed. Again, my body reported that the water was cold. My skin prickled up into gooseflesh sympathetically, but I dismissed the information as easily as a popup ad on an internet browser. The cold on my skin was inconsequential in the face of the emptiness spreading under it.

Free of another forgotten nightmare's sweat, I dressed for my early morning training with Uzran, Captain of the Royal Guard—an Ogre I had once begun to consider a friend. He would be waiting for me in one of the royal palace's courtyards, an expanse of marble flagstones set aside by the Queen for me to train and become accustomed to my new abilities. Half of my day was spent training myself, and the other half was spent overseeing the training of more soldiers to continue the ongoing war with the Gythraul.

My underclothes and gambeson on, I called for the squire assigned to me while I was recovering. Out in the field, most menial jobs were relegated to the preserved corpses animated by Lord Arawn's black caulders, but here in the capital of the Twilit Kingdom, such a thing would be considered gauche. Besides, how else to haze fledgling Tuatha battle-magi, the closest approximation of a knight among Tuatha?

With a stiff bow, a young man entered the room. He had not yet grown to the customary, imposing height of his people, nor did he fully possess their refined sense of grace. Nevertheless, his lithe movements and pointed ears marked him as one of the Tuatha.

"Good morning, Paladi—I mean Gorm Bollham." He stumbled over my recent change in titles. The magic which suffused Other-Realm allowed me to understand not just that Gorm meant Tyrant, but also the meaning of every other word he spoke in what sounded like Gaelic or Welsh here.

"I told you, Kieren, Luce is what I prefer." I held out my arms in preparation. "And good morning to you."

Squire Kieren Shieldson bobbed his head as he made his way across the room to a tall bureau where my armor and weapons hung.

"My apologies," he said over his shoulder. "I know you do not hold with courtly etiquette, but I am slow at unlearning my years of tutelage."

I knew I should have felt something like pity for the young Tuatha. He hadn't chosen to serve me and probably barely understood the monster who gave him the order in the first place, but he had to serve me now, the second human Paladin to be bound with the Gormstone. Hardly the detail to write home about, and that should have made my heart ache for him. All I recognized was the absence of what I should have felt, though.

"Well, we'll work on it," I said flatly. "Just figured it would save you messing up my title all the time." I was trying to say it in an encouraging way, but any such sentiment was sucked away by the Gormstone, and the otherwise playful jibe sounded harsh and cold.

Looking crestfallen, the Tuatha helped me slide the armor over my arms and head after doing a quick once-over to ensure the laces of my gambeson were snug. The weight of the armor—negligible with my enhanced strength—settled across my shoulders, becoming even less noticeable when he lashed a belt around my waist to distribute the burden across my hips.

"I heard Captain Uzran noting your improvements yesterday," Kieren said, fetching the vambraces, gorget, and greaves. "Seems that soon you may be able to best even him in a fight."

"Uzran is still recovering from his wounds at the Valley of Luchath," I replied dismissively. I tapped the spot on the armor over the stone in my chest. "And he doesn't have one of these juicing him up."

Kieren knelt down to fasten the greaves. "Still, it has taken you little time to master much of the art of swordplay. Considering your limited experience, that must be . . ."

The squire's voice trailed off and I looked down and saw a scared, almost panic-stricken look on his face. "You were saying?" I asked, genuinely confused.

"Forgive me, Gorm . . . er . . . I mean Luce. I did not mean to suggest that you are inexperienced in war or to downplay your accomplishments already. I just meant with regard to swordplay, and

I . . ."

I cut off his fearful rambling with a wave of my hand. "Easy, Kieren." I looked down into his wide, purple eyes. "I know what you meant. The United States Army hasn't seen fit to train soldiers in swordsmanship for a while. No offense taken. Now, let's finish up and get down there, alright?"

Squire Shieldson nodded as he finished with the greaves and remained silent as he fitted the rest of my armor into place. He belted on my edgeless training sword and dagger and handed me my trusty M-Core. It was a modern military carbine modified by creepy, mad-scientist critters called Daergs. Instead of standard 5.65mm NATO rounds, it was designed to fire manticore spines impregnated with basilisk venom. I wouldn't be using the weapon for any of the training with Uzran this morning, but before midday, I would head out to train the Twilit Kingdom's armies, and it helped to have the M-Core at hand to assist in educating the troops. That, and I just liked having the rifle with me.

I slung the weapon over my shoulder, thankful I still felt a measure of appreciation and security as it settled into place. The Gormstone hadn't taken that from me . . . yet.

Kieren held up a polished oval of flawless silver so I could inspect myself, and when I gave him an approving nod, he took up my helmet and gauntlets, placing them under his arm. The battered helmet was blackened steel, shaped to give the impression of a leering skull across its rounded surface. I hated the suffocating thing as much for what it represented as for how it felt to wear it. Still, the Queen had insisted that the Gorm presented an aura of "appropriate menace on the field of battle," and to her, training counted. So far, I could refuse to wear the damn thing until right before I started my training with Uzran. I wasn't going to touch it until I had to.

My squire looked me up and down, his eyes sticking as

he regarded my face. "Luce, since I am your squire, I would be remiss if I didn't tell you that you hair and beard are quite . . . dishevelled."

I raised a hand and felt the curling whiskers on my face and the tangled locks of dark hair on my head. When I was in the service, I had kept my face bare and my hair short, but in the months since coming to Other-Realm, I had fallen out of practice when it came to such stringent hygiene. At first I had been busy running across the Kingdom getting ready for the war. Now . . . well, now I just didn't care. Hell, even when I looked at my reflection, I didn't bother to look above the rim of the gorget.

"I don't think Captain Uzran will mind," I said dryly—a limp attempt at humor which Kieren didn't notice. "I suppose we can get someone to clean me up later, if we remember."

"Do you not want me to fetch a comb and some oil?"

"No," I dismissed the idea with a shake of my head. "I don't suppose it will make any difference to the old warhorse."

Kieren nodded and, after opening the door for me, followed me to the training yard.

"Timing," Uzran grunted again as I backpedaled away from a sweep of his sword.

The Ogre punctuated the point with a follow-up blow, looping his blade back and around to stab at my face. Through the round sockets of my skull-faced helmet, I saw the blunted tip of the training sword lancing toward me, and it was all I could do to pivot backwards, interposing my own sword to shove the huge blade away.

Blunted or not, Gormstone or not, if Uzran hit me as

hard as his massive frame allowed, I was not sure I could survive it.

"Timing," he rumbled again, his sword raised to guard position. "Timing is better than speed or strength or anything else. You must learn timing."

I created a little more space, minding my footwork, and began circling my giant teacher.

Uzran, looming near ten feet tall and possessed of a body thick with slabs of muscle, gauged the distance between us, dark eyes narrowing within his helmet. He knew what I was trying to do and he wasn't going to fall for it. The Tuatha magi had repaired most of his injuries, but some of the wounds were deep and required more time to fully heal. The Captain of the Royal Guard still struggled not to limp as he walked, so he could not quickly close distance with an opponent. I knew that if he were fully healed, the deceptively quick warrior would have pressed me until I was out of places to run. But for now, his limp gave me a chance to engage him on my own terms. Though it wasn't part of the lesson, both of us knew that—next to timing—the ability to decide where and how a battle would take place was probably the deciding factor in most any fight, sword or otherwise.

"I am not sure I can teach anything to a student afraid to close with his enemy," Uzran goaded, tusks bared beneath the sweep of his helmet's slotted faceplate. "Maybe that is why you humans are obsessed with things that can kill your enemy over great distances?"

He was trying to provoke me into making a stupid rush, putting myself in position to be swatted down by a larger opponent with a longer reach. He was testing my mind as well as my body, like any good instructor, probing for weaknesses that he could exploit now and train out of me later.

But part of me also wondered if he was probing for something else.

Since I had come back from Luchath, defied the Queen, and got this damned stone lodged in my chest, we had hardly spoken outside of training. That may have had something to do with how he had stood there, head down, while the Queen used her magic to burrow into my breastbone and ram a magical mind control device into it. Or maybe it was about how, when he had tried to speak up, the Queen brought up that Uzran had his entire clan executed for planning rebellion against her. That kind of shame tends to make the proud laconic. But hey, who knows? People do funny things.

Was he trying to gauge how easily I could be provoked? To see if I would lash out at him or maybe seek payback for his betrayal? He knew that if I did and he couldn't stop me, there would be no repercussions—even if I beat him to death with my blunted training sword. I was the Gorm, the iron fist of the Queen, and he was an injured Captain of the Royal Guard one short and curly away from disgrace. I even thought that, despite the Ogre's formidable skill and size, I might be able to do it. The right timing and the momentum that good, old-fashioned rage gives you is a powerful combination. But even without rage, thanks to the Gormstone and Uzran's training, I was getting stronger and more dangerous every day. I didn't want revenge on Uzran. Not really. My heart was too sick with its growing numbness to spare him that much emotional energy.

I made a probing lunge that he chased off with a parry. He could easily have turned it into a cut to my forward leg if I hadn't danced backwards. He followed me with a series of reaching stabs of his own. Two I set aside with the flat of my blade; the last I side-stepped as he overreached in a limping lurch. I swept my blade up and brought it back down again. My sword looped around his over-extended defenses, crashing against his leg just behind the knee and causing it to buckle.

The Gormstone suddenly felt colder in my chest, and goosebumps prickled over my flesh.

The Ogre grunted with pain and frustration as the solid blow drove him to one knee, but not before he lashed out in a wide sweep with his sword.

I raised my own to deflect the blow, but there was so much power in the swing that my sword smashed flat against my body, and I was thrown backwards. I scrambled wildly to stay upright, but it was no good. ith an undignified thump, I fell on my ass.

Uzran was back on his feet, eyes smoldering, making it clear that he knew I had bested him, if only for a second. He looked down at me, an emotion I couldn't quite name swimming in the burning depths of his eyes, and slowly lowered his guard, resting the rounded end of his sword on the flagstones.

I should have felt something then—some strong, emotional response to what had played out in these last few seconds. Maybe pride at getting one over on such a sword-master. Anger that I hadn't taken it further. Fear that he might crush me now in his anger. Curiosity at what feelings were moving behind the veil of the Ogre's face. But I didn't feel anything. Inside me was a vacant, dead space. Here, emotions left only impressions—fading silhouettes in drifting dust—and the cold that leaked in as they dissolved was absolute.

Instead, the data stream rolled in. Location changed. Kinetic energy absorbed. Report received and understood.

2

____

MUSTERED

The armies of the Twilit Kingdom had grown exponentially since I had led those first companies to the Valley of Luchath, and subsequent training had been more in depth for those forces than it had for the old war dogs I had led against Ceterum Cinis's northbound legion. With the major threat of the Gythraul advance stopped temporarily as the rest of the enemy legions slogged their way across barren territory, I had more time to train instructors and oversee the training of the Kingdom's armies.

The muster fields outside Duanon expanded more than once, as more and more soldiers were drummed up or conscripted. The Gloaming Court was spurred to provide support after the dread Ceterum Cinis was humbled in battle. From all across the Kingdom, droves of leathery-skinned Bogguns, pale-eyed Hobbs, and doughty Gremlins streamed in alongside the less populous creatures of Other-Realm—Trolls, Ogres, Fomor, and Sylvankin. I had even seen Goblins billeted in the barracks rather than as part of Grimple's growing number of Finger teams.

Also, more of the Lord and Lady Bwyathardd's beasts arrived to be integrated into our battle planning. The deadly and obedient menagerie of living weapons were part of a growing plan to replace the more mechanized aspects of modern warfare. In place of tanks or airplanes, there would be fierce beasts from the woods of Thistlebough. Lord Bwyathardd came personally at one point to deliver his prized creations—Dragons. Or very nearly Dragons. They were the closest things to the Wyrms of legend I was likely to ever see. I was eager to put these flying, fire-spewing death machines to work. In the next engagement, I would order all five of them into the air, were they would rain hell on the Gythraul.

This should have been a welcome sight, even though it ate up more and more of my time with logistical concerns. The Arch-Monger in Chillspire struggled to produce weapons and munitions fast enough to meet the demands from the front as well as our training needs. Instead, the only thing I could think of as I looked out over the muster field, was how ashamed I should be.

I was training thousands of creatures to fight and die for a cause that my heart was convinced was as corrupt and futile as the nightmares of the craziest conspiracy theorist back home on Earth. Say what you want about politics and governmental abuse of power, but at least at some point, the bad people working in the system would die somehow. Whether it was a car accident after too many martinis, an aneurysm from snorting coke off a hooker's back, or just simple, inevitable old age, the corrupt would eventually die. They may be replaced by people just as bad or worse, but at least there was hope that once Senator Son-of-a-Bitch or General Asshole kicked it, maybe somebody would come along and do a better job.

Not so in the Twilit Kingdom. Queen Meabh, the regal, charming, and beautiful monarch who also happened to be conniving, callous, and cruel, was immortal—like all Tuatha. Barring assassination, she would rule Other Realm to the end of time. The armies on the muster field and those on the northern front thought they were fighting to free themselves from the tyranny of the encroaching Gythraul, but in truth, they fought to keep themselves enslaved to the will of an undying, uncaring Queen and her coven of immortal, sniveling sycophants—the Gloaming Court. Even Gythraul overlords died after a few centuries, but Queen Meabh would not die even after millenia. And though Gythraul were ruthless I hadn't seen any so cold and power hungry that they could dismiss the needless murder of 300 loyal soldiers as a result of their own scheming.

That was why a stone was now lodged in my sternum, but for all my shame and despair, I would fashion her an army to crush all her enemies. I had no choice in the matter.

I went through my day instructing soldiers on infantry tactics then spent time with beastmasters from Thistle-bough, brainstorming ideas regarding the use of their living weapons. So far, the fighting on the northern front had been mostly successful because the broken, rocky terrain did not cooperate with the large formations the Gythraul favored and prevented their heavier ordnance from being brought to bear. That worked with my plans to operate the companies as hyper-developed wolf packs—mobile, surgical, and ultra-violent. But there would be times when I needed more power or retractable precision to work against the Gythraul when engaged in terrain and situations which favored their style of war. As a rule, I planned never to engage them when it was so, but war has this funny habit of taking your rules and twisting them in on themselves.

Flexibility came in part from options, and that was what Thistlebough's creatures were—optional tools to be applied to the circumstances for which they were suited. I just had to find out where they fit with the forces I was already building.

"So, travelwise, how quickly can these things move and still be able to fight?" I asked one of Thistlebough's oddly mutated Tuatha. The Tuatha of Thistlebough, no doubt to please the whims of their bestial lord, bore animalistic features which accented, complemented, or overwhelmed the natural beauty and grace common to the nobility of the Twilit Kingdom.

"They can maintain a march comparable to foot troops if the earth is not too soft," the ursine beastmaster said. He crossed his wicked paws over his barrel chest and looked back at the Dread Morgs who stood, waiting and twitching. "In marshy ground, their weight will see them slowing down and losing too much energy."

"What about on an open stretch?" I followed his gaze to the creatures. They looked like a cross between a grizzly and one of those spiny, armor-plated dinosaurs, but with burly, simian proportions. Dense nodes and ridges of bone interrupted their bristly hides. When I visited Thistlebough months before, Lord Bwyathardd had been all too keen to demonstrate how resistant to projectiles they were. So long as they weren't under heavy, sustained bombardment, these brutes could weather small arms fire long enough to wade in and rip the enemy into literal pieces—weaponized, bestial brutality to scatter those lines of Gythraul like toy soldiers.

Even at rest, their bowed, muscular shoulders twitched and shivered with brutal strength. I shuddered to think what would remain after they were unleashed on a target.

No. "Target" wasn't the right word for anything that fell under those hooked, clawed mitts. "Victim" was more like it.

"On solid, open ground, they maintain a lope that will outpace most infantry," the beastmaster said confidently. "They are good climbers as well, though their weight must be supported. Even in the mountains or other rough, rocky terrain they do not suffer from a marked decrease in efficacy."

I nodded and looked up and down the row of the creatures that had been brought from Thistlebough. Not enough to deploy more than one or two per company, and that didn't include those already in the field. I could assign them across all companies, but hitting the enemy with just one of these creatures at a time wasn't going to be worth the effort. Feeding them, let alone adjusting training to accommodate their utilization in field operations, was no small task, and I needed a more efficient way to use them.

If I used them as hammers, I didn't want one little ball-peen whacking away—no, I wanted a sledgehammer dipped in nitroglycerin. I wanted whatever they hit to be nothing but a red stain within minutes as they punched holes in centuries that the infantry could exploit. I did not want them bogged down and shot to pieces by legionnaires. I needed them to dominate their little pockets of the battlefield and help destabilize the Gythraul battleline, not unlike early tanks.

"How well do they work in close proximity?" I envisioned a snarling mob of the brutes dropping down on a century of legionnaires and turning it into metal-flecked hamburger.

"Numbers and composition matter in that regard, my Gorm," the beastmaster said. "Typically the larger females will gather a cluster of males to her, no more than five. They are trained to tolerate each other, but I have concerns that if you stretch the natural order of things, you may have dominance fights erupting in the middle of your operations."

"That would be unacceptable." I adjusted my vision from a mob to a small pack, five creatures strong. "Do they need direct instruction by their handlers to be effective, or can they be cut loose?"

The beastmaster shrugged. "How discerning do you need them to be with their targets?"

The question, posed simply but loaded with crushing memories, caught me like a right hook across the jaw.

I recalled the twisted and torn bodies of Alfa company entangled in shackles. The Gythraul meant the town hall of Luchath to be a temporary holding area, not an execution site, but the Queen's pet Fiendspawn thought otherwise. In addition to the memories of the bloodless, terrified faces of the soldiers I had already lost came visions of new, freshly-trained soldiers ripped apart with scything, sweeping Morg claws.

"So we should expect collateral damage and possible casualties with friendly units?" My voice sounded robotic in my ears. "That is, if any forces are positioned close enough?"

"Gorm, no, not at all," the hairy Tuatha said, aghast at the suggestion. "We have trained these creatures impeccably. Even in the heat of battle and without handlers, the Morg are trained to discriminate between the Gythraul and our own forces by both sight and scent. I was discussing taking prisoners. Only the diligence of our handlers can guarantee that the Morgs will not kill any target they engage. That is ultimately what we bred them for."

Even the blowhard Lord Bwythardd kept his brute animals in line, but the Queen of the entire kingdom didn't seem interested in restraint. "If and when I make use of these beasts," I said without relish or embarrassment, sweeping my hand along the line of monsters, "I do not plan on taking prisoners." The beastmaster flashed a toothy grin, supporting the strategy wholeheartedly.

That night, like every other night since I received the Gormstone, I sat in the war council tent on the muster field and alternated between reading reports from the front, writing directives, or having Kieren read me missives while I wrote or checked the maps. My armor was piled in one corner, and my gambeson laces were loosened, but my sword and dagger were still belted on, and the M-Core leaned against the table.

Before, I would have met with my second, Uzran, my liaison with the Queen, Lady Bryth Lighttread, my Finger team coordinator, Grimple Guthook, and as many of the company commanders as could be spared at one time. I had wanted to coordinate our efforts, foster a spirit of cooperation, and let people get a feel for each other.

Much of what I had wanted was an organic structure that encouraged commanders in the field to coordinate, but also innovate, playing off of each other to create an agile, adaptive, and aggressive war machine. I had wanted the conservative commanders to know that their more aggressive peers would probably be taking risks in the heat of the battle, not just because the Wee Folk we used to communicate told them so, but because they knew that their fellow commanders were go-getters. Familiarity could see them moving forces to support one another's efforts before the messages made their crooked way through the fog of war. By the same token, the go-getters were empowered to seize the initiative because they knew their more stolid compatriots would back them up. The war machine was to be a living creature, all parts shifting and moving in sympathy and support of the direction set by me, the dictatorial neuron, the brain.

But things had changed after the Valley of Luchath, and I sat in the tent scribbling my signature and stamping out requisition forms as Kieren read reports and requests aloud.

"Tango company requests more banshee shells." Kieren's eyes scanned the unfurled scroll of parchment he pinned with one hand while scratching on his own larger sheet. "It seems they did not receive the full training complement they were promised and will not be able to complete the required ordnance exercises without them."

I looked at the stack of requisition orders I had already compiled, and fought to remember if I had signed one for shriekers to be delivered to Tango.

"Did I already have that in my order stack?" I glared at the stack of orders I had written, hardly giving a thought to what each had been for. Oh, the glories of military bureaucracy.

"I do not believe so," Kieren said, and without another word, he stopped writing on his parchment and with a few quick scribbles handed me another requisition form, this one marked for shriekers bound for Tango. A few strokes of the ink-stained stylus and a little candle wax later, my stack was one sheet taller.

"Next," I grunted, diving back into the seemingly endless tide of forms.

"Captain Uzran requests . . ." Kieren's voice trailed off, and I was forced to raise my head above the waves of parchment to see his eyes darting across the next scroll fished out from the stack at the table.

"Yes?" I tapped my stylus on the form in front of me.

"Captain Uzran asks your permission to deploy to the

front," Kieren said somewhat timidly, unwilling, but forced to be the bearer of bad news. "Barring that, he requests permission to go to the Grand Thaig held on Mount Falchrreg to recruit more candidates for the Royal Guard. He claims that the casualties inflicted by the war will soon leave the Royal Guard ill-prepared to serve at home or abroad."

In the absence of hurt, guilt, or whatever I was supposed to feel at Uzran running away from me, my mind began running through the most recent casualty reports from the front. I knew his pride wouldn't let him lie, but Uzran, like all career officers, had learned the importance of "flexible" communication—flexible in that you had to be a damn mental gymnast to see things the way the writer spun it, but you did what was necessary to look after your men and your objectives.

The Royal Guard provided supplementary command and heavier suppressive support, and though full of hulking creatures like the Ogre captain, they could die. Their fewer numbers meant they could not afford as many casualties. I recalled, in a general sense, that as our forces engaged the legions farther south, greater numbers of casualties than expected had occurred as some commands struggled to adapt their movements and tactics to the demands of the area and dense enemy positions. I could have asked Kieren to look up the actual numbers, but decided against it out of hand. I wasn't wasting time nitpicking over how many Royal Guards were necessary for an effective force at home or abroad.

"When will that thaig-thingy be?" I asked, turning back to the requisition forms.

No matter what had happened between us, if I had been the brain of the gathering that used to fill this tent, then

Uzran had been the will, unflinching and stalwart. If anyone could squeeze Ogres and Trolls out of stones, it was the big guy. Keeping him here wasn't practical, even if I claimed it was important for me to wring more sword fighting lessons from him. I had a good foundation, and what I needed most was practice to familiarize myself with the changes the Gormstone was making in my body and to develop the reflexes of a swordsman.

"Next month at the turn of the new moon," Kieren reported.

"If he gets his things in order and can organize a sorcerer to open a Path for him, then he can go," I said, remembering that our supply of Tuatha battle-magi were running thin from ferrying troops, supplies, and information across the kingdom. Was it spite that kept me from assigning one to him? I knew the Gormstone was eating up my humanity— the Queen had told me as much—but did that include the negative as well as the positive? If it tore the love out of my chest, did it take the hate as well? If it kept me from feeling connection to the world and my fellow creatures, did it keep me from being cruel or petty to them? Right then, I wanted to believe as much, but I wasn't sure if that was just a hollow hope.

Kieren scribbled down the necessary notes and drew another scroll. I was still mulling over the realities of my new nature, so I didn't have my nose buried in reports when I saw his face liven for an instant and then darken as he read the document.

It was a report from Lady Bryth Lighttread. I could tell by his expression. Bryth, an emissary of the Queen and a respected battle-magus, was also a cousin of Kieren's on her father's side. Kieren practically worshipped her and had made it known the very first time I met him. It had been in my bedchamber as the last of my wounds were healing following my receiving the Gormstone. Hardly the opportune time to reveal that he was a devout fan of the woman whom I had just begun to love before she sold me out to the Queen. In no uncertain terms, I told him what I thought of his cousin and that, outside of military reporting, I didn't want to hear a single word about Lady Lighttread. Accordingly, Kieren read her correspondences aloud after he first read them once silently so he could mentally squirrel away any commentary they might prompt. When he read them to me, it was just the facts. I allowed his self-editing, remembering that Tuatha emotions typically ran a little closer to the surface than those of humans, and his attempt to respect my wishes was worth the spare seconds of dead air.

But the concerned glare he gave the scroll was not typical of his usual pre-reading routine. Without realizing it, the stylus was out of my hand, and I had pushed away from the table with both hands.

"Kieren," I snapped with a sharpness that seemed inappropriate, even to my tone-deaf ears. "What is going on?"

"Lady Bryth says things have taken a foul turn along the northern front," he replied a little breathlessly. "Ceterum Cinis's forces retreated into the central steppes where three whole legions were waiting. Three, Luce."

The last two words held a touch of panic, and with a disgusted grunt, I rose to my feet and held out my hand for the scroll.

"Steady on there, Squire." I gave him a you-know-better look as he passed the report to me. "It's not like the legions are marching onto the muster field."

"Yes, Gorm. It's just . . . three legions gathered together . . . The last invasion saw a total of five legions stretched across three fronts. Three legions with more forces making their way from the Isles does not bode well."

"Good thing I'm here then, huh?" I said, the Gormstone eating up what might have been a tickle of true concern before I read the letter.

Gorm Bollham,

We succeeded in driving out the remnants of Cinis's legion two days ago, securing the northern valleys and sealing the way to Chillspire for the time being. This victory was not without some cost, as our casualty reports have indicated, but the soldiers are in good spirits, proud to serve and appreciative of the support from more companies deployed to reinforce our position.

That was Bryth. I was the brain, Uzran was the will, and she was our heart. Not some kind of mushy weak thing, mind you, but the tireless and striving thing that reminded you why you were doing this. For ideals, sure, but those glowing, nebulous things were too cerebral to hold onto in the midst of the fight or the grind of training. Instead she reminded you that you did it because you wanted to live, and you wanted the guy next to you to live, and that was enough to face another day. Perhaps that is why I felt hollowed already. I kept my mind, but my will was a prisoner of war. And my heart . . . I was pretty sure it had been ripped out in the Queen's audience chamber as Bryth stood there crying, knowing what was coming but refusing to do anything to stop it. I continued reading.

But things have become more complicated. This morning, one of Grimple's Finger teams reported that they had scouted farther onto the steppes, hoping to coordinate an entrapping ambush with Delta company on Cinis's retreating forces. Just south of the Kindled River they came across a host of encamped Gythraul. Adjusting their priorities, they reconnoitered the position, unde-tected, and found two entire legions—including artillery and cavalry auxiliaries—in a position that seemed provisionally fortified as though they were waiting. Realizing that an ambush would most likely not succeed, the team returned and reported, sending a WFC ahead to keep the bulk of our forces from advancing further onto the steppes.

I was still looking for the other legion, but I found myself glad for the WFC (Wee Folk Communique) as this could have been something worth panicking about. Our company stumbling into artillery range on the steppes could have had crippling consequences. The enemy having cavalry forces to ride down the stragglers could have put an end to the bulk of our forces on the northern front in short order. We would have to adjust our training exercises to prepare for these kinds of circumstance, with particular emphasis on better ways to incorporate the beasts of Thistlebough to counteract them. We had the mortars with banshee and myrk shells, but that was not enough to compete with the kind of firepower the Gythraul would tote across those plains.

We held back our advances along the foothills in order to assess the enemy position, but before we could effectively redeploy to probe, we spotted another legion marching from the west toward our location. Finger teams and shelling from Bravo company bought us time to relocate along the mountains, so the damage dealt was minimal. Alongside the legion and what our Wee Folk ascertained were artillery auxiliaries, this legion possessed machines which moved across the ground on many legs. They were heavily armored with alchemically treated plates. Manticore quills and Djinn bolts were ineffective against them without sustained, intense fire. This proved dangerous, as they were equipped with armatures which sprayed burning, caustic fluid to some distance. I, supported by the company commanders and Lieutenant Droth of the Royal Guard, ordered a general withdrawal into the mountains to assess and reorganize.

We are holding and reconnoitering, but we require strategic and tactical support to handle this change. Cinis's forces joined the encamped legions where a change of standards suggests he has taken command. Our scouts believe the third legion is moving down from the foothills and will camp on the north side of the Kindled River tonight before crossing over and joining the rest of the other legions. If they do this, it is the belief of the command elements here that they will move eastward through the steppes and be poised to deploy against Thistlebough. Either that, or they will move farther south and head for Cinderstone. We do not possess the ability to stop them, but we will try to slow them down.

Awaiting further instruction and reinforcement,
Lady Bryth Lighttread, Draoi'cogaidh

I put the scroll down on the table, considering these developments.

"What are your orders, Gorm Bollham?" The stylus in Kieren's hand shook just above his sheet of parchment.

Flame-throwing tanks? Gythraul technology—especially their metallurgy and alchemy—had developed, albeit slowly, but nothing I had read or been told hinted that they might have something like this. I had structured the army to maximize its applied force against massed infantry movements supported by static artillery and close quarter, non-mechanical cavalry. This changed the game, and while I wasn't anywhere near panicked, I thought petulantly that it seemed unfair to change the rules just like that. But bitching about it wouldn't change the fact that Ceterum Cinis was gearing up for another shot at me.

I had far more soldiers this time, but with three legions, so did he. I had the same advantage as before—more mobility. My army was organized in modern, small-unit formations, and we had on our side Tuatha sorcerers who could open magical Paths that would allow our forces to travel hundreds of miles in a few hours, even on foot. But Cinis had gained something with this change of venue. He had us in sheer numbers, and now, on the more open terrain of the steppes, he would have room to maneuver his centuries and drive our forces out of what little cover they had.

"We are going to start by mobilizing the bulk of the reserves who've completed their training," I said slowly, constructing a plan one piece at a time. "Two more companies—those at full strength and not just minimum battle potency—are going to deploy to Lady Lighttread's position."

I cleared out the requisition reports and made room for maps of the central steppes which showed me the lay of the land.

"What about the rest of the reserves?" Kieren's voice sharpened with interest rather than fear at this point as he watched my finger trace lines across the map.

The Kindled River wound its way through the central steppes, terminating in the marshy lands of Mistmire—a bulging, soggy tumor that sat between Thistlebough Wood above and the plains of Cinderstone below. I understood why command was pretty sure he would choose one of them as his target, if for no other reason than because marching that many soldiers and heavy equipment across swampland would be miserable going. It made my head hurt just thinking about it. Cinis wouldn't waste his time and resources taking a swamp that he could isolate without much work. But by attacking Thistlebough or Cinderstone, he could deny us further beast support or our animated dead labor source. The question remained—how I was going to stop a juggernaut without being squashed?

An idea began to take shape. It was something so fragile I didn't want to look at it squarely yet, lest it unravel. When an eighteen-wheeler was barrelling down on you, the answer was not to play chicken with it. That was a good way to get flattened. Instead, you led it off the road to get over-turned or you blinded the driver. But could I do that with someone as dangerous and clever as Cinis Cetum?

"The rest are going to deploy . . . here." I planted my finger on a scrubby patch of low mountains thirty miles or so south of where the Gythraul camp was supposed to be.

"Morgund's Bastards?" Kieren squinted around my finger at the map. "Yes, my Gorm."

I sniffed, the closest thing to a laugh I could manage at the peculiar name. I hadn't even noticed it, colorfully written in flourished script below the dirty patch of hill country.

Appropriate, I supposed. I did plan to teach Ceterum Cinis what a bastard I could be.

3

MOBILIZED

Captain Uzran stood outside the titanic gates of Duanon upon the bridge that connected the capital city to the rest of the Twilit Kingdom. It spanned the western river, a vast work of stone defying the surging Purllaeth which churned below in white froth around the pillars of smooth dark stone. He waited for an old friend to arrive, unsure of what lay ahead, but knowing in the deepest reaches of his soul that something had changed in him.

Around the other end of the Bridge of Defiance, sometimes just called the Defiant, earthworks braced with retaining walls of timber and stone created a tiered slope with a central, paved ramp running all the way to the opposite gate from where he stood. An assortment of buildings and corrals dotted the slope, clustering closer the nearer they were to the central road leading to the bridge. A population of traveling merchants and tradefolk dwelt there in various taverns and inns. These part-time residents were integrally joined with the the transportation and courier guilds which moved goods and creatures about the Twilit

Kingdom. Watching the wagons and riders departing briskly while other creatures with drooping heads staggered to inns and stables, reminded him that not all—in fact, *most* —creatures dwelling within the Kingdom could benefit from the use of Tuatha magus to open Paths. Many of them, if they wished to earn their daily bread, prosper, or avoid the ire of their masters, had no choice but to mount a steed, hire a wagon or coach, or set foot to the vast network of roads criss-crossing the Twilit Kingdom. Others took to the docks in the shadow of Tuatha's walls and sought passage on the skiffs, barges, and other vessels to carry them upriver and through the waterways of the Kingdom.

Watching a wagon—one of dozens this morning— trundle along the bridge, he told himself that he had known all this, but he had forgotten. He had spent so much time in service to the Queen that any errand he was sent on always came with the promise of easy transport. "You forget things," he grumbled shifting his stance slightly, an adjust-ment of weight to appease the nagging pains of his wounds.

It was true he had forgotten about such truths until he needed transportation to the Grand Thaig. The Royal Guard's attendance there to recruit among the Ogres, Trolls, and Fomor was a regular occurrence when the kingdom was actively campaigning against the Gythraul. He alternated with attending the Elder Groving to recruit Sylvankin and the occasional Wodewosen, though he had not seen one of the latter since Royal Guard Burrin fell in Ceterum Cinis's ambush of Gorm Valoise's forces a century ago. At the Grand Thaig, held upon the summit of Mount Falchrreg, the clans of the various mountain peoples renewed alliances, settled grudges in ritual contests, and drank copious amounts of alcohol. Uzran had not been there since the execution of his clan. He knew that even if none dared to say them to his face, they would whisper curses behind his back.

Kinslayer. Brotherblooded. Thrice-Cursed.

He accepted that such would be his fate when he chose to report his clan's burgeoning plans to rebel, but he had served so long under the Queen by then that he forgot how the weight of those names would press on him. He forgot the bitter looks laced with damning pity that his mother had given Errgund, an Ogre of their sister clan who had killed his brother in a drunken argument. Life, or what passed for it as he begged the exile's alms among the clans, became a burden for Errgund, but he knew that taking his own life would only deepen his shame. Uzran remembered swearing he would never be like that wretch, but the oath had been forgotten in that moment when zeal for serving his Queen had come over him in a flood of righteous indignation.

The wagon he watched was more than halfway across the bridge now, but Uzran's attention was elsewhere, attending to the memory of those blood-streaked moorlands, once his home.

As the last of his clan's elders were being driven onto the spikes before the dead eyes of their children, Uzran remembered his idealistic oath as a child, and something shattered in his heart. As Nofthal––his great aunt and the last to die––gave her final tortured scream, Uzran felt himself hollowed out, scooped and scraped until only a shell remained. It was his longing to honor his clan that had first driven him hard to join the Royal Guard—to become the finest warrior and most faithful servant of the Queen. Like a hunt-maddened hound he had pursued every glory, volunteered for every assignment, and refused to see that he was forgetting what he had sought in the first place. Standing at the end of that brutal inquisition—truly a fear-mongering purge—he had realized that his life was meaningless, an almost comical overreaction to those first longings for pride and respect.

He returned to Duanon with no hope but to continue to serve and do his duty. Such considerations were the only things that remained through the tragedy, and they were all that could keep him going, or at least, that is what he chose to believe. Then, as now, he had been inexorably changed, but none would say a word about it. None except for the figure he saw in the back of the approaching wagon.

"He is probably going to call me a fool, again," the Ogre mumbled as he walked forward to meet the wagon. A single, grizzled Bovarine driven by a Gremlin with a wide, toothless smile pulled the wagon forward. A broad, cloak-swaddled form bounced along where it sat with its back to him. With a wave from the Ogre captain, the driver hauled on the reins and the slump-shouldered beast gave a groan of protest before finally stopping.

"Izthtillzleepinmylord . . ." the Gremlin began in the relentless, sawing speech of his kind.

"I ain't asleep, you wheezing gutbag," the figure in the bed said in a raw, guttural voice as it shuffled its way toward the open end of the wagon. "How can any creature sleep with yer gratin' voice chewin' the whole way?"

The figure slid free of the wagon, landing on thick, bandied legs. The wagon and its beast both made groaning sounds of appreciation at being free of a body nearly as thick as the Ogre's. Slumping around the wagon with a stiffness and effort that instantly drew Uzran's concerned stare was a burly Troll whose entire body seemed wrapped in bandages from his long, fleshy nose to his broad, unshod feet.

"Droth." Uzran was unable to hide his shock at the sight

of his old brother-in-arms. "What in the Wyrd happened to you?"

The Troll lieutenant's features squirmed under their bandages, and he looked down on his wrapped hands and arms with his good eye before looking back at his captain.

"Not exactly parade ground standards, eh Cap'n," he chuckled, an act that set him coughing thickly before he spat a bloody gobbet over the bridge's guard wall.

"Did you just come from the field?" Uzran's black eyes darting from one injury to another. "You look like you've been lashed to the underside of a millstone."

"A few days ago we met with a new toy the Gythraul brought to the steppes," Droth grunted, scooping his pack out of the back of the wagon with one long arm. "Some machine like a metal worm with too many legs. Damn tough. And if you get close, it'll hose you down with nasty stuff that burns like drake fire."

Uzran saw fresh bloodstains blossoming here and there beneath the bandages. After receiving permission from Lucius to attend the Grand Thaig, he had immediately recruited Droth to go with him. The faithful lieutenant had mentioned being "scratched" in a recent fight, but said he would be along shortly, and Uzran had believed him. Trollish powers of recuperation were near magical, and having seen his friend recover from crippling injuries within a day or two, he had been unconcerned about any "scratch." He wondered at this new Gythraul devilry as he looked at his friend's ravaged body.

"Well, looks like you still haven't recovered at all." Uzran crossed his arms on his expansive chest. "Droth, you are not fit to travel like this."

"How hard is it goin' to be to walk a Path to Mount Falchrreg?" Droth rummaged around in his pack before dropping a leather-wrapped package of small silver bars into the Gremlin's waiting hands. With a buzzing and irrepressibly cheerful farewell, the Gremlin left the two old soldiers standing on the bridge while other travelers parted to give the huge figures a wide berth.

"There will be no Path," Uzran said flatly. "The journey will be by riverboat to Duln's Crossing and then the trade roads on foot."

Droth's expression was not hard to read despite the bandages. Sadness mixed with indignation glittered in the Troll's wine-colored eyes, and a sharply tipped tongue ran across thin, blistered lips. He knew the only reason the Captain of the Royal Guard could find no Tuatha to aid him was their fear of angering the Queen.

"To make it to the Thaig on time will require us to make the last leg fairly quickly, and you are obviously in no shape for it," Uzran said, "so I will go alone."

The Troll stared at him, a forlorn look plain beneath his dressings. "Oh, Cap'n," he said achingly, the pain having nothing to do with his visible wounds, "it's happened hasn't it?"

"What?" Uzran bristled. Droth's last words sounded too much like pity for him to take them with good grace.

"Yer out o' favor," Droth sighed, adjusting his shoulder pack as his head wagged from side to side. "The Queen finally turned on you, just like I told yer she would. Didn't expect it would be about you speakin' up for the human, though."

The words, nearly treasonous yet true, pricked at Uzran's ears. He felt like they were the sort of thing one whispered in a hidden room, not pronounced on a bridge full of travelers. Uzran didn't have to wonder who told Droth the drama which had taken place in the Queen's audience hall after the

Valley of Luchath. He had been serving alongside Lady Bryth for some time now.

"I don't remember you saying that," Uzran said lamely, feeling exposed and foolish all at once. "And it doesn't matter, because it does not affect you. You are staying in Duanon to recover."

"Not on yer life, Cap'n." Droth's eyes shone with daring defiance. "Yer set on goin' to the Grand Thaig, and I am comin' with you. Nothin' you can do 'bout it."

"I am still your superior officer and commander of the Royal Guard," Uzran said sternly, squaring his shoulders as he looked down at the Troll. "I could have you confined to the barracks. I could even have you declared an oathbreaker for insubordination."

Droth had been waiting for the threat and bared his sharp fangs in a smile. "Do it," he said with another gargling laugh. "As my oath was to the Queen, you'll have to take me before her to do it, and won't that be a fine thing to trouble her Majesty with? Disgraced Cap'n bringin' wounded war hero to task for tryin' to serve all loyal-like."

Uzran's glare narrowed to a gouging focus, but Droth's grin remained fixed on his ruined face.

"Whoever told you you were a hero?" Uzran's grim expression dissolved by degrees.

"Lookin' like this, Cap'n, I better be." Droth swept a clawed hand up and down his body. "Otherwise, what's the point of wreckin' a face as pretty as mine?"

"Well, if you're done being a big damn hero, we best get moving." Uzran turned back toward the gate into Duanon. "We need to get down to the docks, or else your burnt ass will be waddling all the way to Mount Falchregg."

Less than two hours later, the Troll and Ogre were on

the deck of a river trawler heading up the mouth of the Purllaeth River, looking out across the muster fields beyond Duanon. There, the armies of the Twilit Kingdom, reorganized into the newest iteration of human ingenuity, readied to deploy to the war on the central plains. The activity of soldiers, porters, and beasts of war was the barely-organized chaos typical of a mass military movement. They were too far from the soldiers to hear the individual shouts or marching songs, but were instead treated to a rumbling, growling sound rolling across the field in waves and passing over where Uzran and Droth stood watching.

That sound, well known to veterans and foreboding to fresh recruits, might be called the waking yawn of War. Mechanical in its pounding rhythms, yet living in its hungry tones, it was the sound of a great, metal-gutted beast that would swallow up blood, flesh, iron and brass, and it would leave nothing but red, leaking slag steaming in its wake.

"Do you miss it already, Cap'n?" Droth watched the procession. "Miss leadin' the charge into the teeth o' the enemy?"

Uzran watched them go, thousands and thousands of young soldiers—a new brood being led to the misty Paths that plunged down War's gullet.

"Part of me does." He didn't take his gaze off the companies falling into line for what must have been a final inspection. "But things are different now. Things have changed."

"What's that, Cap'n?" the Troll asked, standing at his friend and commander's shoulder. Uzran was not sure how to answer.

Yes, things had changed, and not only with regard to his disfavor with the Queen, but also how he felt within. Like that day when he heard the last cry of his clan, something had shifted within him, and the movement was not a sudden wrench in his heart, but a permanent relocation of his soul that had been a long time coming. It had happened by degrees, but he knew that it was because of Lucius Bollham. Since the little runt had taken command, things had begun to rumble and move. Uzran had served a few of the Paladins in the past, and while most had been able commanders of one breed or another, they were too much like himself. He saw them as obnoxious but useful tools at best, or dangerous obstacles at worst. Paladin Bollham had been different if for no other reason than that he seemed to truly care about his soldiers and what he was fighting for. Others had taken up the Pale Banner for pride, power, or even lust after the wonders of Other-Realm, but none that Uzran had seen or heard of had chosen to serve with the sincere conviction which seemed to be driving Lucius.

Uzran had seen this as weakness at first, but as he watched Lucius with growing respect, he could not deny the power of his leadership. Lucius was not overly friendly. He did not guffaw or sing bawdy songs with those in his command, but Uzran had watched him earnestly listen to every soldier when he could, and give each his plain and honest answer. There was a stubborn will to him. Even if he was not running around slapping backs and telling stories, it was because he was dedicating his every moment to making sure his soldiers' efforts and lives were not wasted.

In the Valley of Luchath rage, vengeance, and hatred for his own life had nearly brought an end to Uzran's company and to himself. Death would have been assured, had it not been for the brave efforts of Lucius and a coterie of battle-magi. The change was cemented when he saw the cold, unquenchable fire ignited in the Paladin when he discovered the murderous acts of the Fiendspawn. Those soldiers were not humans, and they had hardly been in Lucius's command for a handful of weeks, yet his wrath was as fierce as any band of brothers could have wished.

In the light of that fire, Uzran saw his own shrunken existence in stark relief and realized that his life, his destiny did not have to be this revenant existence of hollow duty. The Ogre captain hadn't come to understand this revelation enough to stand with Lucius when he should have before the Queen, but even under the shame of that moment, Uzran knew that he could not return to a hopeless life.

"It is me, Droth," he said, responding at last to his lieutenant's question. "I have changed."

Droth watched his commander for a moment before speaking again. "We're not really goin' recruitin'. Are we, Cap'n?"

The Ogre shook his head, but said nothing as he watched the soldiers moving out, wondering quietly what they were going to die for.

4

───────

CORNERED

I stepped out of the muffled embrace of the Path to a world of sand-colored hills stubbled with silvery grass that made me think of thinning wisps on the domes of giant, old men. Despite the visual serenity of the landscape, the sounds of war seemed determined to wake up those giants. Banshee shells wailed nearly constantly overhead, and scatterings of rifle and djinn gun fire punctuated the brief pauses. Through it all, there was the tromp and whistle pattern that I now associated with the presence of the Gythraul legions. Less than a half mile from where I stood, scuttling bands of soldiers withdrew before an advancing tide of armored figures. I watched a mortar team scrambling to pull up stakes as their compatriots in a supporting squad snapped off shots at the marching line of death heading their way. The reinforcements I led were marching right into the middle of a battle.

With no breath to spare for a curse, I used the hagseye to get ahold of my Bogle, Sleepyhead, who was flitting along the column behind. "Arrival zone is hot," I snarled, the magical artifact making my senses swim as it linked me to my Wee Folk liaison. "I want all companies expecting to emerge under fire."

Sleepy started to pass the message along the telepathic network the Wee Folk share, then he paused. I heard his voice in my ear even as I watched the mists of the Path boil away in front of his eyes.

"Master, commanders run away and move other-where's?" The Bogle emerged from the Path, and I saw myself through his eyes, armoured and astride Rhoslyn atop a silver-grassed hill.

I considered the option for a second, part of my brain screaming in panic at the thought of losing so many soldiers to an ambush, but the Gormstone muted the screams into a soft, watery noise. This couldn't be an ambush. Our movement through the Path had been too quick for the Gythraul to assemble a force capable of attacking Bryth's position with the kind of power I was hearing. They had planned this attack already, maybe hoping to crush her and her troops before help could come. If that were the case, I was obliged to ruin their plans.

"Negative, but tell them they need to hit this shit on the bounce." I kicked my Diomedan steed into action, wheeling her around to ride along the hill toward the edges of the unfolding skirmish. I needed some perspective and to get in touch with Bryth, but more than anything, I needed not to be standing on top of a hill with my hagseye in, begging to get shot.

Over my shoulder I saw Romeo and Sierra companies moving in the opposite direction, coming out of the Path at a run. They were moving into a flanking position, just like I had taught them. When the Gythraul bulled up, we played matador, getting to the side to put something sharp into their vitals. I felt a distant sort of pleasure witnessing the fluid way the companies moved to enact the principles I'd taught them . . . but it was a vague, diluted thing. Right then, it was far more important for me to get clear and make myself useful.

I put my heels into the Diomedan, and she accelerated into a full gallop, her unnaturally powerful legs carrying me faster than any humvee could. The soft, almost chalky earth kicked up under Rhoslyn's hooves, coating her black flanks and my sabatons with gritty powder. The stuff reminded me of the dirt in Afghanistan—a lot of grunts called it moondust. It was floating through the hillside in thick, drifting clouds. Plumes of dust erupted where the Gythraul centuries marched, while thin wisps marked the occasional movement of Bryth's troops. Farther to the north, where the hills built into the stony feet of the mountains, I saw a thicker band of dust. It stretched in an arc that seemed about to round the blockier Gythraul dust shadows, and I remembered that both Delta and Golf companies were mounted units. Sure enough, as my vision swept south, I saw another similar band trying to round the horn of the Gythraul formation. Both tried to jab at the enemy's exposed areas, or at least disrupt the measured advance, but the Gythraul line was wide and likely strong enough to drag those flankers back in.

I plunged down a shallow ravine and up onto another hill northeast of my original position. "Sleepyhead," I called fitting the hagseye as I brought Rhoslyn to a halt. "I need an aerial view of the battlefield now." My vision through the magic of the hagseye hurtled through a nauseous blur of images, andI found myself staring up at the pale sky and hearing the whistling wind rising over the chaos of the battle below.

"Look down," I commanded. The perspective, somewhat reluctantly, swung downward.

Past the frail, almost human-looking body and spindly sparrow legs of a Pixie, was the expanse of the battlefield. This high up, with the Pixie's excellent visual acuity, I saw things were far worse for Bryth's forces who were even now scrambling back among the hills. Alongside the centuries marched the fire-spouting machines Bryth had mentioned in her report—machines with the bulky bodies of armored caterpillars and too many legs stamping forward in a rippling slither across the ground. Not only were these hellipedes advancing, belching gouts of blue flame as they went, but also ranks of Gythraul cavalry along the southern flank. Gythraul warriors sat on the backs of splay-legged lizards comparable to midsize trucks, couching lances nearly as long as their mounts. The lances sported three prongs; the central prong was an ugly spike of steel, while the other two were open-mouthed tubes where cones of flame burned.

I knew from talking with my veterans of the previous conflicts that, despite their ungainly appearance, those reptile-mounted warriors could cross the field quickly and unleash a storm of fire and stabbing points. I needed to keep them from catching our troops out in the open while they repositioned. A brutal charge from them could sweep up several squads if they timed it right.

Watching through the Pixie's eyes, I spied Delta's company of Sylvanocerous skirmishers cresting a hill and making a pass at the corner of the Gythraul cavalry formation. The move took the Gythraul by surprise, and the swift, sure-footed creatures sprang up and over the hill like jackrabbits. The gunners on the backs of the Sylvanocerous opened up with bursts measured in time with their mounts' bounding movements. Quite a few of the Gythraul fell, and others were thrown as their lizards writhed in spasms of anger and pain. Despite three platoons worth of skirmishers raking their lines, the Gythraul didn't seem at all inclined to back off. Instead, the attacked attachment of cavalry charged to meet Delta's skirmishers, catching them as they wheeled around the hill they had just come down. Sweeps of flame sprang from the lances, washing over many unfortunate beasts and their riders. The intensity of the flames didn't quickly kill a target. In fact, some of the orange gouts failed to kindle anything more than a few hairs on a Sylvanocerous, but the smoke and fire left the retreating skirmishers in chaos. Like knights out of hell, the Gythraul cavalry plunged through, ramming lances into drivers or beasts, and those not impaled by the lance had to contend with the snapping jaws of the giant lizards.

Cursing, I watched the mauled remainder of Delta's skirmishers peel away and move along the hill. Another contingent of cavalry moved to pursue and might have caught them, but the hill rippled and shifted, like one of the giant, old men had just snuffled and shrugged in his sleep. The Gythraul could not maintain an orderly advance and some went to their deaths as their mounts tumbled and rolled over them again and again down the freshly shifted slope. On the backside of the hill, Delta's seared riders gave weary salutes to a lone, tall figure—one of the battle-magi who had saved them from being overrun.

But even the battle-magi could not stand against the marshalled might of two centuries and two cavalry detachments. With another burst of magical power, he called down sorcerous storm winds to carry him away from the vengeful Gythraul moving to pursue him.

With a command I swung across the broader view of the hills and struggled to hold back a scream of rage. Again, just like in Luchath, the Gythraul had pressed us into a large-scale battle which played to their preferences. The anger quickly subsided, though, when I spotted Quebec and Tango companies emerging from behind the mountains' foothills. Loping along at the fore were the Dread Morgs.

I had an idea. "Sleepy, have Sierra and Romeo take up positions to provide resh covering fire for Delta when they come back toward the center. Traveling overwatch to get into position, then I want platoon lines across those hills stitching up anything that dares to raise its scaly head."

I gave the Bogle a second to relay the orders and checked my distance to the newly-arrived companies with my own eyes before getting back on the hagseye. "Now, get Quebec and Tango nestled on the high ground, and tell all three companies withdrawing across the north to pull back just beneath that new killzone. And whatever battle-magi we have here need to settle in with Quebec and Tango, but I want Kieren hauling ass back up a Path to the companies in the mountains. We are going to run a pain train right up this bull's ass, but I want them heading here if we get run off the tracks."

This close, I could smell the Morg's sweat and hear the breath rasping between their tusklike fangs. I hadn't known it before, but Dread Morgs sweat when they get excited, like when they smell blood and know a fight is coming. It makes their bristly hides slick and sometimes their warty spines will actually drip with the stuff. Surprisingly, it wasn't an unpleasant smell, but the kind of the sharp, spicy scent you get from a fresh bag of mulched cypress. It was distinct, but not overpowering. It helped take the edge off their breath which, as a bunch of carnivores that didn't brush, was eye-wateringly pungent.

I moved among the ranks of the hungry killing-machines and their handlers to find the gathered battle-magi I had called for, hoping there would be enough to pull off my plan. The Morgs squatted on their haunches, their short, thick hind legs ready to propel them into a pounce or a bounding run at a moment's notice. Their heavy fore-limbs, easily twice as long as the hind legs, hung limply in front of them, their dagger-tipped paws resting in the moon-dust. A few raised their snouts to sniff the air and stare at me with pale, silvery eyes as I passed, but most considered the space between their huge mitts.

The creatures' simian similarities made me wonder if they had thoughts or feelings like the apes and monkeys of Earth were supposed to have. I looked into those toothy, ursine faces as I walked Rhoslyn between them, and though I might have seen a glimmer of hunger or curiosity here or there, mostly what I saw was blank, or maybe inscrutable expressions.

When I had first arrived in a swirling cloud of dust kicked up by Rhoslyn's rapid advance, one of the Morgs reached out toward my Diomedan as she stopped. I had half a second to register that this might not be a good thing when my flesh-eating steed snapped her fangs less than an inch from the reaching claws, and the Morg's handler cracked its whip across its back. The creature drew back its hand, suddenly as indifferent to the Diomedan as it was to the thin trickle of blood which ran down between its shoul-ders where the whip had bitten shallowly through thick hide. The handler apologized fearfully, but I didn't bother to reassure him as I dismounted and took Rhoslyn's reins to lead her. I had things to do, and some monster handler's feelings were not a priority.

I found the battle-magi huddled together with the

captains of both companies between the Morgs and the infantry platoons there to support them with conventional firepower.

The battle-magi were all Tuatha of course, their race being the one for whom sorcery is as natural as breathing. They loomed like tall, darkly armored spectres over Captain Muln, a Boggun of Quebec Company, and Captain Luzz, a Gremlin from Tango. Muln seemed to be having some sort of disagreement with the battle-magi, while Luzz stood by nervously, looking like he would rather be anywhere else in the world.

"You start throwing fire and lightning around, you are liable to get my lads murdered," Muln spat in the gravelly, too-big voice that all Bogguns seemed to have. It was the kind of voice that would have suited a burly man, some stereotypical biker maybe, but instead, it came out of a creature that resembled a wiry old man barely more than five feet tall.

"Do you really think we are so careless as to let our curses fall on friendly heads?" one of the battle-magi asked indignantly.

"If you had the mind to be, yes, but that isn't what I am talking about," Muln said, throwing a wary eye over the waiting ranks of Morgs. "If those beasts get turned around in the midst of all your blasting and crackling, who's to say they don't come ploughing back into our positions?"

"That's preposterous," another battle-magus said, shooing the statement away with one foppishly flapping hand. "The beasts are trained, Captain, or weren't you paying attention?"

"I was paying attention when I heard about what happened to Alfa company," Muln snarled defiantly, "and the fact is, we don't know how the brutes will react. They've never been used in battle."

"Neither were the rifles your soldiers wielded in the Battle of Luchath Valley" answered a voice that made a mockery of the Gormstone's numbing venom, dragging my heart into my throat. "Just like the Morgs, we had trained with them but never used them in battle until that day. Should we have refused to use those weapons then as well?" Husky and smooth, like honeyed smoke, of all Other-Realm's wonders, that voice was one of my first, and, God help me, still one of my favorites.

"I am not talking about not using them, my Lady," Muln said, open palms coming up. "I am just advising caution is all, trying to look out for my lads."

"Your lads, Captain, are here to serve the Queen, same as all those under my command, and I have not heard them complain about uncertainties," the Lady's voice continued, uncharacteristically sharp and disdainful. "If you hadn't planned on being on the bloody edge of things, perhaps you should have stayed back at Duanon playing soldier on the muster fields."

Muln's angry retort was cut off when Captain Luzz spotted my approach. He threw up a salute and called out loudly in the growling buzz of his kind, "MyLordGormBoll-hamcomes! Attention!" Muln mirrored the salute while the crowd of battle-magi, not actual parts of the military structure, cut quick bows and stepped back to meet with me away from the rank and file.

As their numbers peeled back I was greeted by the pained stare of Lady Bryth Lighttread. Tall and statuesque —beautiful with a strength and vibrance most Tuatha lacked—she was even more striking in the black field plate of the battle-magi. Hers was noticeably lighter than the others, more riveted chain than plate, and her silver hair was drawn back into a braided chignon. The instant I saw her, I felt an old ember of need spring to life, just as I had felt in my tent before the Battle of Luchath Valley when she had come to me and admitted that she wanted something more than camaraderie between us.

Except it wasn't the same thing, I realized. I still wanted her, oh hell yes I did, but the feeling was wider and maybe shallower now. I couldn't have expressed it any other way than to say that I wanted to devour her. I wanted to take her right then, and I didn't care who watched as I sated myself with her. Pleasure or pain, propriety or shame, none of it would matter as I seized what I wanted in the taking of her body. The beginnings of an ugly, ravenous growl began in my throat before I could choke it into a dry cough, rational thought reasserting itself with more numbing cold.

What was going on?

Whatever the Gormstone left me with was something a lot nastier than nothing, or perhaps I was trying to fill that emptiness. As I walked toward the waiting faces, I raised a hand to press my armor against my chest and felt the pressure build against that hard, foreign lump in my breastbone.

"Gorm Bollham," Bryth said, the title sounding like it stung her tongue, "Bravo, Charlie, and Hotel companies report they are withdrawing under heavy pressure from the Gythraul, but they are luring them along the route you specified."

"Thank you, Lady Lighttread," I did not dare to give her more than a cursory glance as I stepped forward, afraid that the bestial desire would pounce. "So it is Golf company trying to turn the flank on the northern edge of the field?"

"Trying and failing," Bryth admitted, frustration plain in

her tone. "Knobbs says that every attempt by the skirmishers has been driven back and they've taken casualties."

At the mention of Knobbs, I spotted something standing by her armoured calf: a fish-eyed creature not even a foot tall. It had leathery jowls and a long tail which it curled and uncurled nervously in its long-fingered hands. The Grindle saw that it had caught my attention, and its eyes bulged further. It cowered behind Bryth's calf as though I blamed it for the bad reports it had been delivering.

"Tell them to withdraw at speed," I addressed the Grindle directly. "Have them move toward the same route as the other companies."

"What about the forces chasing the other companies?" Muln asked hotly, some of his previous argument still burning in his tone. "What if they get caught up by the bastards?"

"Hopefully they won't," I said, the words as disinterested as the shrug I didn't bother to suppress. "But we need to draw the Gythraul below this line of hills, and we cannot afford to have a few centuries wandering above this position. If that happens, we'll have much bigger problems than just some dead skirmishers."

A chilly silence sprang up in the aftershock of my words, something only the rumble and chatter of weapons fire dared to disturb. It took me a second to realize what I had said to produce such a response. I realized that, before this, I would never have used the words "just some" when talking about the deaths of soldiers under my command.

"WhatzplanthenGorm?" Luzz looked incredibly uncomfortable.

"Well, Captain Muln will be happy to know it won't involve any fireballs or lightning bolts going off around the Morgs," I said. "But it is going to require we time this just right, especially to keep Hotel company from getting left out to dry."

The false sense of sincere concern I tried to inject into that last bit went over like a fart in church, but I forged ahead, undeterred. "You can all make magical mobile mist, right?" I looked around the circle of nodding battle-magi. "Good, because once the bulk of the Gythraul roll in below these hills, you are going to pump out enough to blanket their position and have it start moving south."

"If we wait to engage until then, they will be dangerously close to our encampments which lie in a shallow valley beyond us," Bryth informed me, her face a stiff mask. "I gave the order to strike camp when we spotted the Gythraul advancing, but they will not be clear yet. That is why we have been cornered into this battle from the beginning."

"And if we drape them in mist, how will your soldiers effectively dispose of them?" queried a tall, female battle-magus with a fresh cut scabbing over her left eye. "They will not be able to see through the mist either."

"The infantry platoons won't advance toward the Gythraul until after the mist has begun to move farther south," I answered, jerking a thumb back toward the ranks of monsters behind me, "but by then, you'll be rolling up the carpet for those guys. Time for some Morgs in the mist."

5

___

CRUSHED

There is a pressure to magic—at least battlefield magic—that you can't really hear or feel. But the first few times you are around it, it messes with your inner ear and prickles across your skin.

I felt these familiar sensations play across my body as I stood next to the battle-magi summoning up the mist which congealed in the air in front of them. We were positioned just behind the crest of the central lump in that line of hills, listening to the sound of fellow soldiers running for their lives, snapping off shots at random as they retreated from the encroaching tromp of legionnaire boots. Behind us, the Morgs were herded into position, and became progressively more excited at the scent of blood and violence over the hill. Several sniffed constantly at the air, while others grunted and growled in anticipation.

The mist thickened, and I checked my M-Core over once before popping the hagseye in to get another bird's-eye view of the situation.

Things shaped up nicely on the northern side as I saw Bravo, Charlie, and Hotel sweep south around the cover of the hills to support Romeo and Sierra's firing line. Golf cleared the killzone with the massed cohort surging below the hills after us, no doubt making for where their scouts had told them the encampment was. The formations had been too forward and aggressive for it to be Ceterum Cinis leading. I imagined whoever their commander was, he was eager to prove his mettle by crushing the army that had blocked the great Cinis's march in the north. Right now, he probably thought he was having things all his own way, with his southern forces binding up our lines while his northern forces razed the encampment then swung down to squeeze the stubborn southern line into bite-sized pieces. I planned to show him the error of his ways.

The Morgs seemed terrifying enough, but charging across open terrain at a mass of Gythraul who could dig in behind their sheltering shields while sending up volleys of crossbow bolts was a good way to waste powerful assets. The Morgs would make it to their lines, maybe even kill a century or two, but eventually they would be brought down, bristling with shafts.

It wasn't going to be simple, though. I needed complete coverage from the mist and it was going to take a whole lot of magical mojo to get it. Beyond that, I needed the mist to move with us as we advanced, and that was going to take even more power, but all of this was going to funnel into doing what I had come to Other-Realm for—killing Gythraul.

I didn't want *some* Gythraul dead. I wanted the entire legion running scared over the bodies of their comrades while the rest of our forces took potshots at the rat bastards. And I needed my men to see me doing it, which is why, against more than one round of protest, I had insisted that I accompany the battle-magi as they moved along behind the Morgs.

The hagseye fell onto my chest, and I looked up to see the mist reaching critical mass. We would begin moving very soon.

"You don't need to come with us, you know," Bryth said, walking over to my left, ripples of wind gathered around her hands in preparation. "In fact, given what is at stake, you shouldn't come with us."

I turned back toward the wall of mist, raising the carbine to my shoulder, then held up a fist. Whips cracked and the line of Morgs shuffled forward.

"Lucius, please," Bryth stepped close enough that I could feel the air currents swirling around her, ruffling my hair. "I need you to know that—"

My fist dropped and the waiting battle-magi loosed the pent-up windstorms. I spared half a second to see tears in Bryth's eyes as she did the same, driving the blanket of fog before us. A trio of whip cracks and the Morgs were moving, low grunts rising into growls, then snarls, then roars.

The mists surged over the hill and the Morgs chased after it screaming, their handlers scurrying a whip-length behind. Loosing my own battlecry, I surged in after them along with the battle-magi. And Bryth.

The curtain of mist rolled and churned, driven forward by the magical wind, but not fast enough to stay completely ahead of our advance. We waded through a fog where the sounds of battle echoed around us in a weird, funhouse sort of way. Swallowed up in the mist, I wondered with cold, academic curiosity if the Morgs were truly capable of the violence I needed.

A few minutes later, following screams and roars down

the other side of the hill we found the first corpses, I learned how little I had to worry about such things.

The Gythraul had huddled together at first, interlocking shields and raising crossbows, but it only made them juicier targets. Some of the bodies looked like they had been flattened by trucks, limbs fallen in a splayed tangle and their torsos burst along a gory seam. Around these "points of impact" were more messy, mutilated forms. The air was thick with the smell of blood and spilt bowels; the ground had gone marshy in some places with the crimson juices of so many killed so savagely. As we moved forward, it became harder and harder not to plant your foot in a mashed mass of guts or feel the wet snap of bones through your boots.There were no survivors at first, just corpses and cast-off battle gear—all crushed, crumpled, and torn.

Another dozen yards and the corpses began to spread out, the ranks of Gythraul coming to the realization that their huddled formations weren't working. The belief in the Twilit Kingdom was that the Gythraul were absolutely fearless, and perhaps that was true, but they weren't innately suicidal. Whether because their officers had called for it, or as a general initiative at being slaughtered, the formations had broken, knots of soldiers striking out across the ground. Maybe they were searching for more defensible positions, or perhaps they were just trying to get out of the mist, but either way, we passed them in little clusters and trails where the rampaging Morgs had fallen on them as they ran.

Among the scattered drifts of dead bodies, past the smoking, twisted remains of a hellipede machine, I found my first survivor.

He crawled over the corpses of his comrades, one leg hanging ragged and red from hip to calf, the short, wide sword all Gythraul carried clenched in one fist. His back was to us, and with the strange way that sound murmured and rebounded in the mist, he didn't hear me until I drew the sword at my belt and stood over him. He turned at the sound, but the quick movement curled his whole body around his rent leg. His eyes didn't find me until my sword slid through his armpit, the fine point driven by the preternatural strength of the Gormstone. The metal links of his mail parted with hardly any resistance.

Looking up the length of the sword jutting out of his body, past my arm, he met my eyes. His helmet had been knocked free, and for the first time, I saw my enemy face to face. At first, with the mist swirling around, I thought he was human. His features were blunt but consistent proportionally within human norms and absent the stretched, unnatural grace of the Tuatha. For one long moment, I stared down at a square-featured man with olive skin and close-cropped black hair. It was only as he choked up blood that I saw teeth, far too pointed to be human, and small ridges of scale which ran along his jawline, temples and scalp. Then there were the small back-swept horns sprouting on either side of his brow. The examination complete, I put my boot onto his body, feeling his last blood-drowned breaths through my sabatons, and tugged my sword free.

My gaze swept around and I realized I had fallen out of line with the sorcerers. I could vaguely make out the battle-magi moving ahead of me asone paused to thrust a spear into a kneeling survivor. It seemed that no one had witnessed my action. Then I saw one tall figure, so still as to be almost invisible in the shifting, dreamlike world within the mist. Bryth Lighttread stared at me from across the mounded dead, her expression unreadable. As I looked at her, my feet carried me back into the line, and I realized something—I didn't care what her expression was, because

I didn't care what she thought. I had said no prisoners, after all.

Knowing how long we moved through the mist was difficult. The surreal, muffled experience, not dissimilar to passing along the Paths, was almost hypnotic. If I hadn't been so fixed on staying with the group, it would have been frighteningly easy to stagger around over the dead, dazed and drowsy, the sounds of battle rumbling distantly, like a far-off thunderstorm.

It helped that the concerns of command gnawed at the back of my mind. Had the Morgs stalled out just ahead? Were the infantry platoons ready to open fire from the hill line without killing us below? Would the mortar teams get their measures right? I had left Sleepyhead to communicate between platoons and the mortar and the Pixie spotter I had first used, but I wanted them to hold off until the mobile cover cleared.

The Gythraul beyond the our position needed to wonder what was happening to their brothers inside and not work to get dug in. I hoped that the screening fog opening over a swath of their comrades, the sounds of them being butchered by monsters, and then a thundering volley of rifle fire and shrieker shells would convince them that they were overrun. Fearless or not, confusion and an explosion of violence would send them reeling. At least that was what I hoped.

The battle-magi told me that as we moved farther from the hill, the magic ould diffuse and dissipate gradually. After a few hundred yards, the fog would be spotty enough for those outside the cloud to begin making out shapes and figures, and in another hundred yards or so, targets could begin to be identified.

I had stayed with the battle-magi as we walked in a loose line, pausing to put down a survivor here or there as the mist thinned. I put the point of my sword through the hearts and throats of half a dozen more legionnaires, refusing to waste a round on them when it could be helped. As our magical cover dissipated, I heard more of the butchery, and here and there saw the dread Morgs at work. I watched a monster swing its claws and tear the heads off two retreating legionnaires less than twenty yards from me—frighteningly close when I realized that seconds ago I hadn't seen them at all.

Another dozen steps and the thickened air became filmy and translucent. The sight of carnage was matched with the sound of bestial roars and frenzied cries, punctuated by whip cracks.

Most of the Morgs had kept their handlers, at a ratio of three beasts to one whip wielder, but some ranfree, loping gorilla-like towards the largest gatherings of legionnaires. Some put their heavy shoulders down and bowled into the enemies, scattering armored bodies like bowling pins before laying about with fist, claw, and fang. Others leapt into the air before crashing down like jagged, flailing meteorites. Gythraul bolts hung from their hides, and more than a few looked like hellish porcupines, but not one of them went down even as they were shot, stabbed, and hacked by the desperate legionnaires. Beyond, more Gythraul soldiers piled into the advancing ranks of their fellows, colliding as they tried to reorder themselves out of the reach of the monsters. Other centuries marched in support of those still trapped inside the mist.

The forward ranks of at least two centuries shuffled into a firing line, shields interlocked to the fore and bolts ready to arc over into our position. They would have opened fire already if not for the confusion of so many legionnaires retreating into their ranks. This was it.

My sword flashed up, gory and bright, my voice raised in a battlefield roar, "Magi! Now!"

Hearing the signal, those closest unleashed a final ripping torrent of wind and mist which raced into the faces of the legionnaires beyond. My field of vision cleared, the noonday light shining over a plain between the hills. The first third of the expanse was a churned stretch of carrion wreckage bound by a thin line where the Morgs still worked. The other two portions of the small field were filled with two full centuries struggling to get past the last of the survivors. The scene hung still for half a heartbeat before the chatter of M-Cores and the *whump-pop* of mortars sounded.

The Gythraul held their line as many fell in the first perforating volley of manticore quills. Then the shriekers came down, exploding into sonic whirlwinds, and the Gythraul's battle order began to collapse.

We'd drawn them in close so that those on the hill could keep up the crushing punishment, and the Morgs would pile into them in short order. When that happened, they would be ground into hamburger. Some of their officers saw the writing on the wall and called for a general withdrawal back along the hill. But then Golf company's skirmishers—whom I'd sent sweeping wide around the hills we had sheltered behind—rode the crest of the hill and unleashed a withering onslaught.

The Gythraul had only one direction to go, and, shedding bodies with every yard covered, they withdrew. The Morgs followed hard on their heels with whooping screams and cheers, the skirmishers ran alongside their flight.

"Come on!" I shouted to the battle-magi and turned to make for the line of hills overlooking the enemy's retreat.

I crested the rise and looked down to see the withdrawing centuries crashing into the other cohort that had been dug in trading shots with Romeo, Sierra, and all the retreating companies I had funnelled down to the south side of the battlefield.

The disorderly lines were easy prey for the Morgs. The beasts plunged in, showing not a trace of fatigue after all their bloody work. Shield lines fractured, and the Gythraul became easy prey for the disciplined bursts of carbine and djinn gunfire that awaited. Even the Gythraul's insect-like machines were of little use, their flames only enraging the Morgs who tore them apart with wild abandon. True, a few of the creatures succumbed to their injuries, but even as they fell, the savage beasts snapped and tore at any enemy within reach, some crawling on their bellies to get at another foe. The Gythraul line was coming apart, the entire legion sundering.

I socketed the hagseye and asked for a view of the battle-field, determined not to allow any unwelcome surprises to foul things up. Through the airborne Pixie's view I saw the crumbling centuries take their first staggering steps back on themselves, and even with the Gormstone I felt a fierce, glowing pride spring up.

As the Pixie panned across the steppe, that pride faltered when I spotted that the cavalry attachments—how could I forget about those?—had marshalled into one blunt wedge, nearly two hundred strong. They skirted the westward side of the battle, preparing to roll across the positions of the soldiers who were even now pouring fire onto what was left of the legion cohorts. They would smash through

Golf company, riding through or over them, before they rushed east and then south along the hills.

At the head of the massed cavalry formation, the Pixie's hawk-eyed vision picked out a Gythraul rider garbed in white armor and flanked by a contingent of mounted warriors in scarlet. So the Ceterum himself was going to turn the day, it seemed. I was about to be outflanked, and if I didn't throw a monkey wrench into the Ceterum's plans, I would end up with a pyrrhic victory, at best.

The hagseye fell away. Bryth was coming up the hill, the band of battle-magi with her.

"You guys have any juice left?" I asked urgently.

Bryth looked around for a second and then nodded.

"Good, because I need you to help me kill the Ceterum and two hundred cavalry." I refused to pause when I saw the incredulous looks spread across the Tuatha faces. Instead I pointed at where the cavalry was moving to charge down upon Golf company. "How many Morgs can you paratooper over those hills with that magical wind of yours?"

6

DETERMINED

Uzran and Droth did not make good time after leaving the river on their journey to Mount Falchrreg. Droth's wounds were healing, despite the travel, but the flames of the Gythraul machines had seared a painful venom into the Troll's body, and that cost him much of his strength and endurance. The roads were well maintained, and their packs were not heavy, but Droth could maintain the ground-devouring trot of the Royal Guard for less than an hour before he had to rest. As the sun set on their first day of foot travel, he was leaning heavily on a staff Uzran had cut for him from a hornbeam beside the road.

On the second night, they still had not reached the foot of the mountain though it loomed immense and white-crowned ahead of them. Stepping off the flagstones of the road, they took shelter under the boughs of a large oak. The tree sat a little way into the forest which grew about the soaring peak like a verdant skirt.

Neither bothered to strike a fire as their natural night vision functioned better than anything a lit torch could provide. They gnawed on hunks of smoked meat, each with his back to one side of the old, stalwart trunk. The sounds of the forest closed in around them as they chewed their cold meal. Bird and beast gave the interlopers a wide berth but were determined to be about their nightly business.

"Cap'n?" Droth said over his shoulder as he dug at his walking stick distractedly with one talon.

"What?" Uzran rumbled around a mouthful of meat so stiff and leathery that he was sure it must be either Sylvanocerous mutton or Bovigore shoulder.

"You'd do best to head out on yer own in the mornin'. I am slowin' you down too much. I know I said I could keep up, but bugger me if that damn fire didn't crisp me good. Quit playin' nursemaid and leave me."

Uzran swallowed the meat, uncertain if his chewing had done anything more than wear his teeth down, and rested his head against the tree.

"I told you to stay in Duanon and rest." The Ogre's voice was worn and more than a little rough with irritation. "But you were just too damned stubborn to listen."

Droth shifted his weight on the other side of the tree and Uzran heard more sounds of Troll talons gouging at wood.

"You did, Cap'n, and I certain-as-stone insisted I come, but you were right. I ain't doin' you any good, stumping along like some saddle-sore Gremlin."

Uzran smirked at the image, but raised his head off the trunk and looked over his shoulder toward Droth. "You at least going to explain why you thought you had to come before you throw up your hands in surrender?" He smirked again as he heard the Troll's claws gouge at the wood with a final barb. "And don't tear that crutch apart while you're at it. I'll not make you another."

"This staff be a fair walking stick, but a piss-poor crutch, if we're bein' honest, Cap'n," the Troll lieutenant observed, and blew some of the looser splinters off the notches he'd dug.

"Crutch or no, it'll serve as a club well enough if I have to beat answers out of you," Uzran growled, years of practice putting plenty of menace in his voice where none existed otherwise.

"Liable to break on my hard head, I'd wager." Droth ceased his digging at the hornbeam staff with an effort of will. "Truth is, Cap'n, I had lots of reasons to come with you."

Uzran waited a spell, but nothing save the night chorus came to ear. "Such as?" The first traces of actual frustration sharpened the question.

"Firstly, is to see if I could talk you out of it," the Troll said. "You haven't been to the Grand Thaig in centuries. We both know why, and we both know it's a good reason. So long as you exiled yerself, the clans could ignore yer . . . indiscretions . . . and keep sendin' their kith and kin off to join the Royal Guard. You coming back isn't just threatenin' to upend all that, but it puts the Thaig in the spot where they have to address what you did."

"How is that going?" Uzran asked with a quiet chuckle to himself.

"Well, it's goin' to be a damn sight harder once we part ways." Droth grunted as he settled into a more comfortable position against the tree. "But, I suppose you think you know what yer doin'. That, and you've always been stubborn, with little interest in what I, or any others save the Queen, thought was best."

"Should I apologize to your tender sensibilities?" Uzran snorted disdainfully. "And you can't really be talking about your schemes to displace the Paladin?"

"Well, they call him Gorm now—but what if I am, Cap'n? Might have kept you in favor a bit longer."

"And ended with me dead at the hands of Ceterum Cinis's praetorians," Uzran said flatly.

"Oh, are we not followin' the old 'death before dishonor' credo anymore, Cap'n?" Droth asked sardonically.

Uzran made to answer, but his jaws snapped shut, tusks giving a clack. He didn't have an answer to that question, his recently altered self not having weighed in for a summary judgment.

"What are your others reasons for burdening me with your weak legs and tireless mouth?" He drew out his whetstone and the broad knife he had used to cut Droth's stave.

There was a muffled grunt followed by ripping sounds, then the Troll answered him through a mouthful of unfamiliar meat. "Well, for protection, I suppose," he said matter-of-factly. "You seemed determined to not only lose the favor of the Court and Queen, but also to head to the one place in all of Other-Realm besides the Blight Isles where yer most unwelcome."

Uzran wanted to laugh at the thought of the bandage-wrapped Droth defending him, but the thought of Mount Falchrreg as enemy territory stifled the sound. As a child he had loved coming to the mountain for the Thaig gatherings and the old feasts, savoring the reminder that the old races—Ogres, Trolls, and Fomor—endured in a world that, though unkind, was still their home. It had been a constant source of pride and comfort, but now, as he finally returned to the place of those happy memories, he would be facing the very real possibility that he could be tried and executed. Technically the Thaig council needed to seek the Queen's blessing for such a thing, but they might forget that protocol if things went poorly.

"If things take that turn, I am ready to accept it," Uzran said grimly, as much to himself as to his companion.

"Damn it, Cap'n, why did you ask me along if this was just yer round about way of killin' yerself?" Droth made a lurching attempt to sit upright, then abandoned it with a grunt of pain. "I wouldn't've come if you'd told me you were off to get yourself spiked on the mountain."

Uzran sighed and sank back against the tree. "That isn't the plan, but since you've appointed yourself my protector, I thought you should know." The Ogre closed his eyes for a moment, feeling an incredible weariness settle over him. "I don't want you doing something foolhardy if the worst should happen."

"Plan? Things? What are you on about if it isn't suicide?"

"I am going to make things right," Uzran said, the words simple, even if the task described was not, "and I need you to help."

There was silence again. Uzran and Droth stared at the yawning dark between the trees where the occasional creature flitted or scurried by on some nocturnal errand. "So this isn't a recruitin' trip then?" Droth asked at last.

"No. It isn't."

"And yer not going to leave me to go on ahead?"

"No," Uzran sighed wearily, "we'll be late, but not late enough to matter."

More silence, then the Troll's voice rang out in one last, irritated query. "Well, if yer so dead determined on goin' and need me to boot, why waste all that breath about me not comin' in the first place?"

"Force of habit, I suppose." Uzran smiled, as he settled in to be lulled to sleep by his friend's angry grumbling.

7

BECKONED

It hadn't been nearly as quick as I wanted––snatching up some of the Morgs and their handlers on the rear of the carnage. Some of the handlers acted terrified at the idea of being transported by magic. One went so far as to throw himself on the ground at my feet and beg that he not be asked to trust "such ill-winds." But internally, the countdown was ticking off seconds until the apocalyptic cavalry charge I had no time for debate.

As the rodentious little beast-handler knelt at my feet, I shoved the barrel of my carbine into his open mouth. It was still warm from potshots taken at retreating legionnaires, but it not quite hot enough to sear flesh on contact. The handler gave a terrified squeak around the length of metal puckering his snout, looking up at me with tearful, beady eyes.

"Get up, or get put down." My voice was so low and cold it sounded alien in my own ears. The handler, and his nearby fellows to boot, surrendered with nods of desperate acceptance.

With a few barked orders, we rallied nearly two dozen of

the bloodstained monsters that seemed fit enough for a fresh fight. Bryth asked if it was enough, to which I replied that it would have to be, and gave the order to get moving.

The strain on the remaining eight battle-magi was more than I'd ever seen, and that included the time when they dropped part of a mountain on Ceterum Cinis's legion. More than once in those few hair-raising seconds in the air, I saw bemused Morgs wobble in the draft of tempest wind. Only with a snarling, cursing effort did the responsible Tuatha keep them from plummeting to the dirt some hundred feet below. There was an instant when I wondered if they would have the strength to fight alongside the dread Morgs, but a chilly voice answered my musing with a simple response, as certain as any mathematical proof: if they can fight they may live, and if not, they will die. The arithmetic of war had been part of my life for years, but even with the Gormstone, I found the pronounced equation quietly maddening.

But then we came down on the other side of the hills, fast, and the broadside of the cavalry formation was right there. M-Core in my hands, I snapped off shots at the closest mounted warriors as the battle-magi released their payload of tooth and claw. On seeing the enemy, some of the Morgs tried to run in midair, their limbs churning the magical winds before they came down in great plumes of moondust. Some landed and fell down the slope, but they rolled into the fall like two-ton acrobats, turning the tumble into an arcing leap. The Gythraul had enough time to see what was coming, but, riding in close formation and with forward momentum, they couldn't turn and face the approaching doom. Lances and lizard legs tangled, and the center of the formation stalled and collapsed even before the attack hit home. And when it did, you would have thought a bomb had gone off.

In good old American, gridiron football, when two players collide—I mean really hit hard— a stadium full of screaming fans can hear a distinct popping sound. It makes people wince, then cheer even louder. A Morg is eight to ten times the size of a football player, and with the tempest winds driving them at forty or fifty miles an hour, the sound of twenty-three such collisions happening at once formed a sonic sledgehammer. Or maybe it was just my ears, because instead of a succession of explosive pops, I heard a single, roaring boom.

The nearest line of cavalry, riders and mounts, were smashed into crumpled detritus and either thrown clear or ground into the dirt. It didn't even slow the Morgs as they plunged in. Claws like sickles of bone raked left and right in sweeping attacks, armor and bony scales parted, and bodies burst like rotten fruit. The handlers jogged along behind their charges, snapping whips, but the monsters needed little direction as they reaped a red harvest. Even a few of the rat-faced creatures got in on the action as they fell on crippled survivors with plunging knives.

Some of the riders triggered flame-throwing lances, but tangled in the thicket of their comrades' weapon shafts, eruptions of fire and smoke flashed harmlessly into the air. The lance blasts served to mark where another Gythraul cavalier was dying under the rending grip of a roaring Morg.

The fiery eruptions, combined with the bursts of blood and the screams of the dying, turned the narrow valley into a hellscape, and I took the whole scene in with grim satisfaction as we touched down on the top of the slope. "This is the work of my hands." The words tore loose in that terrible moment of black exultation. For the first time in my life, I reveled in the destructive power of my will, free of conscience and fear of judgment. I imagined that Genghis Khan and Conan might have said something like this. It seemed that the Gormstone didn't eat up everything inside you after all.

"Luce!" A voice screamed, and I was shaken from my musings by what Bryth was pointing out down the line of riders to the forward edge. The Ceterum, his bodyguards, and a few other riders had broken off from the imploding formation. Less than twenty of them remained—not enough to turn the tables—but my pride was offended that the defeated refused to roll over and die. Even if they were in retreat, I could not let him escape. He needed to be punished for daring to face me.

"Cut him off, and get us over there now!" I shouted at the exhausted battle-magi whose noses, lips, and eyes were still dripping red from the exertion of delivering the Morgs. For a heartbeat, I saw resistance, but what they glimpsed in my eyes made them reconsider. With a single, bracing breath, the tension of magic filled the air again.

The tempest winds rose, and again I sailed after the Ceterum and his attachment. Three of the battle-magi pulled ahead of us, darting forward on howling winds, angling for a parabolic intercept course. The Gythraul riders saw just in time and hauled back on their mounts as the battle-magi unleashed curses in a crackling arc in front of the escapees. Jagged spurs of stone and crystal erupted from the dust in a semicircle, forcing the Ceterum and his warriors to halt or impale their mounts on the spikes. Two of the riders couldn't bring their mounts around in time and were thrown to the ground as their reptilian steeds drove themselves onto the waiting fangs of stone. The three battle-magi fell out of the air just past the spines of rock, landing without grace and lying or kneeling on the ground, utterly spent.

Midair, I pumped off three bursts of carbine fire into the knot of huddled cavalry before the winds took me up and over the fence of spikes. Slamming a fresh clip of manticore quills home, I landed to the right of where they were corralled. The riders, the Ceterum in his glittering white armor at their head, tried to shuffle their mounts around the stones. They drew up short as they saw me, flanked by the remaining five battle-magi, blocking their path. We were only a short charge beyond the reach of their fire-breathing lances, but my rifle was pointed right at their leader, and even if the magic of Other-Realm hadn't given us a common tongue, the message was clear.

One of the red-armored bodyguards tried to interpose himself between me and his commander, edging his mount forward. Two quills cracked free from my weapon to nestle in his lizard's chest. The beast gave a gurgling hiss and collapsed, the bodyguard barely managing to roll clear of the carcass. The other riders stirred and shuffled, but their commander held them with a word and an upraised fist.

"Dismount and disarm," I called, my aim returned to the Ceterum.

The white dragon helm regarded me for a few tense seconds then called out from within his enclosing helmet. "You are the Paladin then?"

"Gorm Lucius Bollham," I answered, mildly irritated by how the new title tugged on something sore in my chest. "Commander of the Queen's Armies, Champion of the Twilit Kingdom."

The Ceterum considered my words, looking across the ragged line stretched before him. "I am Ceterum Lacertun, and I can see your sorcerers are spent, Lucius," he said, almost conversationally. "If they had their full strength, maybe things would be different, but as it stands, if we charge, it will be you alone standing between us and escape, and you won't be standing long."

I didn't dare steal a look around, but I had seen the drooping stances of the battle-magi as they landed around me. Too much magic, too fast. I was lucky they were still vertical, and even with a few more riders without mounts or dead on the ground, they had double our number on their feet. "Maybe." I smiled,showing my teeth, "maybe not. But one thing is sure, you won't make it two steps without basilisk venom smoking inside your skull."

Angry mutters rose from warriors around the Ceterum, but a stiffening in his posture was all it took to silence them. "My life is not so precious that I wouldn't trade it for my men," he replied, handing his lance to a rider beside him. "If you share such honor, then I beckon you to face me in single combat. Whoever falls, their warriors give way to the will of the other."

A duel? Was he for real? Right here on the battlefield? He was leaning over the horn of his saddle now, watching me, and I took the moment to snatch a quick look at the battle-magi on either side of me. It wasn't good.

None of them seemed capable of standing upright, and blood ran freely on their faces. Their weapons were in their hands, but hung at their sides, too heavy for their tired arms to raise except at the utmost need. I hadn't realized how exhausted they were—hadn't cared—in my lust to cut off the Ceterum's retreat.

Beyond the riders farther up the valley, I heard the Morgs roaring as more Gythraul died. Could I stall him here long enough for those monsters to get up here and handle the situation for me?

"Best hurry," Lacertun warned, as though reading my thoughts. "Soon your pets will be coming, and we will have no choice but to ride you and your sorcerers down."

"Damn it," I cursed under my breath and stole another sidelong glance at my wilting entourage. Useless now, but each battle-magi was precious not only for their tactical magic, but for their strategic value in the opening of Paths. I had really just put eight of my most valuable eggs in one fragile basket.

"Alright," I called, gesturing toward the massive reptile under him with the barrel of my carbine. "I assume you want me to put this down as you hop off your lizard?"

"Naturally." Lacertun swung one leg over as a show of good faith.

I unslung the M-Core and gingerly handed it to the battle-magus on my right, a crimson-teared Bryth.

"Luce, please," she panted hoarsely, every word a burden. "Be careful."

I suppose the last she knew, I had been about as hopeless a swordsman as you could find, but training with Uzran had changed that. Whether it was the Gormstone or the confidence born of dueling Uzran every day, facing this guy seemed like just another obstacle to total victory. Today, I was smashing such obstacles.

"I will be back for this," I said, turning to the Ceterum and yanking my sword from its blood-clogged scabbard. Uzran had warned me about that, but damn it, I'd been busy.

Ceterum Lacertun was on foot now, one armored fist wrapped around the short, wide sword of the Gythraul legion. In his other hand, he held a round disk of metal, little bigger than a dinner plate, with a raised center where he gripped an internal handle. What Uzran called a buckler,

I thought. He advanced, arms out so I could see his ornately wrought, marble-toned breastplate with rows of coins fixed across the chest.

I moved forward, feeling the comfortable way the sword flowed from my arm, through my hand, and down the length of metal to its stabbing point. I smiled noting that my sword was a good foot longer than his. With a longer hilt, I could take a two-hand stance to rain powerful blows down on him. Already I liked my chances.

"Size matters," I smirked, but the Gythraul didn't even flinch.

"I am not sure if the witch-lovers told you about such things," Lacertun began as we came to the midpoint between our opposing sides. "Each of these commemorates my personal defeat of one of your Royal Guards." He tapped his buckler against one of the coins on his breastplate with a blunt klink. Nine coins glittered in the dulling light of the afternoon.

"I am going to end you," I said flatly, hoisting the sword into guard.

Lacertun laughed and raised his buckler and sword to the ready. "I like you, boy. A shame you'll be dead soon."

Unspoken assent passed between us, and the duel began. Despite his armored bulk, the Ceterum was quick to attack, his stabbing sword lunging in at me, each thrust sheltering under the guarding buckler. I worked my feet backwards, giving ground steadily as I brought my sword around in counter-cuts that drove off the probing sword, never finding purchase as the curve of the buckler deflected the brunt of the swing.

He knew I had the longer blade and wouldn't let me use my reach. If he worked his way inside, he would gut me like a fish. I had to create some space then go to town on him, without losing my feet. A warrior on the ground was a warrior either dead or dying, whether he realized it or not. Uzran had taught me that.

My feet shuffled in the dust as I backed, turned, and swiveled, but he kept coming, his sword darting forward over and over. A second of panic tightened my throat, I felt suffocated by his relentless attacks, entrapped by the ceaseless assault. He was so close and so quick I was going to miss eventually, then he would have me.

Timing. Timing is better than speed or strength or anything else. The instruction cut through my mind's babble, and suddenly I saw it just as Lacertun lunged forward again. There was a rhythm to his advances—a cadence to the movement of his entire body. In a flash that was so clear and distinct—like I was viewing things in freezeframe—I saw when my shot would be. I set aside another thrust and timed a swiveling turn off the next stab.

The blade of my sword turned the thrust aside, but my well-timed swivel drove the hilt of my sword along with my armored fist into the side of his helmet. The Ceterum's head snapped hard to the side with a crunch, and part of the dragon jaw of the sculpted helmet cave in.

Lacertun staggered back, sword sweeping back and forth in warding slashes as he tried to gather his rattled senses. Scenting the kill, I swatted the sword aside and brought my weapon around in an overhand chop which would fall diagonally to the lines of his neck and shoulder. Even if I didn't cleave into flesh, the force of the blow would snap his collarbone like a twig.

Too bad I had forgotten about the buckler.

His half-blind haymaker scudded the lip of the little shield across my cheek and the bridge of my nose instead of my throat or eyes. As it was, I fell back, barely keeping my feet and sword in order as pain exploded across my face and tears blurred my vision. I wondered why my face was wet, and a second later, my nose and mouth were choking on blood.

Shaking my head and spitting into the dirt, I looked blearily at Lacertun. He had torn his helmet off, and from the way one part of his jaw hung lower than the other, I imagined it was broken. His eyes blazed russet and blood-shot with pain and anger, looking like iron glowing in a fire. Nodding though it made him wince, he advanced with sword and buckler up. He was one tough son of a bitch.

I expelled another jet of bloody spittle and moved to meet him. A cold fury sprang up in my belly, filling my muscles with shivering surges of strength. How dare he strike at me?

Before he could close for more pressing stabs, my sword came around in one scything swing. The rational part of my mind screamed "Be careful!" lest I end up gassed from the effort of a drawn-out battle, but the roaring rush of blood in my ears drowned it out. The Gormstone was so cold in my chest that it burned like frigid fire.

One stroke shivered the buckler's edge, the tortured metal catching a little on my blade before letting go and throwing the Ceterum off balance. I pulled the blade upward in a cleaving arc that he tried to deflect with his sword, but his blade snapped, and my swing lodged itself right under his armpit. I tore the point free with a scattering of blood and shorn rings of metal, leaving the Gythraul's arm hanging limp and bloodied at his side. Without pause, I brought the length of my sword level to my shoulder, and thrust. The tip plunged into his throat, just above the gorget, splitting the collared links of mail in front and then the rear as the red tongue of metal burst out the back of Lacertun's neck.

He hung for a second on the point of my sword, made one feeble swing with his shivered buckler, then collapsed with a wet, choking sound. Blood frothed on his lips and between his sharp teeth as my sword slid free, surrendering him to the ground. He met my eyes one last time, flashes of emotion coming and going so quickly it was impossible to track what each one meant. He shuddered once more, pitching onto his side and gurgling up more blood which spilled down his chin and into his ruined throat, and he was gone. Dead eyes contemplated the stained moondust in front of his slackening face.

The burning of the Gormstone subsided, and my arms trembled with fatigue, but nothing else. Anywhere.

The head of Ceterum Lacertun made a soggy melon sound as I drove it down on the spear planted at center of the camp. The trophy stood next to the twisted remains of a hellipede and the detached head of one of the Gythraul's lizard mounts. All around me a hearty cheer rose from my soldiers basking in the gory fruits of our victory. My victory.

The companies from the mountains—Echo, Foxtrot, Igloo, and Juliet—were stationed around the hills surrounding the encampment keeping watch after missing the battle. That left nearly nine full companies gathering in this valley for a brief "celebration."

"Gorm! Gorm! Gorm!" they chanted over and over again as I turned around slowly, drinking in as many of their hungry cheers as I could. God knows it was better than the emptiness I felt otherwise.

I raised a fist for silence, and they quieted, their eyes watching eagerly. Two whole legions may be encamped only miles away from where we now stood, but today, their commander had led them to victory, and they wanted to know that it was just the start. Less than half of them had been at the Valley of Luchath, and those who had knew how close it had been.

"Victory builds on victory; momentum carries conquerors from one height to the next," I bellowed so that all could hear, though I was hoarse from battle. "At every turn, the Gythraul come at us with more tricks and more schemes, but we throw them down time and time again." They couldn't contain themselves, another cheer rose up, ragged and brazen.

"Two legions have fallen at your feet now, and we are only getting stronger," I shouted once they finally fell to self-congratulating murmurs. "Every day more of your brothers-in-arms emerge from training, ready to join the fight, while new weapons from the Far-Hold bring us more opportunities to crush those who dare to stand before us." I swept my arm toward the remaining dread Morgs now shackled and tended to by their handlers; they paused to snap their whips by way of salute. The beasts, many still with bolts and skorpion shrapnel lodged in their flesh, looked up dumbly before continuing to lick their wounds.

"If a few Morgs, supported by honored battle-magi, can turn an entire legion to flight, what hope do all the armies of the Blight Isles have when we drown them in fire from the skies and ordnance from the ground?"

The gathered soldiers knew, and proudly shouted the answer . . . "None." Their voices grew rabid. They were going to grease the coast of the Forgotten Sea with Gythraul blood, just watch.

"I told those of you with me from the beginning that a new age was coming, didn't I?" I raised my hands high. "I know some of you doubted, but I said that the time had come to throw off the old ways and seize victory with two bloody hands. Do you still doubt my words?"

My hands swept down to the Gythraul kneeling beneath the empty gaze of their Ceterum's head. Their faces were set into grim, downcast expressions, but one or two looked around furtively. You could smell their fear. The Twilit Kingdom's policy on prisoners of war had changed with whoever led them in this centuries-spanning war. They awaited their fate on their knees. The crowd quieted after I raised my fist, and I stepped down from the mounded earth under the war trophies to stand over the first rank of defeated legionnaires.

"Now, to handle the leftovers," I said, letting the laughter and jeers wash over the prisoners. "Can you tell me?" My voice was filled with a venom that was as absent in my heart as it was hot on my tongue. I looked down at the captured soldiers. "Did they show mercy when they invaded your lands?"

"No!" the soldiers snarled in unison.

"Did they stay their hand when they came upon your friends fleeing for their lives?"

"No!" they roared, their cries forming one bestial voice.

"Did they listen to the calls for peace when your loved ones were at their feet?"

"NO!" they screamed, ready to explode.

I turned from the kneeling legionnaires to look at their inward-leaning faces; they were holding their breath.

"Then why should we?"

I was debriefing with the captains of the companies present at the battle when Grimple Guthook strode into the command pavilion. The screams of the Gythraul and the laughter of my soldiers followed her inside before the flap fell back into place, reducing the sounds to muffled babbles.

"Yer idea of a party, Luce?" She hooked a thumb back the way she came. Her amber eyes were unreadable, but something in her voice expressed a mild, almost bored disappointment.

"My idea of rewarding the loyal," I said coolly, standing up from the table where maps of the central steppes were stretched out. "Maybe instead of being critical of my command methods, you should explain why you have been out of touch with Bryth and now me for the past few days? Oh, and while you're at it, explain why you didn't give any signal that an entire legion of Gythraul were on the move?"

Grimple shrugged as she came to lean against one leg of the table, cocking her head over its surface to give the maps a sidelong glance before looking back at me.

"Thought they were just repositionin', my teams were elsewhere, and anyways, that seems like a report I should make to Bryth." She sniffed and then pretended to look around the tent with concern. "Where is Twinkle-Toes anyway?"

"Recovering from magical fatigue after the battle *she* fought," Kieren said at my shoulder, his tone sharp and shrill, "and while she is your *superior* officer, Gorm Bollham is commander of all her Majesty's forces, so answer the question, scumborn."

Despite myself I smirked at Kieren's zealous defense of Bryth's honor and mine, but then I saw the cold, humorless smile on Grimple's face and knew I needed to settle things down fast. It didn't matter that she was four feet tall and barely more than eighty pounds; with a smile like that, Grimple was going to kick the shit out of Kieren.

"Squire," I said with clear authority, drawing not just his

attention but that of everyone else in the room, "'please escort the captains to the Quartermaster's tent for some wine, and finish the debriefings there."

Kieren looked like he was about to fire one parting shot at the Goblin underboss but thought better of it. With a stiff nod, he bid all the company commanders to follow him to some refreshments. Murmuring assent and distracted words of farewell, the captains shuffled out with their attending staff. Grimple and I were left in the tent with two of the animated dead standing off to the side in case we should need their services.

"I knew working with an underboss would have its own challenges," I commented, looking where she stood with her arms crossed, leaning against the table, "but I would have thought someone like you would at least understand the importance of hierarchy and respect."

Grimple snorted up a wad of phlegm and spat it toward the corner before rolling her eyes. "Bugger me, Luce, I figured that rock between your tits would make yer cold, but I didn't figure it would make yer a stiff prick, too."

I smiled out of habit rather than actual amusement and leaned over the table towards her.

"I am not going to threaten you, but I am not going to waste time bantering either," I said flatly, hoping she didn't press things further. "If you didn't come in here to report for your screw-ups, what did you come here for?"

Grimple blew a raspberry and gave a petulant shrug. "Well, you're no fun anymore," she said with a pout, her tone more childish than I would have thought possible for her rough voice. "Cold and prickly as the Queen's quim— that's the new Luce now."

I wanted to laugh at that one, but the Gormstone had eaten up the part of me that could laugh naturally unless I was watching my enemies driven before me. Now a soft, hissing sound between my teeth was all I could manage. "I am still waiting for the part where you tell me what you were doing before, and why you are here now," I said after an abortive flirtation with the hissing thing.

"Well, my Gorm," she sketched a dainty curtsy before resuming her slouch, "I was runnin' my teams around the Kindled River, thank yer very much, tryin' to gather info and stir up trouble like a good li'l Goblin commando, when suddenly one of my Finger teams got themselves captured."

I quickened at that, not caring so much that some Goblins were at risk, but more at what the slippery creatures might share to escape from such a situation.

"So you were mounting a rescue then?" I watched her expression warily, looking for any sign of subterfuge. In the days before the Gormstone, Grimple was the latecomer to the war council, and while competent and ingenious in her unconventional way, she seemed the one most capable of deceit and the one I had the least reason to trust. Nothing had changed since then, other than learning that she wasn't the only liar.

"Wyrm's hole, no!" she exclaimed, rolling her eyes again. "What a bung-popper that would've been! No, I asks Cinis what he wants for the return of my boys, I does."

Sometimes lacking normal emotional responses comes in handy, and this was one of those times. Before I might have grabbed her and shaken her angrily for communicating with the enemy. That would probably have resulted in losing a finger or five, and I was relieved that, though agitation was simmering somewhere in what was left of my psyche, I could use my words in response to her declaration. "What did he ask?" I asked, stonily.

"To meet with yer, of all things," Grimple said, sounding bored. "Beckons yer to a parley or some such nonsense."

That was unexpected, and it took me a second to form a reply. "I meet with him, and he'll let the team go?" I was incredulous. "I trust Cinis as much as a fart when I got the runs."

Grimple nodded and shrugged. "Told 'im as much, so he says he's goin' to make a pledge of good faith, and then just like that, he returns my boys safe and sound, quick as yer like."

That wasn't nothing, given the fits that Grimple and her Finger teams gave Cinis and his legionnaires as they retreated from the mountains to the steppes. The Ceterum knew even a single team could be responsible for the deaths of hundreds of his men, and they would eagerly report on anything they had seen while in captivity. Cinis must really want this sit-down, but why now? "Was all this before or after the battle today?" I asked.

"More during, really," Grimple said picking at her nails with a thumb. "Seems he knew you were comin' and you'd win somehow, and wanted you to know that Ceterum Lacertun's attack was not his plan. He still wants yer to meet, before the rest of his forces and our forces show up. Says if yer wait till then it will be too late."

"Too late for what?"

"Didn't say." Grimple rose from her slouch and looked up at me, arms still crossed.

"Why does he want to meet?"

"Didn't say."

I looked down at the Goblin who just stared up. She tapped her foot impatiently.

"Well, what do you want me to tell him, already?"

8

EXPOSED

The meeting place was a steep-sided, flat-topped hill with aspirations to be a full-blown mesa one day. It was almost a day's ride west from either of our camps. On a map, you could see that it was actually a good deal closer to our farthest positions, but it was as close to neutral ground as I was going to allow.

Though Grimple's teams and reports from Wee Folk for miles around confirmed that–– besides Cinis and his two bodyguards––there were no other Gythraul, I found my back itching as if a target was painted on it. "So help me, Grimple, if this is a trap," I growled under my breath as I walked toward the cliff where the Ceterum and his body-guards stood.

"Enough of yer grousin'," she chided absently and pointed toward the waiting Gythraul. "Get over there and see what the nice, li'l warlord wants."

I looked at my entourage and was comforted to know that if something did go foul, Cinis and his legionnaires would be dead in an instant.

The Ceterum said he would bring two bodyguards and

hadn't objected when I promptly told him I would bring more. Just for spite, I wanted to bring an entire platoon, but I supposed if Cinis saw that many soldiers on the hill, he would scuttle back the way he came. Instead—besides Sleepyhead who went everywhere with me—I settled for a marksman team from Echo company, four of the best war-painted little psychos I'd ever trained, as well as Hurrahn, the Fomor Royal Guard, and finally Bryth. I didn't ask the recently-recovered Bryth to take that last position, but on the day we left, the other battle-magi were suddenly absent or indisposed. Cursing all the way through the Path, our little party made its way to the hill.

"We still all clear, Sleepy?" I asked the oversized, bright-winged salamander draped around my neck.

"Clear, Master," he gurgled softly, his head bobbing a little before settling back down on my shoulder.

Ever since the Gormstone, I hadn't let Sleepyhead this close, but I wanted instant access to the network of Wee Folk viewers and informants, and the Bogle was determined to enjoy his old spot, no matter the reason. As we walked toward Cinis—the team from Echo positioned themselves around the hill— I wondered if things had been hard on my little Bogle since the Gormstone. Intellectually, I conceded that they had been, but followed with another question—why should I care?

"I don't think Ceterum Cinis means to deceive us," Bryth said softly as we advanced. "If anything, he is more at risk of being declared a traitor by his own for doing this. In all the annals of our people, there is no record of peaceful meetings with any Gythraul leader. Ever."

"That may be true." I looked over my shoulder into Bryth's face. "But it seems lately I am having a hard time trusting anyone." Bryth stiffened and lowered her gaze.

We marched in silence until we were a stone's throw from where Cinis stood, his white armor glinting in the pale morning sun. His helmet was off, and his almost- human face greeted me with an easy smile that spread across open and intelligent features. It was the first time I had seen him unmasked.

"Greetings, Paladin Lucius Bollham," he called in his rich, silky voice. "I truly appreciate the honor you do me in meeting peacefully."

I had my M-Core in my hands, and while I didn't raise the barrel, I put the stock up to my shoulder meaningfully before I spoke. "Whether it remains peaceful is up to you, Cinis." I fought the urge to look around the hilltop one more time. "Why don't you say your piece, so I can tell you where to stick it. Then we can leave here quietly and go back to killing each other."

"Very diplomatic," Grimple muttered. I didn't need to see her face to know her eyes rolled with disgust.

"Could we, perhaps, have this conversation at a distance where we don't need to shout at each other?" Ceterum held up his hand plaintively. "As I am sure you have confirmed, you have us completely at your mercy."

"Sleepy, we still good?" I whispered as I stared across the dusty stretch at the slippery Ceterum.

"Yes, Master, no enemy," the Bogle said with a chirping croak.

"What about your teams, Grimple?" I didn't take my eyes from the Gythraul.

"If anythin' was stirrin', Cinis would be dead already," Grimple said confidently. "And before yer ask, I already got the all clear sign from the shooters from Echo."

Even if I didn't trust Grimple enough to confirm with

Echo's marksmen, I figured Hurrahn or Bryth would say something if she was lying, and neither said a word.

"Alright, fine," I huffed.

The others followed along beside me, and I felt the air thicken as Bryth gathered magic to her. For all her talk of Cinis's sincerity, she wasn't taking any chances, either.

We moved to within spitting distance of the Gythraul, Cinis still holding up his hands, his helmet's draconic visor watching us impassively. The hand bearing the helmet gestured to the ground between us.

"May we sit together?" he asked cautiously, his smile replaced by a somber, concerned expression.

"If you want to plant your ass in the dirt, go right ahead." I nodded at the aforementioned earth.

"No need for that, Paladin." He pointed and his two bodyguards produced triangular camp chairs—the kind composed of stout sticks with a stretch of canvas between them. With carefully modulated movements, they gingerly placed the two chairs in front of us.

"Please, join me." Cinis lowered himself into the seat.

I took one last look around, casually ignoring the encouraging nod Bryth gave me, and moved to take a seat. The chair was lower than an average man would prefer, and so for someone tall like me, it was a struggle to sit without falling over, much less be graceful about it. As I stiffly settled in, I noted Cinis discreetly looking elsewhere, politely refraining from witnessing my awkwardness. What a bastard, huh?

"Again, Paladin Bollham, I am honored to meet with you here," Cinis said once I seemed unlikely to topple off my seat. He sounded like he was about to dive into a practiced speech, but I cut him off before he could build up steam.

"It's Gorm, now," I corrected, not really caring about the title but glad to keep my enemy off rhythm, "not Paladin."

Cinis paused, staring at me, his fingers beating a little tattoo across the helmet on his knees, then he bobbed his head deferentially.

"My apologies, Gorm Bollham, I was not aware of the change." He sounded so sincere that I wanted to smack him across the face. "I heard a similar title only once regarding a former champion of Queen Meabh, but you must excuse my ignorance of its significance. I assume after your victory, it is a promotion of some sort?"

I realized that he was honestly asking a question and resigned myself to being more civil than I had first intended. Being belligerent and taciturn was only going to drag things out and give him more opportunities to screw me over.

"Of sorts, yes," I lied. "But that is not why we are here, Cinis, so I would be more comfortable addressing that point."

His bodyguards stiffened, and his smile turned glassy, but for the life of me I couldn't tell what my offense was.

"Yes, to the point then," the Ceterum said, the artificial sheen of his smile melting into another genuine, if sharp-toothed, grin. "Gorm Bollham, I asked to meet with you after offering evidence of my sincerity and good faith, for one single purpose. It is one about which you will no doubt be incredulous, but I must assure you, I am sincere in my desire to bring this conversation to an arrangement acceptable for both of us. I pledge this to you, as a commander I have grown to respect."

I sat watching him for a heartbeat, then gave a slow nod to continue.

"I wish this conversation to be the opening dialogue for

the negotiated surrender of the Estranged Republic to the Twilit Kingdom."

Wow.

Bryth gave a soft gasp of disbelieving surprise behind me, while Grimple issued an amused chuckle.

"Well, tickle my tits," the Goblin hissed amid laughter that threatened to break into a full-blown cackle.

"Are you serious?" as I supposed to be angry because he was mocking me, or grateful? I settled for surprised. "You want to surrender?"

"Not just me and those I command, but our entire government," Cinis said with a sweep of his arm. "I am here to end the war that has claimed so many of both our peoples."

Of all the things we might talk about, this was not one I had considered.

"And you are ending the war by surrendering?" I was hardly able to believe what I was hearing.

"Yes, Gorm Bollham." Cinis answered, and we both sat there for a moment studying each other.

Ceterum Cinis sat quietly, and though he was composed and smiling, his posture was stiff and his pointed teeth worked against each other. He wasn't happy, but he was doing his damnedest to keep a calm, cool face.

"I have to be honest, Cinis," I began, and again I saw the tension in his bodyguards. That is when I realized I had not used his title once, while he had never *not* used mine.

"I mean, Ceterum Cinis," I began again. His men visibly relaxed at the courtesy. "I find this a little hard to believe, even with your insistence and show of good faith. For months I've been told how your people have an iron will, and though they are not the battlefield bogeymen some described, they are proud and determined at least. You want me to believe they are just going to roll over?"

Whatever goodwill I had won with the bodyguards by using the title vanished. Their bodies twitched with agitated energy after I mentioned rolling over. But true to form, Cinis took it with a smile.

"My people are proud, and while this surrender would not be unconditional, our people have known since we were driven to the Blight Isles that this day might come."

Not unconditional. I knew this wouldn't be that easy, and maybe I was sniffing a bit too much of my own press ink, but the growing desire for dominion since the last battle chafed at the idea of the defeated putting conditions on accepting their status.

"Tell me this then, Ceterum Cinis," I asked, staring defiantly into his dark eyes, "knowing that your people are ready to fold, why should I bother with any of your conditions?".

The bodyguards twitched some more, and I saw more glass in Cinis's expression before he calmly replied.

"Because not all of my people are willing to surrender." His smile slid into a kind of grim earnestness. "The truth is that while I have enough influence to sway many on the Senate, the kind of support needed to guarantee an end to this war will only be possible if I can bring assurances that the surrender will cause as little humiliation as possible."

"If you wanted peace, why did you start a fresh round of invasions?" I pressed, suspicion honing my words.

"In part because it is has become a tradition, and in part because our Senate needed to see that the often proclaimed victory was no closer than it has ever been," he said simply. "We have been fighting for so long that, to many, it is just the way things are. I think after these last two defeats, I can get them to see that, if anything, we are moving further from any such victory."

A thought came out of my mouth before I could stop and think it over. "So you lost the last two battles on purpose?" I felt my face redden as much with the petulance in my voice as at what the words implied.

"Never!" Cinis bristled. "Whatever my aspirations, I would never have let you slaughter my men to make a point. I faced you as I would any enemy of the Republic."

Maybe it was the fact that he actually called his soldiers men, or hearing the word Republic again, but a half-formed suspicion squirmed in the back of my mind. The Gythraul, like the Tuatha, were not natives of Other-Realm.

"If things are so desperate you are willing to give up on thousands of years of war, why should I be worried about your people making further attacks?" I tried to quiet the nibbling thoughts. "If it is just a matter of time, why shouldn't I wait you out?"

Cinis nodded, accepting the point, but pointed east toward the Kindled River. "I have two full legions and the remains of two others—more than a full cohort," he said, his voice flat and without menace, yet still a touch chilling for all that. "Even now, another legion bearing the most potent and terrible weapons we possess, is preparing to cross from the Isles within a week. Another legion holds the Isles, and if the reserves and home guards are called up, a further two legions could be mustered within a month."

I was doing the math in my head—three to four thousand strong each—to my nineteen companies. The numbers were small compared to the bloated armies of Earth, but here, they were plenty to keep me busy. Either way, that many legions marching across the continent guaranteed we wouldn't be able to stop them all before they inflicted serious damage, and that assumed they didn't get wise to our game and turn the tables.

"I am not threatening you, Gorm Bollham," he said with impeccable, icy calm. "I am explaining the realities of what we both face. My people have stockpiled arms and supplies to wage war for another century, maybe two, but the Isles and what lands we could reach beyond them are stripped bare. The Senate knows that our time has grown short, and if I cannot bring them a chance to surrender in honor, those with fatalistic ambitions, those like Ceterum Lacertun, will lead my people on a last desperate march across your lands."

The apocalyptic vision he was painting, if honest, did indeed seem bleak. I couldn't fathom what advantage he gained by lying to me about this. He was smart enough to know we weren't going to let them all go with a good-game-pat-on-the-ass. Disarmaments, refugee camps, and forced relocations were the best they could hope for, and given what I'd set loose in my men a few nights ago, even those would be a miracle.

"Alright," I raised a hand to rub a spot behind my eyes that was starting to ache. "What kind of conditions are we talking about?"

A rigidness I had assumed was just part of his posture seemed to melt off the Ceterum at my question, and the look on his face was nothing short of thankful relief.

"The specifics will no doubt take months to arrange," he began, for the first time showing a more genuine, slightly lopsided smile. "But the main concerns will be that our people, once disarmed respectfully, are given the means to leave Other-Realm and return home. Aside from supplies to tend to the basic needs of our people, we will turn over our wealth and any other resources we possess as payment for opening the Path to the lands we left many generations ago."

My growing curiosity over this made the words rush out of me with a speed that would have been embarrassing if I hadn't been dying to know. "And where is that, may I ask?"

Cinis gave me a strange look, part surprise, part caution, as though he hadn't expected the question and anticipated some trick. "It has been some time, nearly two thousand years as we count time, but surely your Queen remembers."

Queen Meabh? Why would she know where these invaders came from? Despite myself, I stole a look over my shoulder at Bryth, who pinned Cinis with a penetrating stare. Noticing my look, she broke off her glare and gave a perplexed shrug. I shook my head with disgust as I turned back to the Ceterum, taking passing note of the way Bryth bristled at my head-wagging.

"What is that supposed to mean?" I asked, taking my turn at being confused and suspicious.

The Gythraul commander looked between me and the rest of my entourage and then back again.

"Forgive me, Gorm Bollham," he said, eyes still wide with surprise. "I had thought all your people were taught concerning our coming to Other-Realm. From childhood we have been told the story, and though I expect the details differ, I thought our origin was common knowledge here."

"Apparently not," I said, some agitated heat coming into my tone. "All I know—and to my knowledge this is all anyone knows—your people invaded Other-Realm years ago, though no one knows where you came from or how you got here."

The surprise on Cinis's face transformed into a recoiling outrage, and I thought he would stand up and attack me. His bodyguards muttered sharp words between their teeth, though they were so quick and low I couldn't catch anything except that they were profane exclamations. Cinis regained control with obvious effort, his armoured fingers scraping, metal on metal, as they clenched his helmet. When he finally spoke, his voice was measured and bore the same rich sibilance, but each word was rigid, and he finished each sentence like he was biting off a piece of something foul.

"Our people did not invade this land. We were invited, by our revered First Praetor, Marcus Titus Caelius, with the blessing and magics of his once-beloved Meabh, Queen of the Twilit Kingdom. Our ancestors left Britannia after faithless Agricola sacrificed many of our forefathers to his vanity and incompetence."

Britannia? Agricola? Senate? Republic? Century? Legion? I attributed my slowness in connecting the dots to the suspicion and nerves which had occupied the bulk of my thought process throughout this encounter.

"Wait a second." I held up a hand. "You mean to tell me that before your people came here, you were Romans? As in *Romans from Earth*?"

"Well, most were not true-born Romans, but men from Gaul and Hispania who served in the Imperial Legions," Cinis explained, his outrage ebbing as understanding broke over me with aching slowness.

"Gorm Bollham," Bryth said warily, her voice tight.

I waved her quiet, and leaned toward the Ceterum. "So your people were men, soldiers, from Earth?" I spoke with careful and deliberate emphasis.

"Yes, though it was not only men, and not only soldiers that came when the First Praetor brought our people here in the beginning." Cinis sounded almost relieved. "Men, women, and children settled on the western shores of this land, invited by Caelius and the Queen."

"Lucius," Bryth said her voice sharp and strained, but I had no time for her in the face of exposing what was right in front of me. My hand flapped again, and I think I may have barked "Quiet!" at her.

"If you were invited then what happened—"

"LUCE!" Bryth nearly screamed at my shoulder. "Something is not right!"

"What?" I roared, rounding on her. "What could be so fucking important right now, Bryth?"

I saw Grimple quicken a second before a hot, roadkill stink crept into my nostrils.

"Fiendspawn!" Bryth shouted as one of Ceterum Cinis's bodyguards lurched to one side.

I made a fumbling stagger to my feet as the lurching bodyguard collapsed to the ground, twitching and convulsing. A black, chitinous worm flailed about underneath the back of his helmet. Ceterum was up with his short sword in hand before I could haul myself upright, and yelled out a warning to his other bodyguard who was advancing on the thing attached to his brother-in-arms. The red-armored soldier turned in time to throw up an arm as another black, sinuous creature flew toward his face. Its head, a nest of stabbing, tearing hooks and barbs, crunched around the Gythraul's vambrace and the two fell to the ground in a twisting, grappling heap.

"Fireteam!" I screamed, but a quick sweep of the plateau revealed that three were down, unmoving in the dirt, and the last one wrestled with a creature like a dark, spiny python.

How had this happened so fast, so quiet? I recalled the creature that begat these monsters, its huge and silent coils, its terrible and vicious strength. These things were watered down imitations of their progenitor, but standing atop this exposed hilltop, they might be the end of us all the same.

Cinis tore his eyes from his struggling bodyguard, taking in the scene, and, for an instant our eyes met. I saw his sword rise as blame and hate burned in his betrayed stare, but something in my face must have spoken before my words could form. He looked at me with one part understanding, one part pleading.

"Form up on me, protect Cinis," I yelled a split second before a black shape launched itself at him.

The Ceterum saw the attack coming and met the leap with the tip of his sword. The blade punched through the thicket of ripping spurs to tear the back out of the creature's head, but its death throes tore the weapon from Cinis's grasp. The Gormstone hummed with icy power, and I sprang between the Gythraul commander and two more would-be assassins rising from the ground, snake-like. I popped a quill into the first, its whole body curled around the ragged wound in its midriff where basilisk venom smoked and spat, hissing bubbles of ichor. Then its partner flew at me.

No time to adjust my aim, my left hand snagged the creature just below the gnashing nest of bony hooks that passed for a head. The creature's jump had been aimed over my shoulder, toward Cinis, but as soon as I touched its carapace it began to twist and reach for my face, hissing what sounded a hell of a lot like profane curses.

Somewhere behind me came a giant rush of displaced air then a thunderous crumpling of flesh, bone, and metal giving way to something very heavy, moving very fast.

A strength I couldn't have possessed flooded into my left hand and I squeezed. The rough shell-like exterior gouged at my hand, then surrendered and gave way until ichor spilled over my hands, hot and sticky. The bristling head reared in a hissing screech just before it erupted upward in fireworks of inky gore that separated the rest of the body from the cracked pieces of chitin I held in my hand.

Those pieces fell to the ground an eye-blink after the rest of it landed in the dust, and I took up my carbine and swept it around the plateau. Hurrahn, Bryth, and Grimple had stepped to Ceterum Cinis and formed a rough fighting square. The bodyguard who had the Fiendspawn burying itself in his skull was on the ground, his head, neck, and spine pulped, with a goodly measure of Fiendspawn mashed into the ruined meat and twisted metal. Hurrahn must have been the source of the sound. His mace dripped with blood and ichor.

The bodyguard who had been grappling with the Fiendspawn, got to his feet, cradling the mess of his forearm and vambrace as well as his dripping and broken sword. The last third of the blade was still lodged in the head of the Fiendspawn, pinning it to the ground like a bug to a specimen board. The bodyguard, blood dripping from his tucked and wounded arm, stood beside his charge.

I couldn't see anything else, but that meant nothing, not with this kind of enemy.

"Sleepy," I snarled. "What happened?"

The Bogle didn't speak for a moment, but when he did, there was a child's slow, tear-gathering sadness to his answer. "All dead, Master," he said shakily. "Sleepyhead thought they quiet because no trouble. Quiet because they dead."

"The Fiendspawn killed all the Wee Folk we had watching the hilltop?" I asked, half wondering why I cared enough to ask the question. It wasn't like they had been helpful anyway.

"Call, but no one hears," Sleepyhead sobbed, and his whole body quivered on my shoulder. "All alone!"

"Pull it together and make yourself useful," I snapped irritably. "Get airborne and tell me what is going on."

Sleepyhead sniffed back another sob and with a shaky, "Yes, Master." He gathered himself to leap into the air.

As the Bogle took flight, I saw the remaining Echo marksman stumbling to his feet, the Boggun holding a hatchet dripping black in one hand while the other wrestled his rifle strap onto his shoulder. Even across the plateau I could see his whole body rising and falling in panting breaths. He kicked a twitching pile of chitinous coils once the strap was in place. Nothing besides us moved across the hilltop.

"This wasn't me or my people." I spared a look toward Cinis, who had recovered his sword and was putting his helmet on one-handed.

The Ceterum broke from fastening the dragon-faced helm to meet my eyes, his stare boring into me from inside the visor slits. "I believe you," he nodded, and stole a glance up at Hurrahn who loomed next him, an armoured heap of muscle. "I suppose if you wanted it, I would be dead already."

"The stink of the Fiendspawn has diminished," Bryth said, and I felt a ripple of probing energy spread out from her. "I do not sense any more of them on the hilltop."

"If you can sense them, why didn't you give us more heads up?" I asked accusingly, suspicion sharpening each word. "I've got three dead soldiers and half a dozen dead Wee Folk!"

"Unless they are very close, I can only sense them if I am looking for them, specifically," she explained defensively, her voice more defiant than hurt. "I had no reason to think they would be here."

"What about your teams, Grimple?" I asked, wanting to vent my rage.

"With the Wee Folk gone, I can't contact them, but I'm thinkin' they're still around but distracted," she said, eyes taking the hilltop in with a predator's expectant stare. "Unless there are a whole bunch more of those things coming, there is no way they could've taken them all out without some ruckus."

I didn't like the answers, and I didn't trust either of them, but right then, it was a moot point. It had happened, and those of us still alive had to get out of the open if we wanted to stay that way.

"Bryth, get a Path ready to take us back to camp," I ordered, picking up the hagseye and fitting it over my eye.

"What am I looking at, Sleepy?" I asked gruffly, seeing the hilltop where we stood. The aerial view swept into the barren land that I had thought would serve as the perfect killzone for the fireteam. Between the dead lizard steeds of the Gythraul near the base of the cliff, nothing moved across the open ground. Like Bryth, I hadn't accounted for the Fiendspawn and their ability to slide between shadows or swim through solid ground like eels through water.

The Bogle widened his search, and revealed movement at the edge of the expanse, close to a rocky outcropping. A tall figure with exposed skin the color of burnished bronze stepped forward and was swallowed up in rush of white, shimmering fog.

"A Tuatha taking Path," Sleepyhead observed numbly.

"Nadder," I spat. "Sleepy, get down here quick. We are leaving."

I let the hagseye fall and looked up to see the fog of a

Path curling around Bryth's feet. Ceterum Cinis and his bodyguard viewed the act of sorcery with a mixture of disgust and awe as tremors of magical energy raced invisibly through the air.

"We'll arrive at the edge of our camp. and I'll have a detachment of Royal Guards escort you from there," I said. "Your rides are dead."

"I expected as much." Cinis nodded gravely. "It is what I would have done."

WIth a final incantation, Bryth completed her spell. A wall of coiling white vapors like cirrus clouds stretched in front of our group.

"Ever taken a Path before?" I met the gaze of widening eyes within the dragon helm.

9

CAUTIONED

Lady Bryth Lighttread stood upon a rampart of earth, arms crossed and looked past the waist-high palisade to the steppes leading to the Gythraul encamped on the north side of the Kindled River. The dark stain of their tents and trenches had spread since those on the south side had forded the river. As she looked at the mounds of earth and rows of sharpened stakes, she remembered Toulouse Valoise, the first Paladin to be made a Gorm by her father's artifice.

She recalled his proud stride as he marched before the thundering artillery emplacements, now relegated to defending the home front when once they had been the point of Valoise's spear. Like a divine musician orchestrating a thunderstorm, he directed fire and belted out encouragement in equal measure. When the enemy was good and pummeled, he traded his square cap for a helmet, and—with a reflexive hunch that he explained was part of an effective "trench scurry"—joined the massed waves of soldiers squatting in the trenches. With a laugh and one last mouthful of wine, he led them across no-man's land and into the battered lines of the enemy. He sang one of his bawdy battle songs, and she screamed the words right along with him.

She remembered once––as the Gythraul withdrew from a fiercely held position––standing beside him as he boomed out laughing orders in a voice too deep and powerful for his narrow, sinewy chest. She had looked into his dark, blue eyes twinkling with will and fire, and fell in love that instant. "Nothing can quench that fire, that life," she had thought. "His body is mortal, but oh, those eyes, and that spirit—they belong to a god."

So she had loved him. Quietly at first, but when the fire of his eyes had burned away all her self control, she came to him, and with those same eyes twinkling, he took her into his arms without a word.

Later, after they had lain together in his tent, hearing the boom of the cannons which had become as commonplace as a thunderstorm, he had held her face in his hands and told her she was "*Ma Cherie.*" The words rolling from his tongue sounded softer and more beautiful than the simple meaning they conveyed. They had pierced her heart fixed themselves there, as warm and tingling when his lips hovered above her neck and spoke them.

"Yes, an immortal in a mortal shell," she had told herself, even as her Toulouse fought and squabbled with her father and the Queen over his plans to offer terms to the defeated Gythraul. "Nothing can quench that fire."

Then the squabbles turned sour, and her father's dread discovery, the Gormstone, was used for the first time. She learned that before the will of Queen Meabh, all fires could be extinguished.

She wept to see what was done to her beloved, and then wept harder because he hadn't comforted her, but instead looked at her with cold disdain. Her love was right before her, but he would not hold her, would not kiss her, would not whisper the name of her heart into her longing ear.

She had wanted to hate her father and the Queen then, but they had come to her, each in turn, and told her how it broke their hearts that they had been forced to this. They had only done so because the Paladin would not relent—would not yield to his oath. Hadn't Toulouse chosen his will over his promises to the Twilit Kingdom, even over his love for her? Hadn't he chosen to defy his rightful leige rather than carry out the will he was sworn to serve?

It had torn at her heart, but little by little, their words had won her over. Though her soul had ached to the point of breaking, she had found herself able to take up her duties once again, serving her father, her people, and her Queen. In the midst of losing her father to Ceterum Cinis's ambush, she felt relief at the passing of Gorm Valoise. Perhaps that was why she could not truly hate the Gythraul commander. With one stroke, he had freed her from the burden of seeing her lost beloved walking around like the living dead, and she could lay her conflicted feelings for her father to rest. She had felt a stab of shame at the realization when first she made it all those years ago, but now it was a truth she could accept.

History repeated itself, and once again the man she had fallen in love with had the Gormstone eating up every ounce of what had once made him beautiful. Even more darkly comical was that he was returning to Duanon even now to speak to the Queen of peace with the Gythraul. She knew, of course, what would happen when he met with Meabh. She would have known even if Lord Nadder hadn't made his assassination attempt against Ceterum Cinis.

When she could stand to think on him directly, she imagined Luce knew as well.

Just as the evolution of how she had come to see Ceterum Cinis, her understanding of who Queen Meabh really was had been a laborious process. Since she was a child, even before her commonly-absent mother had been killed by the vengeful Wyrms and her father had become the Queen's consort, the Queen doted on Bryth. She called Bryth the child of Our heart, in her strong, imperial way. When Meabh spoke that over Bryth for the first time, it carried the power of a royal edict, and her young heart thrilled at the thought. A child of the Queen—a princess by another name. She sat at her surrogate mother's feet or stood at her side as she witnessed her wisdom, power, and grace in giving all of herself to protect her people and sustain her kingdom. In time, Bryth had come to think of Meabh as her true mother, and the Tuatha who bore her as simply a fondly-remembered but ultimately disappointing relative.

It was once she came of age and joined the ranks of those who would stand—and rightly so—to do the Queen's will that she had the first inklings of something being amiss. Yes, she saw past the schemes, deceptions, and outright cruelties. She reminded herself that whatever her Queen did or bid those who served her to do was for the good of the people and the realm, even if at first they could not see it. As if through a membrane of conviction, she saw everything in light of the assurance that all of this was for a noble purpose—some great good that only a being as wise, experienced, and powerful as Meabh could see.

But with Toulouse, she had nearly pierced the membrane when the first tears started to form. Now, with Luce, it hung in tatters. She saw the ugly truth; the Queen was cruel, petty, and doggedly paranoid beneath a facade of regal command and noble sacrifice.

The bitter truth now loomed in her life, as unavoidable and intrusive as the Gythraul encamped along the horizon, but just as was the case with the Gythraul, ignoring the truth was pointless. For the first time since she watched her mother leave Duanon, she felt very small and alone.

"Makes yer feel tiny, don't it?" asked a rough voice.

"What?" Bryth warily turned from the vista to see Grimple Guthook, also looking out across the steppes at the Gythraul.

"Seein' a battle line formin' or just watchin' any of your enemies gatherin' against you," the Goblin said, sparing a glance upward at Bryth. "Makes a body feel shrunken and outmatch'd—leastwise it does fer one like me. Maybe, it's different with the likes of yer."

"Grimple, that sounds almost like you've been afraid," Bryth frowned at the underboss curiously. "I don't think I've seen you take anything seriously enough to be afraid."

Grimple laughed, a shallow and sharp-toothed sound, and crossed her arms. "Just because a thin's frightful doesn't mean t'ain't funny. In fact, it's often t'other way round."

"Perhaps." Bryth gave a humorless laugh of her own. "Though what I would find it far more entertaining than looking out there and seeing enemies would be to hear from Duanon that I'm looking at refugees."

"You'll be waitin' here for some time." Grimple turned her back on the Gythraul with a disgusted grunt and leaned against the palisade timbers. "We both know what's coming back from Duanon."

Bryth nodded then intoned the next words like a liturgical prophecy, staring at the enemy encampment. "The

Gorm comes to be the fist of the Queen, and that fist is going to fall on those wretches."

The pair stood for a long moment, considering the proclamation, each a prisoner to her thoughts. At last, Grimple cleared her throat, the uncertainty in her voice a testament to her discomfort on the subject. "Eh, well, do yer think everythin' that Gythraul was sayin' is true? I mean about them bein' invited here by the Queen and all?"

"Maybe." Bryth found she did not care if Grimple was aware of her revelations about the Queen's character. "I wouldn't put it past the Queen."

"But how's she kept it a secret this long?" Grimple'sher voice was agitated with disbelief. "Yer Tuatha live forever, less somethin' kills yer, so wouldn't one of yer kind be around to point out how it were her fault to start with?"

"All the elder Tuatha died in the first conflict with the Gythraul," Bryth said, her shoulders feeling heavy. "All the great lords and ladies of old, the Queen's own household—all gone—until the only ones left were those who came of age in the midst of the invasion. They were children when the fighting started, and as their fathers and mothers fell, they became more and more reliant on an elder for guidance and leadership . . ."

"And the lie was born," Grimple sighed.

"Exactly."

Another silence lapsed until it was Bryth's turn to break it with a quiet but burning exclamation. "Damn her!" she growled, a low and feral sound. "Damn her for lying to me all this time. Damn her for making me believe in her. Damn her for using me, first with Toulouse and then with Lucius . . . And damn her for . . . for . . ." The primal anger gave way to pain before she knew what was happening, her voice trailed off as she fought to keep a sob bound within her breast.

"For takin' both of them from yer," Grimple finished for her and looked up into Bryth's eyes, glittering now with tears she wouldn't shed. "Damn her for that, especially."

Bryth nodded but could not speak, knowing it would open a floodgate she was unsure she could ever close.

Grimple watched her, amber eyes inscrutable though her features seemed bent in a sympathetic frown. Bryth took turns looking at the Goblin and back at the Gythraul before settling on the vacant middle distance, where nothing and everything that had ever happened moved along invisible loops of memory.

"Is he lost forever then?" Grimple asked, her voice surprisingly and uncharacteristically hopeful.

Bryth gave as small a sniff as her dignity would allow and returned wholly from considering that vacuous realm of despair to stare down at Grimple.

"What?"

Grimple stood a little straighter and repeated. "Is he lost forever then? Luce, I mean."

Bryth made a disgusted sound. It was an absurd question. Grimple must be mocking her. Then again . . . the Gormstone had been created by her father. At first, he claimed it was to be a method of interrogating captured Gythraul. The process which created the stone required great feats of alchemy and magic, far too difficult for any but the most skilled magi, and its components were so rare as to be legendary. General creation for use as an interrogation tool was out of the question, and even worse, the Gythraul reacted poorly to the stone, withering almost immediately if they even survived having it implanted in their bodies. Yet in his frustration, her father offered the stone to the Queen as a means of taming the errant Paladin Valoise—or at least removing the threat he posed. Instead of destroying him, it worked just as her father hoped, and the Queen gained complete control over the will of her wayward servant without losing any of his skill, knowledge, or instincts. The Gorm was a living weapon bent to the will of the Queen, forever.

It had never occurred to her through the entire drama of events that perhaps the process could be undone.

She supposed it should not shock her that such was the case, given that both Lughan Redfinger and Meabh had been the foundations of her life. When they spoke in absolutes, she believed them with a childlike certainty, because that was what she had been to them for so long. It was also how she still thought of herself when in the Queen's presence. They knew best, and what they said was as true and real as though she had seen and touched it herself.

When they said the hold of the Gormstone was absolute and insoluble, was that really true? Given what she knew about magic and all its precepts, did she know of any instance where it was so permanent? For every spell, there was a counter-spell; for every curse, a counter-curse. Wasn't that how she had learned magic—how her father had taught her? Perhaps it was time to grow up.

"Perhaps not . . . after all no spell is inherently insoluble" she said cautiously, feeling a conspiratorial thrill race up her spine. "But that would require information and expertise I don't have, and I don't know any sorcerer who would willingly help us."

Grimple nodded and stood quietly for a moment, considering what had been said. When she spoke, her eyes slid to the Tuatha in a sidelong glance. "What if say I knew someone? Someone who is interested in freein' yer lovely boy. Might yer be willin' to work with 'em?"

Bryth looked over at the Goblin, the enormity of what

had been implied settling between them. To say yes was to take the first step on the road to something that years ago she would have rather died than consider—treason. Considering a means to unbind Lucius from the Queen's power was a direct act against her will, and in the Twilit Kingdom, the Queen's will was the law which bound everything together.

One stray word is all it would take to condemn her as an oathbreaker and a traitor, but at this point, did she care? What difference did it make if she voiced what was already festering in her heart? Practically, a good deal, but given the many terrible things justified with pragmatism for the sake of the Kingdom, perhaps she was done being practical. "Who might this person be?" Bryth asked after her moment of consideration, her voice falling to a whisper, her eyes darting left and right.

"Easy now," Grimple chuckled, her voice still as easy and conversational as before despite Bryth's sudden change in manner. "I need to know yer in for whatever lies ahead before I give yer anythin' more. After all, Bryth, this be the sort o' thin' that sees us gettin' visits from Nadder and the blackworms."

Bryth shuddered remembering the aetheric stink of the Fiendspawn. They were as loathsome to her magically attuned senses as they were horrible to look at, but she squared her shoulders and nodded. "Yes," she said, the words seeming too small for the meaning. "If Luce can be freed, I will do whatever it takes."

"Even if it means betrayin' Meabh and raisin' your hand against her?" Grimple pressed, her usual levity evaporating.

Bryth swallowed but fixed Grimple with a hard look. "Does 'whatever it takes' mean something different among your people?"

Grimple smirked showing the edge of her sharp, small

teeth. "Fair enough. Just checkin'." She rose from her slouch against the palisade. "Well, I'm off to see that the Fingers are back up to snuff. Nadder didn't kill 'em, but he glamored 'em up in knots, for sure."

Bryth frowned, unsure at the sudden change of subject. She opened her mouth to demand the name of the one who would help her free Lucius from the Gormstone, but stopped and looked around, suddenly afraid. Had they been discovered by unseen eyes and the surreptitious Goblin was trying to make a break? Or––the thought came with a strangling clutch of fear––had this been a test of loyalty? Having failed, would she find herself buried under a tide of ripping and shredding Fiendspawn?

"Is this . . . are we . . . being watched?" she choked out, her eyes roving wild circuits while the rest of her body remained as motionless as a fowl sensing a predator in the brush.

"Always, in one way or another, I imagine," Grimple said with a shrug as she started down the earthen ramp. "Burden of leadership and all, but no need to panic, eh? In my experience, by the time yer ready to panic, it's already too late. So save time an' keep yer head about yer."

Bryth wanted to follow her down the ramp, a thousand suspicions playing out in her mind, but she remained where she stood, watching the underboss strut away. "And the friend?" she called, unable to contain herself.

"In time." Grimple did not bother to look over her shoulder. "But just to keep yer awake, yer know her already."

10

DISCOVERED

Captain Uzran and Lieutenant Droth passed beneath the sable horns of an elder Lindwyrm as they stepped into the hollow mountain basin where the Grand Thaig was held. The horns swept back into a massive fanged skull, the entire artifact a memento of a time before the Tuatha, when the People of the Stone—the Ogres, Trolls, and Fomor—fought to make a place for themselves between the Ancient Wyrms and the Darklings. According to legend, this skull was taken by Arzgund after he allowed himself to be swallowed by the degenerate cousin of the true dragons so he could tear the armored brute apart from the inside out. On the roof of the skull's mouth, a cleft was visible. There the Ogre hero anchored a flint spike attached to a length of Bovigore gut so that, when victorious, he could pull himself back out of the giant creature's depths.

Uzran remembered the first time he passed beneath that skull suspended by ropes dozens of feet above his head and searched for the cleft in that yawning expanse of bone. There he found not one cleft or divot in the bone, but several, the legacy of the ancient monster's violent eating habits and belligerent prey worked out in radiating holes, cracks, and seams. Some were patched with rough nodules of fresher bone, and others gaped, creating shadows that may have been inches or feet deep into the skull. He remembered standing there, a lone Ogre child in a flow of traffic to the mountaintop, trying to guess which one was Arzgund's until his mother realized he had fallen behind and came for him in righteous maternal fury.

"By the Wyrd, you wicked whelp, scaring me like that!" she said, taking turns striking the side of his skull and embracing him to her broad bosom. "What were you thinking? I had to leave your brothers and sisters with Grummah. We'll be lucky to find she hasn't traded them all for drinks and a new dress."

Uzran had not thought it a fair assumption her mother made against her aunt—the Ogress was a sharp bargainer and would have gotten at least two new dresses and a smock with the drinks. He hadn't said anything, knowing his mother would not be interested in his opinion of her sister or why he had stayed beneath Arzgund's Skull. His mother, like many Ogresses, was run ragged tending the home and children while her husband sought his fortune and sent back what he could. She had no time or patience for her son's ramblings about old heroes, nor his conviction that he would one day join their ranks. At best he expected to receive another bludgeoning about the ears as she groused about him needing to have a pack of children before he could set forth into the world like a true hero of old. At worst, she would try and beat the foolish notions out of him right there beneath the Skull, not caring who witnessed. The People of the Stone tended to be a harsh, loud lot, and none would bat an eye, though after a particularly solid strike one might yell encouragement to his mother in passing.

So he shrugged and muttered an apology that earned him a few more cuffs, and she frogmarched him back to the rest of the family. As she did so, he looked back at the hanging trophy and made a silent pledge to return with one to equal that immense skull. Someday he would stand shoulder to shoulder with the likes of Arzgund the Mad, Fellig Spike-Tooth, or Nazla the Bone-Queen.

Centuries later, Arzgund's Skull appeared as immense as ever, even though he knew it should seem smaller now that he was older. He thought maybe his perspective hadn't changed because the promise he'd made all those years ago was unfulfilled. The Skull was a reminder, now more than ever, that he had not become the hero he longed to be.

Instead, he sneaked into the Grand Thaig like a thief or an outcast, his cloak's hood pulled low over his face. Some hero.

"So what exactly is the objective here, Cap'n?" Droth asked as they walked, a pair of roadstained travelers amid the sparse flow of foot traffic passing in or out of the basin. The Grand Thaig had begun two days ago, and the noise echoing out of the wide, scaffold-buttressed hollow meant that Mount Falchrreg was full to bursting.

"Lay low and wait for a chance to address the Elders before everyone, probably during one of the Grudge-Settlings." Uzran's voice was little more than a whisper, his head and shoulders bowed to make himself as small as possible.

"And then what?" The Troll ground his knuckles into the fresh scar tissue that webbed his face in lines of pale grey on blue-black. In the time it had taken to reach the mountain, his wounds had healed over. The bandages were gone, but

Droth was hardly less conspicuous. One of his kind sporting a serious scar was rare, and one with a network of them was extraordinary. In most cases, a Troll either healed clean or died from his injuries.

"Then I try to convince them." Uzran stole a look at his friend's ravaged face. "Give an impassioned speech to win them over and call them to arms."

Droth rolled his eyes and made a sound in the back of his throat, making clear what he thought of Uzran's plan.

"You've spent too much time around the human, Cap'n," he grumbled, shaking his head. "There is no way you're goin' to convince that bunch o' withered bastards to throw in with some half-mad bid at rebellion. You *do* remember who it was who helped raise the Elders as the council over all the People of the Stone, don't you, Cap'n?"

He remembered. He was more convinced than ever that it was the Queen's support for the Elders all those years ago which kept them sending their champions to the Royal Guard even though he had violated his people's most sacred precepts. Before the Tuatha—before Queen Meabh—the People of the Stone had fought tooth and nail with the Darklings, the Ancient Wyrms and even each other to hold little patches of land in the mountains, hills, and canyons of eastern Other-Realm. Seeing the opportunity to acquire powerful, resilient shock troopers in their war with the Darklings, the Tuatha had come, with Queen Meabh spearheading the effort to raise a gathering of Elders. There were twelve members in all, from the oldest and most powerful clans—four for each: Ogre, Troll, and Fomor. Bound together by oaths of fealty to the Queen and to what they decreed as the People of the Stone, a title they created for the three races, their preeminence as a governing body was quickly and violently cemented.

And now, after millenia of being in power, he was going to ask this most recent crop of Elders to put all that at risk to come to the aid of one treacherous criminal.

"If you want to skitter off now, I am sure you can make it back to Duanon and rejoin the war," Uzran said. "At least before your superior officer knows you've run off."

Droth's head wagged and he rubbed at his ravaged face again. "Bastard," he grunted. "Let's just get in there and get this over with. I swear . . . survivin' that damned fire, just to be executed here."

"Maybe they'll let you take the Trial of the Guiltless?"

"And die in agony? I don't think so."

"Suit yourself," Uzran grunted, leading the way as they marched down into the cloven mountaintop roaring with hungry life.

The paths around the basin were narrow—at least for creatures built on the scale of the People of the Stone. They weaved in and out between the booths and tents scattered thickly across the area. In places, it was so close that to pass by the merchant stalls, one had to sidle past sideways or ask shoppers to step aside or be trodden on. The alternative was to barrel on through, hoping to get clear before screamed curses and flying fists could be brought to bear. From the noise, there were equal portions of both occurring.

The Grand Thaig was a raucous and lively place. Drink and food flowed freely and sometimes forcefully, punctuated with bursts of profanity, laughter, and violence. The walls of the basin reverberated with the sounds of celebration, and even face-to-face conversations had to be shouted. The People of the Stone gathered together in such numbers only rarely. It was often remarked that it was just as well, because if they did otherwise, Mount Falchrreg would soon split apart from the sheer amount of noise they made. Combine that with frequent fighting and general violence, and any meeting place would crumble.

Actual killings or cripplings were forbidden by the Elders, but brawling and violent contests of strength and belligerence were commonplace, and accidents did happen. Navigating to a booth to purchase a drink or pausing to hear a tale-spinner share a traditional epic of the great heroes could quickly become a shoving, kicking, or punching match, and only some could be considered good-natured roughhousing.

For their own safety, the smaller folk of Other-Realm—the Bogguns, Gremlins, and Hobbs—were not admitted. Goblins sometimes crept in, but they strove to avoid notice, knowing that the only attention a Fomor would pay to a Goblin was to scrape the fool from the bottom of his foot. Tuatha were not forbidden, but rarely showed any interest, and in the long memory of the People of the Stone, the Sylvanfolk and Wodewosen had never deigned to set foot anywhere near Mount Falchrreg.

The Grand Thaig was for the People of the Stone, a celebration of their spirit and strength, and so the mountain was theirs. Despite the impossibility of what lay before him, Uzran smiled as he navigated his way through the crowds. There was infectious vitality in the air—a vibrance not found in the elegant balls of the Gloaming Court or in the quaint festivals of the common creatures in the rest of Other-Realm. Whether it took the form of a bellowed laugh rolling over a low drinking table or a snarled curse growled during a brawl (knocking a merchant's stall flat) there was an irrepressible life and personality to the event. It was a chaotic, wild energy that embraced life's vagaries—sorrow and joy, pleasure and and pain—with an abandon that was like nothing else Uzran knew.

It had been long since he was among his own kind, apart from the regimented life of the Royal Guard. He found he had forgotten much of who his people were. Now, immersed in it all, he felt a heady, almost drunken euphoria steal over him, making his grin broaden even as tears beaded in his dark eyes. He was home.

He looked up, wiping his eyes, and saw Droth returning between two booths, one selling skewers of seared meat, the other offering roasted mushroom caps as wide as soup bowls full of murmoth curd. The Troll fetched two horns of mead, one in each over-large, clawed hand.

Uzran waited for his friend to bring the welcome liquor, eager to wash some of the road and his worries away, when he spotted trouble brewing. In the space between the mead stall and the two food booths was a small yard with a jumble of tables and stools where buyers could squat and enjoy their purchases. At one table, two young Ogres and a Fomor took hearty bites off their skewers and played at a game of dice. One of the Ogres, a prize bull of his race, seemed increasingly unhappy with the way the dice were falling. With each poor toss, he bellowed curses, and his arms flailed in paroxysms of outrage. Navigating his way around a table full of glowering Trolls, Droth would pass right by the volatile dice game.

"Droth!" Uzran shouted, stepping out from between the booths as the agitated young Ogre threw his arms wide at another foul turn of the dice. Mead splashed over the raging bull's hand and arm, some spattering his face, which instantly furrowed into an ugly, snarling knot.

"Shithead."

Even over the raucous sound of the Grand Thaig in full

swing, Uzran heard Droth's thoughtless expletive, and so did the table of dice players.

"Shithead!" the young bull roared, rising to his feet with a speed and force that sent his stool tumbling away. "Who you calling shithead, you ape-armed, assraker?"

Uzran paused, wondering if Droth could defuse the situation, then spied the other two at the table climbing to their feet, eyes bright with drink and expectation. Even if Droth had the temperance to shrug it off, it would do no good. They were young, drunk, and spoiling for a fight. There was only one way this could end. Cursing, Uzran worked his way toward his outnumbered friend.

"What was that, you stoneless whelp?" The Troll glared up at the youth who stood even taller than Uzran. "I saw your slackjaw waggin', but it just sounded like that slappin' sound your ma and I make when you're not around."

The Ogre and his companions gaped at the crude audacity of the scarred lieutenant before their massive leader's face darkened with murderous rage. "Maybe you'll hear better when I pound myself through one ear and out the other," he threatened, leaning into the Troll's face.

Droth brought the empty drinking horn around in one long-armed loop, crashing it against the Ogre's head. The horn splintered into a spray of black shards, and the young bull staggered to one knee. Droth downed the other horn of alcohol as the other Ogre and his Fomor friend leapt over their stunned leader.

Uzran shouldered past more bystanders, desperately trying to reach his friend without starting his own brawl, when he saw Droth slam a fist into the belly of the second Ogre youth after ducking his wide swing. The dice-player-turned-brawler released his wind in a single, wounded gust, but with Droth's attention elsewhere, the Fomor smashed into the Troll with a flying tackle. Droth was relatively short and broad, like most Trolls, but his low center of gravity failed him when the Fomor's ram-horned head crashed into the lieutenant's scarred nose. Blood spurt from his cucumbery snout, and Droth tumbled backwards under the Fomor. Once astride Droth, the Fomor reared back his bludgeon of a skull and slammed it into the Troll's face.

"Get him up," the massive leader roared. Obediently, the other Ogre and the Fomor hauled Droth to his feet. Uzran's lieutenant fought fiercely, his elbows, knees, and heels crunching into faces and joints. He had almost broken free when his whole body seized around a pain that came from no physical blow. His fighting slackened and for the first time, Uzran feared that Droth's battle wounds were far deeper than either of them had guessed.

Droth was suspended between the two lackeys as the leader drilled his huge, knobby fist into the Troll's face. More blood sprayed, and fresh wounds opened on his thin lips. Another two pummeling blows, and his long nose sat mashed and crooked on his face.

"Tell me about you and my mother now!" The massive Ogre roared in the lieutenant's face to the snickers and snarled encouragement of his mates. "Go on, tell me!"

Droth spat blood, and then bared his teeth in a defiant grin. "She . . . does this thing with her tits that'll change your life." He chuckled through his split lips. "'Least it changed mine."

The Ogre responded with a wordless roar of hate, but before he could rain down more blows, Uzran piled into him at a dead sprint.

Head bowed and shoulder tucked, Uzran drove into the huge youth hard enough to cause his bulk to wrap around the captain's charging body. Feet off the ground, the brawler was carried three strides past his companions and Droth and thrown down onto a table. Splinters and crushed drinking vessels hurtled outward in all directions. Not content with that, Uzran stomped on the dazed young bull's belly, putting his knee into the huge chest and pistoning his fists into the impact-slackened face. One, two, three, four times, the captain's fist crashed down before he stood up to survey his handiwork. The young Ogre's face was a swollen, cracked mash of flesh, blood, and tusks, but breath still bubbled on his lips and nostrils.

Uzran turned to cow the other youths into submission when someone smashed him across the back of the head with what was left of a drinking horn. It seemed the occupants of this table had not appreciated having an entire Ogre dropped in the middle of their gathering. His vision swimming, Uzran saw Droth throw off the Fomor, who careened into the table full of Trolls from earlier, then the world exploded into a whirlwind of fists, feet, and snarling faces. How long they fought or even whom they fought was something that Uzran and Droth never sussed out, but they managed to arrange themselves back to back, punching and hurling aside anyone that came within arms reach.

"CEASE BY ORDER OF THE ELDERS!" A tectonic voice thundered through the chaos.

Uzran hammered his fist down on an oncoming Troll's skull as the brawlers began to separate.

"CEASE NOW OR FACE THE FURY OF THE ELDERS!"

Uzrand and Droth, still back to back, turned and saw a phalanx of warriors in boiled leather armor standing with cudgels at the ready. In front was a tall, almost lanky Ogre with a pictograph mountain tattooed on his broad, bare skull.

"Damn it!" Uzran hissed through his bloodied, swollen lips as he recognized the Master of the Elder's Sentinels before him.

"Wait, isn't that . . ." Droth began, but then the Master Sentinel spotted Uzran standing at the center of the frozen chaos, his concealing cloak ripped free long ago.

"Well, greetings, Uzran Thrice-Curse!" the tattooed Ogre said, his voice dripping with false geniality. "It is long since you honored the Grand Thaig with your presence."

A ripple of murmurs, none of them friendly, raced through the soldiers and brawlers, the latter taking a step away from Uzran.

"Greetings, Kugin." Uzran suddenly felt tired.

"I haven't seen you for years," Kugin said in saturated tones, tapping his iron-banded club against his shoulder as though in thought. "In fact, I don't think I've seen you since you ordered the murder of my wife. Is that right? Has it been that long?" The question hung in the air—a hook waiting for Uzran to hang himself on.

"Your brother-in-law?" Droth hissed incredulously.

"Well, I guess I know we'll be going to the Grudge-Settling," Uzran sighed as the Sentinels waded toward them at a gesture from Kugin, truncheons raised.

"You have the worst fuckin' ideas," Droth swore before they were both thrown to the ground.

11

WELL-INTENTIONED

I stood before the Queen's throne, digging deep to muster every ounce of hateful will I possessed in hopes of defying her, if even for second. That was all it would take to put a manticore round through her heart.

In the meantime, I needed to keep her talking. "If I had known you intended to kill Ceterum Cinis, things might have gone differently." She lounged, resplendent in the bone-white construction of her throne, which seemed to grow from the floor up toward the ceiling.

"I am not criticizing, just suggesting that I should be informed when you plan to assassinate a target I am negotiating with."

"And what made you believe you could speak on Our behalf?" The Queen's blue eyes shone with a dangerous, watchful light.

"Nothing," I said, without concern. "I went to listen to what he had to say and determine what advantage could be gained. Even though I am your champion, I had no plans to speak for you on diplomatic matters." That much was true, if for no other reason than I could never have dreamed what Cinis had actually called me there for.

"And you had no intention, once Ceterum Cinis's purpose was revealed, of attempting to broker a peace with those savages?"

I knew, with a certainty that ached like the cold stone in my chest, that what I said next had to be honest. Even if I considered deception, wanted it in my heart of hearts, the Gormstone wouldn't let me.

"I . . . I hoped to begin the process, yes." My voice betrayed the brief struggle of my kidnapped will. "Once Cinis spoke of surrender and peace, I hoped that I could bring an end to the war that way, and then be . . . be allowed to go free."

"Free?" Meabh said the word as though it was unknown to her. "Whatever would that look like for you, Our Gorm? Would you find a quiet corner of this alien realm to settle down in, or would you ask Us to return you to that filthy, blighted world where you are a war criminal?"

Right now, neither sounded palatable, but I knew the question was only meant to demonstrate how much she had me by the nose.

"I don't know." I pushed on to my own questions in the hopes of buying time for a miracle. "But I did learn much about what the Gythraul believe about their coming to this world. Though I am not sure how much of it is true."

The Queen leaned forward, her eyes glittering. "What tales did that snake whisper into your ear, I wonder?"

"He told me that the Gythraul were people from my world originally," I carefully modulated my words to hold neither accusation or disbelief, hoarding my sparse emotional resources for something else. "That they were what we call Romans in Earth history books—soldiers and their dependents brought here by your invitation and that of a man named Marcus Titus Caelius, whom Cinis claimed was your consort."

The Queen leaned back, the light in her eyes changing into something strange and distant. Her head suddenly came up as her whole body tensed, and her eyes, hunted slivers, darted around the emptied audience hall.

Seeing no threats and no doubt feeling my eyes on her, Meabh met my stare and allowed her lips to part into a thin, amused smile, the paranoid glare gone as quickly as it had appeared. "Does that shock you?" Her voice was low and a touch huskier than usual.

"Which part?" I asked flatly. "The fact that you were responsible for bringing the Gythraul—or the people who would become them—to your realm, or the fact that your boy toy was a Roman legionnaire? The former sure, but not the latter, I guess. Seems good, old-fashioned manmeat is in high demand around here."

Normally, it would bother me to talk about Bryth like that, even considering all that had happened, but the Gormstone left only the memory of what that guilt might have felt like.

"We suppose you have a point, but if you had met Caelius you would have understood," Meabh said with something like genuine warmth. "Among all those We have ever taken as consorts, he was closest to Our Beloved."

"Beloved?"

"Yes, Our royal husband, the King. We stepped together onto the roads between realms to this savage place." The Queen's voice grew distant. "That first crossing took much from Us, not the least of which Our memories of home and Our reason for leaving. But most terribly, it severed Us from

Him. We remember his face, his voice, and the way his hand felt enclosing Our own."

I stood dumbfounded as her naked feelings and memories spread before me, realizing only later that this was probably the first time she had been able to talk like this since the last Gorm. She was only able to be honest when she knew the listener was enslaved to her by magical chains. I might have felt bad for her if I hadn't been so busy hating her.

"Caelius was mortal, but he looked at Us and held Us in a way that We could almost imagine he was Our Beloved," Meabh said, her voice and focus hardening incrementally with each word. "So when he asked to bring some of his own people here, We acquiesced for the sake of Our Beloved's memory. Yet, in spite of Our graciousness, he returned Our gift with scorn and treachery."

"What happened?" I asked, feeling the accumulation of angry will gathering to a lethal point within me. I needed just a little more time and that spear of ice would snap free and plunge into her.

"He went back to your world and found those who would follow him back—soldiers and their ilk. People who were embittered about their lot and looking for a second chance. Does that sound familiar?"

"Vaguely," I muttered.

"They came in a sniveling herd, but We welcomed them and loved them for the sake of the affection We bore Caelius," she said.

I almost believed her, even knowing what she was capable of.

"Even when Caelius began to spend more and more time apart from Us to tend their incessant needs and whining, We were patient and longsuffering. But a fresh conflict grew among some of the Ancient Wyrms stirring from their sleep. We called on those ungrateful wretches to take up arms for Us as they had once done for lesser masters, and they refused."

A seething, ancient hatred came into her voice, and it took an effort of will not to take a step back. "A greater treachery arose when they poisoned the mind of Caelius against Us," she spat, her words echoing in the empty chamber. "Then he dared to appear before Us and challenge Our word, the word of a being who was ancient when your miserable ilk dwelt in caves like vermin. We did not have the Gormstone then, and so We had no choice but to destroy him for his insolence and curse his people. We condemned them to bear the image of those they did not have the courage to face in Our name.

We should have destroyed them, but We are merciful, and the Ancient Wyrms required our attention. When We had brokered peace through the Unbound, We sought to punish their treachery appropriately, but in the intervening time, they had taken up arms against Us and marshalled other dissidents to their banner. Many jealous Tuatha rose up against Us as well, desiring the throne for themselves. We were pressed by two bitter enemies, but We would not surrender our rightful rule even if We would be required to burn all of Other-Realm to ash. It is Ours—now and forever. It is a perpetual affront to Our throne that their filthy feet once nearly stood upon the very walls of Duanon, but We drove them back with Our few remaining loyalists then rebuilt what their treachery had ruined."

I stared at her, my mind reeling at the full extent of what she was responsible for—the tragedy which had been playing out senselessly for nearly two thousand years. She decried the actions of others, but at so many turns she had made the wrong choice—the petty choice—and she had learned nothing from it all.

"After that you began to bring the Paladins in?" I was flabbergasted that after the near-apocalypse she had brought on herself she would consider bringing one more human to Other-Realm.

"We were lonely and could not trust any of the remaining young and hungry Tuatha, so we sought another who might replace Caelius," she said with a defensive petulance that contrasted grotesquely to the image she presented upon her lofty throne. "Arcturus could not love Us as Caelius could, but We trusted our glamors to ensnare him and assure his faithfulness as Our general. So yes, that was how the Paladins began."

"So the whole 'needing the warlike peoples of Earth' line was just bullshit, then?"

"A useful by-product, though hardly our chief aim," she replied archly, fiddling with a jewelled bangle on her arm. "A useful fiction to swell the egos of capable but small-minded men who would keep the actual power of the Kingdom armies out of the hands of scheming Tuatha within Our court."

I shook my head, and the movement drew the Queen's eyes to me like twin blowtorch flames, blue and ravenously hot.

"Are you crushed to learn the truth?" She leaned forward, her voice obscenely eager. "What do you think now that you see how foolish and deceived you were? How does it feel to know you danced to a tune I have been played for over eighteen centuries?"

My tongue loosened at the question, and I felt words coming to my mouth sharp and hot. This might be my chance.

"What do I think?" My rhetorical question stoked my anger, gathering steam and will. "I think that you are, without a doubt, the most petty creature I have ever been unfortunate enough to meet."

She arched an eyebrow and glared but made no move to interrupt, not that I was planning on giving her such an opportunity.

"You have power like the myths from Earth give to gods, but you have them all enslaved to a mind that is small and selfish and ugly. You are petty, fickle, and so damned shrunken. It would be bad enough if you were just another narrow-minded, self-serving human or Hobb, or whatever the hell else walks on two legs, but you have the magic and the eternal life that should make you better than everyone else. But it doesn't. Instead you waste it all on vendettas and schemes that are beneath you."

Momentum built inside me, each word a drop on that angry icicle I was building to skewer her with. In her arrogance, she hadn't even had me disarmed when I came to her court.

"You should be wise and kind and patient, because hell, why not? You are immortal and can snap your fingers or say a few words and change reality. Your needs are met as soon as you are aware of them. You've lived long enough to learn patience, to see how things work out. Everything which drives most people to do the wicked, stupid shit they do . . . you have no excuse for. You should be better—you should be more! You should be what I thought you were when I first saw you!"

I was shouting now, one finger pointing at her accusingly, while the other hand quietly tightened around the grip of the carbine slung over my shoulder. "You should be someone worth honoring, worth following, worth dying for, but you aren't! You're pathetic, and that's why you have to die!"

With a herculean effort, I threw everything I had at her hold on me—every last ounce of anger, disgust, hatred, and defiance. The final droplets were freezing to that frigid spine of rage, hardening into a blade to tear her grip loose, just for a second. That was all I needed.

My hand clenched the grip of the rifle and I willed my arm to raise, but nothing happened. It wasn't straining or pulling against some incredible force. My arm simply would not raise, and little by little, I felt my fingers unfurling from their grip around the M-Core. Another few seconds and my accusing finger fell, defeated, to my side. I stood impotently, shame and disbelief dragging my eyes to the floor.

"Did you think you could simply will yourself free?" the Queen asked with a brittle, mocking laugh. "You—a weak, whimpering lump of insecurities, fears, and doubts? Did you really think you could raise your hand against a goddess?"

I didn't want to answer, but the Gormstone sent runners of ice out from my chest and the words came out anyway.

"Yes," I confessed miserably. "I believed I could take control, if only for a second."

"And in that second you thought to raise your hand against me," Meabh crowed, her normally rich, smooth voice cracking in exultation. "How delicious! How incredibly, utterly doomed!"

I bore her gloating with my head bowed, wishing I could turn the gun on myself, but at the thought, more lances of frigid power shot through my skin and soul. It was pointless.

"Look at me," she commanded, and my head rose without my consent. "Now that you better understand the extent of Our power, you shall listen well to what We bid you do," she said, obviously savoring each second she held me pinioned by her will. "You shall depart here and speak nothing of that which has been shared with you. You shall return to the steppes with the rest of Our army and crush Cinis's legions. It matters not if the Ceterum survives, but if he is captured, We wish him brought back to Us in chains. Once the Gythraul threat is dealt with, you will withdraw your forces from the steppes and prepare to redeploy elsewhere."

"Even if I destroy all of Cinis's forces, more are coming." I surrendered myself to the only thing I could do in that moment. "Another legion is on its way, and more will come after them. The Gythraul are fighting for their lives now.'

"We know this." She brooded quietly before going on. "Leave the Goblins behind with orders to slow any further incursions. We have learned that with your victories, more of the underbosses have begun funneling their teams to Grimple's command in hopes of receiving a stake in the land you promised. Tell Grimple she must keep the Gythraul at bay or Our arrangement is forfeit and she and all her kind will be considered traitors."

"And if she defies me right then and there?" The words tasted bitter in my mouth. "What then?"

"Then you treat her like a traitor and create an example for the rest of her spineless ilk," the Queen said hotly. "The Goblins are used to such changes of regime, and besides, they are only meant to slow the Gythraul while you serve Us elsewhere."

"Elsewhere?" I asked, the coldness choking concern and numbing my humiliation into a dull ache.

"The fiefdoms of the Far-Hold have enjoyed far too much independence for far too long," she said with a smile as cold as the ice spreading through my chest.

12

CONDEMNED

The Cavern of Meeting sat beneath the basin of Mount Falchrreg, separated by a dozen feet of solid stone at its highest point. It could only be reached by taking one of the three tunnels which opened up on the sides of the mountain nearly a hundred feet below the basin floor. The tunnels were natural formations that had been further excavated and reinforced to accommodate the traffic of the large-framed People of the Stone. A gate closed the mouth of each tunnel, and each gate was appointed for the use by different groups which came to the revered mountain.

The largest gate was located on the eastern face, ten feet or so below the level of the others Called the People's Gate, the vast majority of those attending the Grand Thaig passed through it to reach the underground amphitheatre that was the Cavern of Meeting. Its tunnel was spartan, only constructed to ensure that large numbers of bulky individuals could pass in and out in with relative ease.

The second and most easily reached gate was the Elder's Gate. A set of stairs had been worked into the mountain's rocky bones, switchbacking from the northern lip of the basin. It served as the point of ingress and egress for the Elders who served as the municipal authority for the People of the Stone. It was a smaller portal, and the tunnel was never as wide as the People's Gate, seeing as it had only to serve the twelve Elders and their immediate families, but it had side corridors which led to furnished rooms and antechambers where the Elders and their kin could rest. They were not the fine, pampered living quarters of the Tuatha, but they were far better accommodations than most coming to the Grand Thaig received. The assembled masses simply slept on the slopes, sometimes with a tent but just as often without.

The third and smallest gate sat on the northeastern face of the mountain, a quick scramble across a wide cliff from the Elder's Gate. It was here, to the Sentinel's Gate, that Uzran and Droth were dragged after being stripped, beaten soundly, and bound by the guards under the command of Master Sentinel Kugin. The tunnel of the Sentinels was nearly as bare and simple as that of the People's Gate, with the exception of one smaller tunnel that drew off and down toward the Cavern of Meeting. It ended, opening up into a small guardroom with a pair of long, low alcoves appointed for sleeping. The room contained a simple wooden table and stool, and a door made of thick, interlocking bars of iron. Beyond those bars was a low-roofed cavern wide enough for half a dozen People of the Stone to be in without crawling over each other, though they would have to crouch down to walk about. It was into this rough-hewn prison both offending Ogre and Troll were thrown.

The two comrades lay in the dark room, catching their breath following the bruising trip down the stone stairs of the Sentinel's Gate. The light from a pair of guttering torches at the head of the guardroom and a small oil lamp on the table just managed to penetrate, in a wavering orange glow, between the narrowly fitted iron bars. It was a good thing, too, because though Uzran and Droth were as nighteyed as any other member of their race, in the pure darkness of the underground, they were as blind as any other creature. With the faint illumination filtering through the door, they could make out the bare surroundings of the enlarged cell, noting a few cast off rags and a sunken place that looked like it was commonly used as the midden. The air was stale and cold, but the cloying smells of urine and feces were faint, guessed-at memories. The Grand Thaig was held only once a year, and they were the first to be held here.

"Funny," Droth grunted as he lay on his side, swollen cheek pressed to the soothingly cool floor. "I seem to remember more people in that fight than just you and me, Cap'n. You figure they'll head back to round up the rest o' those brawlers?"

Uzran, bound in heavy, iron shackles, raised both hands to probe gingerly around his swollen eye socket. The tissue was hard and hot, with little give to it.

"If Kugin went up there to do anything, it will have been to buy a drink for every last whoreson that took a swing at me."

Droth gave a chuckle that ended in a wince as he felt his lips split and bleed anew. "Hope this Sentinel racket pays well," he said moving his lips toward the floor. "Because that's goin' to be an awful lot of drinks."

Uzran's fingers had left the eye, which was currently swollen shut, and now ran gently over the rest of his skull. He discovered four new bumps to go with the somewhat knobby topography that had formed in his many years as a

Royal Guard. Alongside the bludgeon-raised hillocks, he found a large gash which traced its way between two knobs like some kind of red valley. There was also a spot on his temple where his thick skin had been so abraded—Kugin's grinding boot he imagined—and the skin was so raw that his fingers came away wet when he touched the injury.

Lowering his hands and feeling his feet—which were also bound—he began to worm his way toward the door across the uneven floor. He groaned as his cracked ribs and battered spine protested, but eventually he slid up against the door, the one ear that wasn't throbbing pressed to the space between the bars. He heard retreating foot-steps and low murmurs coming from back up the tunnel. He turned his head, pressing his one good eye to the slot, and looked around the vacant guardroom. On the table, their cloaks, weapons, and belts had been left unceremoni-ously in a pile, but otherwise the bare space was undisturbed.

Had they really left them unguarded? Granted, there was not much they could do in their current location, but still, it was bad form to let two prisoners sit unattended and unobserved. Perhaps the Sentinels were not the organiza-tion he remembered.

As Uzran adjusted his position to get a better look a the guardroom, his manacled wrists struck the door with a dull, metallic clang. Uzran winced at the sound, but lurched suddenly backwards as something hard and heavy struck the bars with a spiteful crash.

"Away from the door," a thick, gravelly voice commanded.

The guard left in charge must have been pressed close to the door to listen to his new charges when Uzran acciden-tally hit the door. He supposed the guard's angry knock—

probably with his cudgel—was as much an act of mean-spiritedness as it was shock.

"Good to know if one of us takes ill in here there is a sympathetic ear at hand, eh Cap'n," Droth mumbled into a fresh patch of cold stone. His former spot was smeared with blood and spittle.

"I don't imagine we'll be here long enough for that," Uzran commented, wriggling his way back toward where the Troll lay. "If Kugin doesn't beseech the Elders for a special session of Grudge-Settling, I don't know him from a Gremlin fish-monger."

"That keen to see you dead, eh?" The Troll rolled onto his back with a pained moan.

"He's been waiting for this day for over a hundred years." Uzran smiled ruefully in the dark. "He can be forgiven his hastiness."

"Oh, Cap'n, Cap'n," Droth sing-songed mournfully as he craned his neck toward the Ogre. He winced and settled back to consider the rock roof. 'Makin' friends every place we go."

"You didn't have to come," Uzran muttered absently, feeling his body's every ache and pain, wondering if he could sit upright.

"Would you quit gnawing on that ol' bone," the Troll said with tired exasperation. "I'm in the thick of it with with you now, no two ways about it."

Uzran sighed and let out a tremendous breath. He sat up with painful slowness. Looking at how close the roof was as he sat on the floor, the Ogre imagined that to walk about, he would have to bend nearly double to keep his legs from bunching underneath him in a perpetual, cramp-inducing squat. There was more headroom closer to the door, but he wouldn't be able to stand up straight until after that iron portal finally opened.

And when that happened, he would be led to his death.

"Sentinel?" Uzran called to the guard beyond the door. "Have any water you'd be willing to part with?"

There was no reply for some time then both Uzran and Droth looked hopefully at each other as they heard the sound of liquid pouring into a vessel. A moment later there was a rasp and clatter, and a small, sharp squeak as a panel in the iron bars slid upward. An earthen bowl slid through the space, splashing slightly as it bumped along across the uneven floor.

The panel slid down, another rattle, then a shunted rasp, and the cudgel rapped twice across the bars.

"Go ahead," the voice said, but Uzran was already squirming toward the bowl.

Despite his thirst, the captain made certain his lieutenant, who seemed far worse for wear, took the first few swallows. The Troll didn't protest, slurping the water gladly before he settled back against the floor, eyes closed. Taking a few thankful mouthfuls himself, the Ogre shuffled to the door and set his back against the wall to the right of it.

"Thank you," Uzran said, loud enough to be heard in the other room, but not so loud as to be shouting. "I know there are not many who would be willing to give any kindness to me. Not on this mountain anyway."

There was no reply. As carefully as he could, keeping his shackles clear of the bars, Uzran leaned over and peeked into the room. His broad back bent over the table, an Ogre squatted upon the stool and made an inventory of his prisoners' effects. Their weapons and Droth's walking stick were on the right with their belts and coin purses on top of them. On his left Droth's cloak was rolled up into a neat bundle.

Uzran couldn't see what the Ogre was doing with his hands, but there was a rustle of fabric, and then Uzran's cloak sat next to Droth's in a matching bundle.

"Has Kugin said what his plans are for us?" Uzran watched the guard take up his belt, one swollen lip brushing against the icy surface of the iron. "Any instructions?"

"Away from the door," the Sentinel grunted over his shoulder, but made no move to get up.

"When is the next Grudge-Settling?" Uzran pressed, edging a little closer, though mindful of his bruised mouth. "Is there to be one tonight?"

The Sentinel emptied Uzran's coin purse into his palm, counted the coins, slid them back into the coin purse, and wrote on something on the table.

"Kugin does not tell the likes of me his plans," the guard snorted off-handedly as he rolled Uzran's belt into a tight hoop around the attached coin purse. "But I heard him calling one of the Senior Sentinels to make for the Elder's Gate ahead of him."

Uzran pulled back from his view of the guardroom as the Sentinel took up Droth's belt. The news was what he was waiting for, but its impact was more profound than he expected. He felt like an anvil sunk into his belly, and the pain of his smashed face was forgotten as he felt his mouth grow dry and his throat tighten. This was it.

Before the sun rose on a new day, he would be dead. He would make his appeal, hoping for some mercy from the uncaring Wyrd, but he knew it was a fool's hope. This was how he would die . . . not as a hero with his trophy hefted beside Arzgund's Skull, nor as warrior falling in battle among the mounds of his defeated foes. He would die as a common criminal, dragged before the Elders to hear his name rightly cursed and disparaged before he found his skull falling beneath Justice's Maul. Childhood oaths or no, this was to be his end.

"Well, that's that then," Uzran said numbly.

"What's that?" Droth said with a snuffle, coming out of a light doze.

Uzran looked over, smiling in spite of himself at the Troll's ability to sleep anywhere, his proficiency outmatching even the veteran abilities of the other Royal Guards. Once, in what felt like another lifetime, after Droth had fallen asleep in full armor in a muddy trench in the middle of a pouring rain, the younger Guards had taken to calling him Old Lind, after the legendary wyrm-spawn who slumbered for ages in the caverns beneath the mountains. Though Uzran had never used the nickname, it seemed as apt now as ever.

"Kugin's meeting with the Elders." Uzran shook off the fog of reminiscence. He wouldn't spend his last moments in a stupor of nostalgia. When he died, he would meet his end with his head as high and his eyes as clear as the Wyrd allowed.

"Well, he's not wastin' any time then," Droth said, the words having a similarly sobering effect on the Troll. "How long we got?"

"I'm not sure," the Captain confessed, resting his head against the wall behind him. "It'll be over before sunrise for sure. Kugin doesn't want to chance that the Queen or one of her emissaries sweeps in and saves me. Not that she would now, anyways."

"That's good then. They're goin' to be in a rush, and that means they'll make mistakes. You just need to make sure that you angle them into condemning you to death before they denounce your place among the clans."

Uzran didn't raise his head from the stone, but his eyes swung to look at Droth.

"What?"

"Trial of the Guiltless," came the answer, but it was from the Sentinel in the guardroom. "If they condemn you to death, you can demand to face the Trial, but only if you are still considered one of the People of the Stone."

"Balls," Droth swore quietly under his breath.

"You should learn to scheme more quietly," the guard's voice said from beyond the iron barred door. "If Kugin or one of his cronies had been in here, your plan would be over before it began."

There was sourness in the Sentinel's pronunciation of his leader's name that neither Droth nor Uzran missed. Uzran sidled over and looked through the gap into the guardroom. The Ogre had finished his inventory, everything arranged in orderly fashion on the left side of the table, and he sat on the stool, head bowed. The Captain couldn't say exactly how he knew—the stoop of the shoulders or the tenor of the Sentinel's voice—but he could see the warrior wrestling with a decision. It was the sort of decision one made quietly in private, and then carried it out to whatever end when the time came, fair or foul.

"And what will you do with such knowledge, Sentinel?" Uzran asked cautiously.

There was a long silence, heavy and thunderous in the ears of all three. "I know your crimes, Thrice-Cursed," the Sentinel said slowly. "I know that you deserve to die for what you did. You cannot deny it."

"I don't," Uzran said in a voice so soft it barely carried to the Sentinel beyond, but when it reached his ears he nodded.

"And yet you came here anyway," the guard said, his

struggle coming through in his words. "You came, and though you were caught up in a brawl, when Kugin came, you did not draw your sword. Some may think that was because you are craven, but I . . . I wonder what it is you wish to accomplish."

"To free our people from a yoke we took in good faith." Uzran's words escaped like steam from under a kettle lid. "A yoke that has grown heavier and heavier, and whose burden I have only increased in all my years. Now, with my eyes opened to my own sins, I come to awaken our people."

"So you come to overthrow the Elders, then?" the Sentinel asked, his flat tone unable to keep out an edge of accusation.

"No," Uzran said with careful deliberation. "I have something far grander in mind."

"Which is?"

"I want to overthrow the Queen."

Droth swore fluidly in one long, low, hissing breath. Despite having known more or less what was in his friend's heart since they left Duanon, he was unprepared to hear it said so baldly.

"Treason against the Twilit Kingdom?" The guard threw a look over his shoulder that was one part reviling shock, one part stunned admiration. "That is certainly grander."

"She is not the Kingdom." Uzran pressed his face against the bars, heedless of his damaged lips. "She has led us on with lies, and that is one of them. A hundred thousand falsehoods have been woven into the lives we lead, and all of them are cords tying us to her. The decrees about where we shall live, the tithes to the Royal Guard, the fact that none of the People of the Stone have ever been part of the Gloaming Court, and so many other things which we accept because we are assured she is great and good—they need to end."

"And you are the one to do it, eh? The one to save us?"

Uzran took in a ragged breath before answering. "I am the one who will try," he said, a grim, unyielding certainty in his voice. "I do not expect to succeed or even survive, but I hope that others' eyes will be opened. I have been part of the reign that kept us bound in lies strong enough that we surrendered our lives to those unworthy of our trust. Now, after all I have done, I can at least try to tear down what I helped build."

The Sentinel gave no answer, his eyes inscrutable, and turned back to consider the table before him, speaking no more.

Kugin did not come himself, but he sent so many Sentinels to march Uzran and Droth to the Cavern of Meeting that they got in each other's way as they moved through the tunnel. The captain and his lieutenant were dragged out of the cell and onto their feet, where coarse rope nooses attached to poles were thrown around their necks. They struggled to stand up straight as the hemp was drawn tight around their throats, and they saw their guard speaking with another Sentinel—a thickset Fomor whose brow was tattooed with two dark lines between the ridged base of his horns.

The Fomor stared at Uzran, and when the warden finished, gave him a sneering smile.

"Not likely, Thrice-Cursed," the Fomor called with an ugly laugh. "Not bloody likely."

Uzran and Droth exchanged crestfallen looks, and then they were dragged down the tunnel toward their doom.

The Cavern of Meeting, an immense amphitheatre of stone domed by a ceiling of dripping stalactites, yawned before them as they were hauled out of the stony passageway. The walls of the cavern had been worked into broad, tiered platforms connected by short stairs, and it was all lit by tall, smoldering braziers. It was on these platforms that the People of the Stone gathered in their thousands to watch the spectacle.

Uzran's head turned slowly, taking in the space, amazed as much by the relative quiet as by the vast numbers present. An expectant hush settled over the entire cavern, with the barest murmur of gathering intensity sliding beneath the surface. That murmur became a rolling hiss, and he felt as much as saw their eyes turn toward him. Ogre, Troll, and Fomor, male and female, child and wizened grandparent . . . all eyes looked down on him, glittering hungrily in the light of the braziers.

"You certainly have an audience, Cap'n," Droth choked out as their handlers goaded and tugged them to the left of the tunnel from which they had emerged.

The People of the Stone watched and muttered, their usual raucousness absent in the face of the grave business of the Thrice-Cursed, a legendary figure of revulsion among them. No Ogre, none of the People of the Stone for that matter, possessed such storied accomplishments as a warrior, barring the mythic heroes of old, but none had ever committed so grave a sin as to betray his parents, his kin, and his clan. The living boogeyman whose minions had collected their sons to fight and die gloriously on far-off battlefields stood before them bound, beaten, and dragged before the Elders like a common criminal. They had no cheers, no jeers, only a pervasive morbid curiosity. So they stood, and they watched.

The northernmost edge of the circular cavern was not constructed like the rest of the tiered platforms. Instead, lumpen, mossy boulders arranged into twelve primeval thrones—four for each race—rested upon a single, trifold stage. These seats on their platforms rose two dozen feet into the air on smooth stone walls, and it was from this height that the Elders looked down upon Droth and Uzran. Four wizened Fomor sat on the right, four leathery Trolls on the left, four grizzled Ogres in the center, and each held a long, iron staff topped by a mallet head of burnished bronze.

Standing in the center of the stone floor in the midst of the threefold stage was Kugin, his armor and cudgel gone. Knots of sinew bunched and slithered across his frame, naked from the waist up, and when he saw Uzran's approach, he broke into a wide, toothy grin.

The tattooed Fomor stepped spryly away from the group and whispered into Kugin's ear. Kugin's smile squirmed into something else, a kind of hateful fear, but then it twisted back again. He regarded Uzran in his shackles, straining not to gag from the rope around his neck.

"Clever," Kugin snarled over the Fomor's shoulder. "But I'm not afraid. You won't worm out of what's due. Not now."

Uzran, heart sinking to his stomach, knew that for all Kugin's self-righteous declarations, this had nothing to do with avenging his wife, Uzran's own sister. It may have once, but hate had performed some terrible alchemy, and it was something far darker driving the Master Sentinel. Uzran's eyes sank at seeing another casualty of his arrogant adherence to his "honor and duty."

The stands filled with excited murmurs and whispers as they pointed at the events unfolding on the floor. Each word was spoken a little louder than the last to be heard over others, and the resulting din threatened to spill over and wash the entire Cavern in a cacophony of gossip and speculation. There was a tremendous crack of metal on stone, and the chamber quieted as thousands of eyes turned to regard the Troll who had struck the stage with the butt of his staff.

"Who comes now before the Elders to settle a grudge?" the Troll bellowed in a voice so thick and raw it took Uzran a moment to understand the words.

Kugin stepped forward and raised both arms before the Elders, turning in a slow circle as he spoke. "I, Kugin of Clan Fyrll, stand before you with no weapon in my hand and my skin bared in peace."

The Troll who acted as speaker for the Elders waited until Kugin faced them squarely before speaking again.

"We see you and give testament to the truth of your words," he intoned, and each Elder stamped the butt of his staff on the stony platform. "What is your grudge, Kugin of Clan Fyrll?"

Kugin lowered his arms, but raised his eyes to look boldly from face to face among the Elders.

"My grudge is set against the one you see now bound before you," he called out, his voice echoing throughout the Cavern, "though I am but one of many who could bear this grudge to you, respected Elders. My grudge is that of a warrior offended, of a People blasphemed, and a husband robbed of his precious bride. My grudge is against Uzran Thrice-Cursed for the murder of Clan Druhn!"

The crowd's murmuring was beaten down by another clash of iron upon rock.

"Are you who Kugin of Clan Fyrll claims you are?" the Troll Elder asked.

Uzran raised his head, not in pride, but out of desire to meet his death with his face to the fore.

"I am."

Another ripple of rising sound was driven back by the descending staff.

"And is there merit in this grudge, or do you renounce Kugin of Clan Fyrll's claim?"

Uzran turned his gaze and met Kugin's leer. "I renounce nothing he has spoken."

"Neither the merit to bring the grudge, nor the charge of the grudge itself?" The Speaker's tone pressed a subtle warning toward Uzran, who already knew what the outcome would be.

"Yes." Uzran couldn't help but notice the many barely-masked smiles among the Elders looking down on him as the crowd bubbled with competing voices. He was making this easy for them.

"You acknowledge that you, Uzran Thrice-Cursed, formerly of Clan Druhn, are responsible for the murder of your entire clan?"

"I do," Uzran answered, and the quiet response carried over the swell of voices.

The staff descended twice before the gathering quieted.

"Very well, Uzran Thrice-Cursed, formerly of Clan Druhn, the Elders recognize you as condemned by the grudge of Kugin of Clan Fyrll."

All twelve staves voiced their assent. Uzran felt the impact of those twelve condemning blows upon his heart, but they were welcome. It was like they struck away crust from his soul— something he had carried for so long that he hadn't realized was suffocating him under its tarnishing weight.

"Elders," Kugin's voice rose before the echo of the staves had died away. "My Sentinels have reported that as humble as this kinslayer may seem now, he has come with artifice to escape what is justly deserved."

Uzran's heart rose to his throat. Was Kugin going to prevent him from speaking before the entire Cavern of

Meeting? Had he really come here to die for his shame and nothing more? He had always known it was a possibility, but now he might experience it as certainty. If he attempted to speak out now, the staves would crash over and over to drown him out as the Sentinels beat him into silence.

The Speaker leaned forward, red-rimmed eyes squinting at the Master Sentinel. "What artifice is this?" The old Troll turned a suspicious glare on Uzran.

"I have learned that, like a craven, he wishes to be disavowed from the People of the Stone, and thus granted exile," Kugin pronounced, turning a disgusted eye on the accused. "Rather than face his end bravely like those he himself put to death, he seeks to slink away under a rock."

Not that he would make it that far. Uzran imagined Kugin added that part to his accusations because he, like everyone else in the Cavern, knew that exiles could be killed without consequence. It would not be the spectacle Kugin wanted, but Uzran knew that if exile was his sentence, he would dead before he left Mount Falchrreg. But Kugin's attempts to ensure justice gave Uzran a glimmer of hope.

Uzran waited silently, wordlessly thanking the guard-room Sentinel, whatever his reasons may have been.

"Then what do you wish the Elders to consider?" The Speaker slid back to rest in his mossy throne.

The old Troll, like the other Elders, seemed bored now. All knew what would unfold and all were eager to have it over with.

"I would see them both put to death," Kugin cried with a feverish intensity.

"Hey," Droth cried, moving forward and straining at the rope around his neck. "You haven't even said two damn words about me, and now you are sentencing me too? What kind of shit-gobbling grudge is this?" A Sentinel drove an elbow into the lieutenant's belly, and he collapsed to his knees.

"Apologies, respected Elders." Kugin turned away from the winded Troll. "In my zeal for justice, I allowed myself to spring ahead of proceedings. For now, I am asking only for the execution of Uzran Thrice-Cursed. A second grudge can be settled after his fate is decided."

Kugin twisted around to spare Droth an ugly, self-satisfied grin, and the kneeling Troll spat blood onto the floor.

"Very well," the Speaker said, and after a moment of gathering nods from the other eleven Elders, he turned back to look down upon Uzran. "The Elders do here sentence Uzran Thrice-Cursed, once of Clan Druhn, to death. He shall be taken to the summit of Falchrreg and—"

"Trial of the Guiltless!" Uzran roared in his thundering battlefield bass.

The murmurs in the Cavern fell to gaping silence, and all eyes darted back and forth between Uzran and the Elders.

"You already confessed!" Kugin snarled, rounding on Uzran. "The Trial of the Guiltless can-"

"Be invoked at any point by the head of a clan on behalf of any of his clan, including himself," Uzran said flatly, turning toward the Elders. "I invoke the Trial of the Guiltless for Uzran of Clan Druhn."

"You are not the head of Clan Druhn!" Kugin frothed, stepping toward Uzran. "You murdered your entire clan!"

"As the last remaining member, and having never been exiled, I stand as the only one who can be the head of my clan," Uzran replied coolly, his face never turning from the Elders. "And as head of Clan Druhn, I invoke the Trial of the Guiltless for Uzran of Clan Druhn."

Kugin screamed in rage and came at Uzran with

clenched fists. Uzran, shackled, hobbled, and with a rope around his neck, bowed his head and took three enraged blows before he lost his footing. The Cavern exploded into shouting and echoing cries. The Sentinels belatedly pulled their maddened leader off of Uzran as the Elders drove their staves down again and again.

"This changes nothing!" Kugin snarled, his face pressing savagely into the side of Uzran's bruised and bleeding head as the Sentinels struggled to haul him back by his arms. "You're still going to pay, Uzran! You're still going to die screaming, Thrice-Cursed!"

13

ENSNARED

I sat on Rhoslyn's back and watched the Army of the Twilit Kingdom mobilize. This was all of it, with the exceptions of one understrength company left as an honor guard at Duanon, and some raw recruits that were just now showing up for training. The massed forces of Queen Meabh, brought together from across the realm and organized according to the schemes of yours truly, now moved to unleash hell on the Gythraul. I felt a twinge of pity for my enemies, outmatched as they were, but feeling much of anything was getting harder since meeting with the Queen.

I came back to that emptiness the way a tongue comes back to the socket where a tooth used to be, but just like the tongue and tooth, the probing didn't bring it back. You felt the absence—the awareness that something should be there—but that was it. That had become the extent of my feeling, except for that terrible, dark exhilaration I still felt at the memory of standing in victory at the last battle.

The valley occupied by Bryth's command and the relief

forces was not large enough to accomodate the rest of our troops. I stood on a rocky hill that imitated the mountains north of our position and looked down on several pocket valleys between the rough hills, watching packs of swift figures kicking up clouds of moondust. They raced outward, dark against the chalky complexion of the hills, and my elevated position let me see a general shape forming. The stretching horns of a crescent were already angling to encompass the wide, bristling rectangle of the Gythraul camp situated along a stretch of the Kindled River to the south.

Ceterum Cinis had dug in, and the scouting reports from the Finger Teams and our Wee Folk spies said that they had serious artillery watching the broad avenues of approach across the rolling steppes. Anything coming within sight of their hastily erected spotting towers was going to take a horrendous beating. I hadn't seen those war-machines in action yet, but according to all I had heard and read, they were nearly as capable as modern American artillery in turning the land for miles around into a pitted hellscape with frightful speed and precision. Which is exactly why we weren't going to start with a ground assault this time.

I watched the five Drakes from Thistlebough climbing into the sky, hearing their immense wings beating the air.

I supposed as a dedicated grunt I should have been bothered that the crux of my battleplan used airpower, but even before the Gormstone I'd felt nothing but gratitude for the thundering, shrieking death machines that zoomed over my dirt-pounding ass. Sure their pilots were a little too full of themselves and made you want to knock a few of their teeth loose, but as the guy on the ground, I could appreciate it when an impregnable enemy position exploded into fire and pureed insurgent. One less deathtrap I had to stick my head into.

I imagined the other companies felt similarly when I told them the battle plan because no objections or criticisms were raised, though I hadn't bothered to ask. Even if we hadn't had the Drakes, there were enough mobile and potent elements to the army that I knew I could slug it out with Cinis and come out on top. This was just more efficient.

Once I crushed the Gythraul here, I would be busy elsewhere in the Kingdom, and it would go a lot smoother if I kept my forces mostly intact.

"I still cannot believe that those things are part of the army," a weary, feminine voice called behind me. I turned and saw Bryth coming up the backside of the hill on her own Diomedan. Dressed in a studded doublet, leather-faced breeches, and with her cloak gathered around her shoulders, she looked drawn and sickly, despite having spent the past week resting. Her recovery since the battle with the Morgs was incomplete, so I gave her a spot as a command attache in this battle. She would stay behind the conflict zones I'd plotted out, coordinating information and maybe providing magical healing if the medical auxiliaries got swamped.

"The wheels turn, and war waits for no one," I said with a shrug as she pulled alongside me. "Humans have been fighting from and in the air for a hundred years now. It's past time your world caught up."

"Yes, but you don't understand how . . ." she began and then stopped, staring at me.

I stared back waiting.

Bryth looked at me with a sad expression that I didn't understand and shook her head before looking back at the

Drakes soaring toward the Gythraul. When she spoke, her voice was rougher and heavier.

"So the Drakes will strafe their artillery positions," she said in a detached, precise tone. "Then as they reorient to repel, a squadron of battle-magi will deliver Morg squads along the banks of the river, where we think their infirmary and supplies have been placed. Is that correct, Gorm?"

"Yes. Torn between those guns and the injured and basic supplies, I knew which I would choose, but we can hope that Cinis is more sentimental, and moves to save the artillery. Either way he loses, though."

Bryth's throat clicked as she swallowed hard next to me.

"I suppose," she said stiffly, turning to give me a sidelong glance. "And if he moves the bulk of his forces to engage the Morgs, what is the plan to extract their handlers and infantry support teams?"

I felt my eyebrows knit as I frowned. "Weren't you at the briefing last night?" I asked, confused. She had been quiet through the whole thing, sitting in the corner with her eyes looking bruised with weariness, but I had hoped she was at least paying attention.

"I was there." There was a brief fire in her eyes that reminded me of something I couldn't explain—some ghost of a feeling such a sight used to provoke. "I was there, but you never explained how you would orchestrate an extraction for the handlers and fireteams."

"Because there is no plan for extraction," I explained. "The Morgs are meant to fight until they run out of things to kill, or they die. The handlers and fireteams can make their way across the Kindled River if they are incapable of holding their positions."

"Crossing the Kindled River at this time of year is

dangerous," Bryth protested. "Doing so under enemy attack is suicide. What happened to no suicide missions?"

Had I said that? Something like it? It sounded familiar, but it didn't matter now.

"Things change." I shrugged. "I have enough Morgs and soldiers that I can spare a few to keep the Drakes safe. I only have five of those, and I won't find more anytime soon."

Bryth sat stunned, mouth hanging slightly ajar, and stared at me with widening eyes. She looked ridiculous, and when she didn't speak, I returned to watching the troop's movements. In a few more minutes I would relocate so I could keep an eye on the tactical situation, though I supposed I could always rely on Sleepyhead who was presumably circling above the battlefield, clear of the Drakes.

"It's happening even faster with you," Bryth said in a soft, breathless whisper. "That damned stone! You wouldn't be talking this way if it weren't for that thing."

"Probably," I grunted as I watched a squadron of Sylvanocerus skirmishers crest a hill and slip out of sight. They were moving quickly, and I made a mental note to check in a few minutes to ensure they didn't wander to within reach of the enemy artillery. A few handlers and fireteams of grunts was one thing, but those skirmishers and their djinn-guns weren't growing on trees.

"Aren't you fighting it?" Bryth asked at my shoulder, and I felt her leaning toward me in her saddle, almost close enough to touch. "You can't just give in to it, Luce, please. No enchantment is unbreakable, no spell irreversible, but you have to want to be free. All the magic in the world won't matter if you don't want it undone!"

There was a growing hysteria in her voice, and though the words she said made sense individually, it was getting harder to understand what she was talking about. Was she really talking about undoing the Gormstone? Did she really think she could pit her will against the Queen and succeed? Was she talking about betraying the Queen?

The idea crackled through my brain like a lightning bolt and before I fully processed what was going on, my body twisted in the saddle toward Bryth. The sharp, snake-like movement made her recoil, and her steed shuffled backwards, but not before I shot a hand out and closed my fingers around her forearm. Bryth took a quick, pained breath as my fingers tightened, causing the flesh to dimple, and she was forced to lean closer to me or risk separating her shoulder.

I gave Rhoslyn a hard nudge, and with a protesting whinny, she sidled closer to Bryth and her retreating mount. "It is treason to speak like that, Bryth." The words came out flat and mechanical.

I saw it happening and had an inkling of why, but for the life of me I couldn't remember when I had decided on this course of action. My chest ached with cold and my fingers, my arm, and my mouth seemed to be moving without bothering to ask my permission.

"Lucius, please . . . Luce, this is not who you are," Bryth said stiffly, her face tightening at the force my hand applied to her arm. "The stone ensnares you, but you must resist."

She didn't pull away, but she didn't succumb easily either—her whole body seemed taut and unyielding.

I felt the cords of muscle in my arm flex with unnatural strength, and Bryth bit back a cry of pain. I wondered absently why I was hurting her. Did I really need to?

"Treason against the Queen, even with careless words, deserves punishment." I looked into her face and saw the first flash of real fear, even though my tone was that of a man reading a traffic sign.

"Luce, please, stop," she hissed through grinding teeth. "This isn't who you are. This isn't what you want!"

What I want? I pulled back and stared at her, and my conscious mind raced to catch up with decisions my body was making without it. What I wanted seemed a novel thing cutting through the haze, and as I looked at her, something hungry and terrible woke up. In a glance it sized her up, noting miniscule details, from the bags under her eyes to the swell of her breasts pushing against her doublet. That thing inside of me saw weakness and softness and it—I—wanted to take her. As psychically bankrupt as I was, I still knew it was wrong and reprehensible, but a will—not a voice really, but some alien intelligence that was partly but not wholly mine—filled the inside of my skull.

Punishment. Gratification. Acceptable.

Moving with their own terrible will, my hands gripped above both her elbows and I tried to haul her out of her saddle and onto my horse.

"Luce, no, stop!" She twisted in my grip.

I pulled her from the saddle, but lost my hold on her and she fell to the ground heavily. Her Diomedan turned on me with a surge of fierce loyalty, snapping its fangs and rearing to lash at me with hard, sharp hooves. Rhoslyn, confused and full of frightened anger, defended herself with her own teeth and hooves, and I let myself slide from the saddle to escape the battle between the two flesh-eating equines. I hit the ground on my feet, momentum forcing me to roll my armored body to dissipate the force, but I was back up and advancing toward Bryth in an instant. I felt nothing other than a cold burning at the skin of my chest.

Bryth, who fell much harder than I did, was getting to

her feet as she crawled clear of the fighting Diomedans. Her cloak was torn and coming free of its broaches. She saw me coming and turned, raising one hand that had been bloodied by her fall between us.

"Luce, enough!" she shouted, managing to get one knee under her. "I don't know what it is doing to you, but you need to stop this now! Please!"

This? What was this? I questioned myself, though part of me knew—the part that had been screaming in the corner since the Gormstone was placed in my chest. It knew what was happening before she had seen the truth in my eyes.

But my conscious mind couldn't accept it, even as my body followed the will of that ruthless, me-not-me intelligence.

I swatted her bloodied hand away, and shoved her back onto the ground. Behind us I could hear screams and snorts as our mounts beat and tore at each other. I drove down on top of her, my hands on her shoulders, my knee coming down between her legs.

She was fighting now—squirming, striking, and twisting to get away—but I was bigger, heavier, and, even without the Gormstone, I had always been stronger. Now her resistance was almost childlike in my grip.

"Luce, stop!" she screamed. "Stop!"

Her screams mirrored the shrinking voice inside my head, but an unholy accord had been struck between the cold fire in my chest and the darkness inside of me. I gathered both her wrists in one metal-clad hand as I bore of more of my weight on her, forcing her legs further apart.

"Luce, I love you!" she sobbed. "Don't make me, please! Don't! Please!"

A pained shriek split the air, and the heavy impact of flesh and bone on earth sounded behind us.

My free hand reached out and pulled at the throat of the doublet, clasps coming away with sharp metallic *pings* as I ground myself deep against the laced seam of her britches. She squirmed and kicked, thrashing and crying, but the top of one breast was already exposed, and the doublet and smallclothes beneath parted under my ripping grasp.

Why was I doing this? How could I be doing this?

"STOP!"

The words tore from my own throat, ragged and hoarse, and for just a moment, my hand relaxed its violating grip, and I looked into Bryth's eyes. That shrinking, cornered voice had broken through, and for one glorious instant, the cold and dark inside of me retreated. I didn't know how she could, but I needed her to see that, to see me, before it came back and took her. Already, I could feel that intelligence asserting itself through my clenching fingers.

"I love you," I sobbed. "I don't want to, I . . ."

But then the cold had me, and my voice flattened into a coarse whisper. My fingers bit into her skin and clothing. "Hold still and shut up."

There was pressure in the air, and then my whole body suddenly arced backwards. Even through the numbing effects of the Gormstone, I felt electric agony snapping along every synapse in my body.

I must have flown several feet through the air, because when I gathered myself enough to sit up, I saw Bryth stagger to her feet well out of arm's reach. One bloodied hand was raised toward me in a warding gesture while the other, sporting livid welts about the wrist, pinned her torn doublet closed against her chest.

"Stay back!" she said, and I felt energy for another punishing curse gather around her.

I made as if to stand, but my legs didn't cooperate, flopping flat and nerveless in front of me. Through the insulating numbness of the Gormstone, I felt pins and needles prickling through my limbs.

"I didn't want to," Bryth began, but then her eyes shifted to something beyond me and she gave a quiet groan.

I followed her gaze to the body of a Diomedan. Bryth's mount lay on the ground, its throat a gaping, ragged mess below a skull crushed into unnatural angles. Rhoslyn was nowhere to be seen.

A series of percussive booms sounded, far off, but deep enough to make my molars ache as they echoed through the air. Less imposing but still distinct, the sauroid roar of the Drakes pierced through the echoing thunder. The battle had begun.

Bryth and I locked eyes, and when I spoke, her face hardened into an angry, defiant mask.

"Run, traitor," I commanded, cautiously putting first one leg under me and then the other. "I will find you and finish this soon enough."

"You won't have to find me, Luce." Her voice was strong even though tears sparkled at the corners of eyes. "When I am ready, I'll come for you."

14

ENCIRCLED

In the end I used the hagseye and a nearby pixie to locate Rhoslyn. The Diomedan was bleeding and bruised from her fight, but she had survived worse, so I took hold of her reins, threw myself over her saddle, and drove my heels into her quivering flanks.

Dealing with Bryth had cost me precious time and attention that, in retrospect, should have been spent attending to the battle.

As the Diomedan's preternaturally quick gallop took me over and between the hills toward the central plains, I caught glimpses of the Gythraul encampment. Large plumes of black smoke snaked across the sky as the sinewy bodies of all five Drakes slithered through on unfurled wings. I watched as they bent their horned heads and disgorged sweeping columns of venomous green fire from fanged mouths. The torrents of drake-fire danced and spun like cyclones, touching down among the Gythraul, detonating ammunition stores and setting soldiers alight to run screaming through the chaos.

Bolts from the Gythraul crossbows shot upward, most

falling short, while the few that reached the drakes rebounded off the creatures' scales and armored plating. It had taken the Arch-Monger some time to create a light-weight, heat-resistant alloy that still offered significant protection, but as before, the bubbling mind of the Daerg rose to the task. Concentrated fire from the skorpions could prove to be the undoing of the Drakes, but the skorpions were slow to mobilize, and the fiery beasts would be away before taking any real damage.

In frustration, one of the Gythraul artillery fired, barking its incendiary, shrieking payload into the sky. The airborne monsters easily avoided the blast, though the shot was so poorly timed they were never in any real danger. The Gythraul guns, the gunners' training, and the munitions used were all meant for firing on land-based targets, and the adjustment to aerial targets couldn't be effectively made in one battle. If I relied only on the Drakes, eventually the Gythraul would get lucky, but I didn't intend to let them adapt.

I crested another hill and rode down a slope into a deep valley, sheltered from the sight of the battle and any enemy patrols that might have slipped out and around our attack pattern. Giving Rhoslyn her head, I used the hagseye to see Sleepyhead's perspective of the ongoing assault.

The Drakes peeled away, content with the molten handi-work left in their wake, while Gythraul centuries glared upward and flinched away from the passing shadows. As the Drakes sailed back toward the hills, I saw the entire Gythraul front lean forward, expecting our forces to make a ferocious advance now that their dreaded artillery was in shambles, but they waited for something that wasn't coming.

Finally on the full offensive, I would crush them my own

way, using my army of wolfish companies to rip and tear at them from every direction. Ceterum Cinis would learn exactly how outmatched he was.

I looked over the Gythraul camp, using Sleepyhead's aerial perspective to watch the riverside. Past rolling plumes of fire on the Kindled River's surface, I saw a whirl of a pale dust and several dark shapes moving through the air.

The few legionnaires stationed near the infirmaries and baggage train did not see them until the battle-magi drew the first Morgs over the burning waterway, and by then it was too late. The hulking beasts took off into the forest of tents and palisades, uprooting what they could not flatten outright. The infantry fire teams following them put down the Gythraul defenders not killed in the initial rush and then used their incendiary grenades to great effect, destroying caches of supplies.

A smile spread across my face as the Morgs, loping forward with a gorilla-like knuckle-gallop, smelled the blood and death of the infirmaries and locked in for a full-on charge. A few stupidly brave legionnaires held their ground in front of the pavilions, launching bolt after bolt into the oncoming monsters, but it was pointless. The two-ton brutes smashed through them like they were bowling pins and fell upon the infirmary stations in a storm of tooth and claw.

The pavilions bulged and buckled as the Morgs set to work. Some of the physicians and more able-bodied wounded scrambled or crawled away from the collapsing expanses of canvas, only to catch manticore quills from the waiting fireteams with their chests.

The spirit of vengeance I had awoken in my soldiers that night with the Gythraul prisoners left no room for mercy or quarter. We had them encircled, and now it was about tightening the noose until every last one of them was dead.

To their credit, the Gythraul scrambled defenders to the rear quicker than I expected. Two entire centuries, each with a skorpion, ran in loose formation back between the rows of tents. The heavy, shrapnel-spewing weapon, combined with the massed fire of two hundred or more legionnaires would take a heavy toll on the Morgs and their support teams. But those legionnaires never got there.

The sound of the shots was lost to the general clamor of death and ruin already resounding across the plain, but the effects were clear enough when three of the forerunners for the centuries pitched over sideways into the dirt. That might have been enough to slow the advance, but when the downed bodies suddenly erupted with lances of pale pink ice, those nearby were forced to ground to avoid being impaled.

With a stumbling realization the centuries slowed, just in time for another three to collapse and explode into a nest of stabbing, raking lengths of ice. It took another three crumbling and blasting out in killer icicles before both centuries went down on their bellies, crawling among their own tents. Now and again one legionnaire would raise his head a little too far or cross a stretch of open ground only to collapse and bloom into a dozen piercing shards. The rescuers were pinned, their skorpions standing impotently among the tents as their wielders tried to see where death was coming from.

The truth was that it came from three different Finger Teams that had infiltrated some of the lower rises on the steppe just outside the encampment. From their camouflaged nests, the Goblin teams used the Daerg adaptation of the Beretta M82 anti-material rifle. Nine had been found in the arms and equipment taken from Baumholder. It took the devious creatures of Chillspire some time to work something out for the Light 50, but eventually, they had concocted a devastating new gun. Using Jotun bone spurs laced with Yeti hair, the Daerg had devised an ammunition that not only punched into a victim at extreme velocity, but also took the water in the body and expanded it into needles of ice. The Gythraul rescue effort stalled thanks to these weapons which The Daerg called Ballistic Jotun Rifles. The Goblins had taken to calling them Frost Pops.

A rescue force of nearly two hundred Gythraul was pinned down by nine Goblins with Frost Pops. My smile that began when the Morgs started tearing into the infirmaries broadened.

I took out the hagseye and checked my actual position, finding that Rhoslyn was cantering along, her head drooping slightly. We followed the valley floor as it led toward the last line of hills before the open steppe land. The bulk of my forces stretched across those hills, waiting for their chance to take a pound of flesh from the already bloodied legions. Before I took the hagseye up again, the shadow of the Drakes spread over the valley floor.

The beasts didn't bother to look below, their conditioning driving them toward the roosts set up a quarter mile to the east. The Ancient Wyrms, I was told, were machiavellian masterminds when not enraged. These bastard offspring were far simpler, functioning with an intelligence more like that of a grade schooler, albeit one whose mind and responses had been shaped by an exacting beast trainer like Lord Bwyathardd. They could follow simple two or three step instructions faithfully and differentiate friend from foe—which was essential—but otherwise the drakes were just beasts, shadows of the extinct dragons they descended from.

Their blackened armor resembled a crocodile's scutum, I noted, watching them pass overhead, oblivious to their master below. Those beasts would redeploy soon enough, but for now they would rest and eat while the rest of my war machine set to work.

A chorus of shrieks cut through the air, and I socketed the hagseye in time to see banshee shells crashing down on the Legionnaires' ranks on the northwestern flank. Some of the platoons on the outer horn of the broad pincer formation had moved close enough to open up with their mortars. The guns on that side of the Gythraul camp had suffered ammunition detonations, and not a single one of their artillery pieces there seemed operational.

The shells, empowered by the deathly wails of unquiet spirits, exploded in swirls of dust and withered legionnaire flesh and armor. Here and there, Gythraul staggered back, clutching rotting, shrunken limbs, but in most impact sites, nothing was left within the blast radius except the husks of enemy soldiers in corroded armor. With the keening bursts, they aged centuries gracelessly, their bodies and equipment buckling under the strain.

Ceterum Cinis and his legions accepted the first shelling without response, the centuries on the northern line holding their ground doggedly. But he drew half of a cohort from the center of the line to move toward the beleaguered rear of the encampment. I saw what he was doing, and it was a two-fold ploy. He thought that he could lure me into taking advantage of the gaps in his line, or barring that, catch my reinforcements to the Morg teams as they moved in. Except I wasn't going to waste my time with either.

With that many legionnaires, not even the Frost Pop

Goblins could keep the Gythraul from moving in to kill or drive the Morg teams into the burning river. The Morgs would die bloody, with Gythraul around them, but they were as good as gone now, along with their handlers and support teams. Yet taking that many soldiers across his encampment would leave his center very thin—an inviting target for a massive Morg-led advance with skirmishers and infantry coming in behind. With the battle-magi and some myrk shells to cover our advance, we could dive in, splitting their position wide open, and create an avenue of escape for the forces up against the river.

Ceterum Cinis counted on me to care about what happened to those raiders I sent to hit him from behind, hoping it would drive me to take a bold risk. Problem was, I didn't care at all.

The battle—which some of the grunts were already calling the Last Battle on the Steppes—drew to a close as the light faded on the second day of fighting. More than one abortive attempt to break free or reposition took place—especially through the night when the Drake runs and mortar bombardments were understandably less frequent—but every try cost Cinis and his legions more soldiers. He had known he was going to lose before, but he hadn't counted on the Drakes, or on his own artillery becoming so impotent.

On the morning of the second day, as the silvery dawn turned the steppes into a rolling plain of alabaster and pearl, I was surprised to hear the remaining guns of the Gythraul roar in defiance. Their burning salvos—immense fireballs that streaked through the skies like meteors—fell just at the foot of the sheltering hills. Over and over they plowed into the powdery topsoil before bursting into gouts of flame and a viscous, magma-like spray. Some of the hills actually deformed into seared little craters, but we were too far out. Achingly close . . . but not close enough. A few casualties occurred, of course, and one unlucky squad coming back from patrol passed between two hills as a stray shell fell far afield of the main zone of fire, and they disappeared. Not one of the squad survived, but it was nothing compared to the devastation that ineffectual shelling was doing to the Gythraul.

The officer in charge of the artillery auxiliaries—or maybe just his gunners acting on their own impotent rage—threw a fit. No impact could be seen from their efforts, and then it was all too clear that all their firepower was useless. When I launched another Drake run and bombardment on the sectors with disabled guns, what was left of the remaining legions knew they'd lost. Each Gythraul was making peace with his coming death after that, or he was a fool.There was no other outcome than this.

I stood next to Lord Fian, liaison with the battle-magi, and Hurrahn, Royal Guard Standard Bearer, in the crook of two hills watching the sun sink toward the Gythraul camp. "They're crumbling," I said. "They are going to make one big push and then fall apart."

Lord Fian smiled wolfishly at this, the tattooed dome of his head crinkling as he raised his eyebrows. "Why wait for that when we could strike the blow ourselves?"

"There is no need." I gave an easy shrug. "That would be wasteful, and this is not the only battle ahead of us, no matter what the rank and file say. Ceterum Cinis will hang himself soon enough, and there is no reason that I should risk my forces to hurry things along. "

"No need to risk since the Morg teams," grunted Hurrahn, a Fomor with an armored helmet that covered an entire side of his head to hide his mangled socket. "*They* seemed worth risking to hurry things along."

I turned from the view and looked up at the horned giant. "Obviously," I said, my face twisting into a frown. "Otherwise, I wouldn't have ordered it. Is there something bothering you, Hurrahn?"

The Standard Bearer who had traveled with me when I first rallied the Lords and Ladies of the Far-Hold stared down at me with his one good eye. As my own emotions atrophied, my ability to understand and respond to the emotions of others succumbed to rigor mortis.

"It's just . . . seeing them out there." Hurrahn stretched one long arm toward the row of crosses behind the ranks of Gythraul which still stood. "It gnaws at me that we let the Gythraul do that to them, my Gorm. Some of them are still alive."

I looked where he pointed and saw the rows of crucified creatures—the remains of the Morg handlers and infantry support teams. At dusk the evening before, Cinis had taken the captives from my hopelessly fated raiders and nailed them to crosses made from the poles of the trampled infirmary pavilions. Through the night and into the morning, you could hear their screams echo across the plain.

"Of course it does," I said sharply to the Fomor, extending my own hand toward the dead and the dying. "They are put there especially to provoke you to do something stupid. That is why I am in command and you or Captain Uzran are not."

Hurrahn's good eye narrowed inside his helmet at my mention of the Ogre, but when he spoke, his voice was empty of all irritation or bile. "What are your orders, Gorm?"

"How are we doing on myrk and banshee rounds?" I

turned to look back over the Gythraul. They had started adapting to the Drake runs, so to keep them confused, we had launched shells which burst into clouds of impenetrable dark to obfuscate the Drake movements and their gouts of strafing fire.

"We can maintain bombardment at the current rate into tomorrow, but by then our supplies will be running short," the Fomor reported.

"I have sent two platoons to take one of Lord Arawn's daughters and a host of dead to fetch more," Lord Fian said promptly. "I imagine we will be resupplied well before daybreak."

"Good." I nodded absently as I thought. "Hurrahn," I said without taking my eyes off the enemy position, "an hour after full dark, I want a spread of myrk and banshee shells across the entire front. Their guns are done for, so we can advance close enough for that under cover of night. Actual casualties aren't as important to me as confusion. I want it to feel like we are hitting them with everything we've got. Cinis will think we are coming to finish him off, and that is when he will try and pull off his last gambit."

"Will we? Move in to finish them off?"

"No. We are going to wait and watch to see what he tries. Again, no sense in risking what we don't have to. Inform the company captains of the plan, tell them to keep their platoons in overwatch. I want everyone in on this."

The Fomor bent his head and tromped off to do his duty.

"What if Cinis retreats across the Kindled River?" Lord Fian said with a nod past the Gythraul camp to the fire-spitting waterway. "It would be difficult, and they would lose many if they rush the crossing, but at this point, that may be Cinis's plan."

"That is where your magi and the Drakes come in." I

met the Lord's glittering eyes. "Have your people ever heard the story of Moses and the Red Sea?"

Cinis did not disappoint. He was no Moses, but he gave it his best.

Even before the bombardment started, our Wee Folk informants, their beady eyes as good as any night-vision goggles, reported the Gythraul were moving. They started by summarily executing the few survivors hanging from the crosses, then quietly dividing up and reorganizing. By the time we started dropping shells on their position, they stood as five roughly equal cohorts—all that was left of the legions they had come with. A division of lizard-mounted cavalry were reported moving between the cohorts before the clouds of myrk and cyclones of banshee screams swept over their position. After that, the intelligence reports became garbled.

When the torrent of abuse trickled off, two things quickly became apparent. First was that Cinis was beating a retreat toward the Kindled River. Four of the five cohorts, now ragged from the shelling, moved along the rear of the camp to the narrowest point in the river. Second was that, whether they were a brave sacrifice or suicidal mutineers, the other cohort and a full division of cavalry were charging out of the drifting clouds of myrk toward the platoons on the open steppes. Maybe they wanted to buy their comrades time or have a chance to strike at their tormentors, but either way, they were coming.

And they were dying before they could even hope to inflict casualties. Frost Pops tore into the close cavalry formation. Bloody shafts of ice that perforated the unlucky bloomed among them, breaking their charging wedge into a staggering blob. I had ordered the Finger teams into new positions in anticipation of just such an event.

Gythraul knights struggled to control their mounts and continue the charge as two flights of skirmishers raced along either flank and stitched their amorphous line with djinn-guns. Rapidfire bolts of lightning snapped and crackled up and down the line, leaving corpses to tumble to the ground, smoking in the after-image flashes.

Three entire platoons had advanced in the dark, crawling on their bellies, and it was their bursts of rifle fire that finished the cavalry. The manticore quills punched through armored bodies and scaly hides; the basilisk venom they carried ate at the flesh beneath, driving soldier and beast to thrash and flail, splintering their cohesion. Royal Guard attachments assigned to infantry squads or platoons shared their own explosions of djinn gun fire. The chargers became knots of individual warriors desperately trying to escape.

A few managed to skirt around the oncoming foot soldiers who were already slowing, perhaps realizing how completely they were outmatched. Given time, they might run away, beating a quick, desperate retreat toward the river, but that was only if my soldiers gave them that chance.

And with a vengeful animus shining in their night-shadowed eyes, that wasn't an option. Frost Pops and the closest squad of infantry rifles pinned them down, and then skirmishers came, and then the rest of the squad's platoon, and then the other platoons.

I removed the hagseye, the perspective from the Night Gab I used was quickly overcome by the relentless muzzle flares filling the night like a legion of dying stars glinting with deathly light. In those dazzling moments, I watched the Gythraul fall in droves, and that same thin smile slipped over my face.

My senses back in my own body, I stood on the opposite side of the Kindled River, watching the Gythraul passing over its burning surface. Confused at first, I saw legionnaires squatting in close proximity on stretches of an undulating metallic surface. Their advance across the water, which was punctuated by jets of flame every so often, wasn't quick, necessarily, but it was steady, and if I allowed them to cross uncontested, a good number of them would make it.

Instead, I lowered my upraised fist, and the Drakes, hunkered down on the banks, opened their toothy maws and blasted flames across the river.

It was a trick to coordinate the large reptiles, their handlers, and the magi correctly along the opposite bank. Too close, and their overlapping fire would be wasted. Too far apart, and we risked a coherent force of legionnaires forming up on the opposite riverbank.

Watching the sickly green flames roll across the hellish, smoldering surface of the Kindled River, I felt confident that there was no danger of the Gythraul forming any kind of real threat. Their armored heads raised in a mute horror that their snarling visors couldn't express, but when the tide of fire came for them, their screams were testament enough.

Some would make it to the shore. With this many it was unavoidable, but I had entire companies mobilizing to other crossing points miles up river where they would scour the countryside for survivors. Sleepyhead marshalled together Wee Folk spies with promises and threats so that any gathering of more than five legionnaires would have a shadow waiting to lead my hunters to its position.

I stood on the shores of the Kindled River and basked in the waves of heat and screams which rolled up from the simmering waterway—my handiwork. The enemies of the Queen were crushed, and with the exception of a few minor casualties, my army was intact. That dark exultation at seeing my defeated enemy almost stole over me, then in the rolling fires, smoke, and steam, a gleam caught my eye.

The smoldering flames of the river had turned his armor from alabaster to a rosy shade of pink—except when jets of drake fire painted it a wan green—but I recognized the white armor of a Ceterum. Two such armored figures had nearly reached the shore at the very edge of the southern-most Drake's position. One matched the proportions of Cinis, thick and bandy-limbed, while the other was a towering figure, standing a head and shoulders above Cinis. He wasn't thickly built, but he was solid enough for his exceptional height.

The undulating raft reached the shore with the two Ceterums and a half-dozen bodyguards, their red armor matching their infernal surroundings. As the raft was about to strike the shore, it reared and slithered up the bank, driven by short, pumping legs. The Gythraul were using the hellipedes to cross.

I didn't realize they could do that, but it didn't matter. I doubted their caustic fire would bother the Drakes, and without support from the legionnaires, they were easy enough to isolate and destroy.

"Fian!" I shouted into the night and waited for the magi's pale face to emerge from the dark.

"Yes, my Gorm." His eyes were fever bright as they reflected the flames on the river.

"Look." I pointed toward the hellipede on the shore with white and red-armoured Gythraul hopping off its back. "Ceterum Cinis and another commander are making their escape. Get me over there now."

If I had Rhoslyn on this side of the river, it would have been a quick trot for her, but it was a waste of the magus's energy to transport her. She had collapsed not long after I rode her into the hills to conduct the battle. It seemed the fight with Bryth's Diomedan had taken a greater toll than I thought.

"Should I not just direct one of the Drakes to finish them?" Fian asked, a queer anxiety showing in his eyes.

"The Drakes are busy, and I want both commanders taken captive, not dead. They'll be a chain-wrapped gift to our Queen."

"Very well, my Gorm," Fian said, with a reluctance I found surprising. The battle-magus had never balked before, but perhaps the idea of being so close to an actual enemy that could fight back was not to his taste.

As if to confirm my suspicions, after fitting his peaked helmet on his bare head, the battle-magus bellowed for others to attend him. Two other magi sprang from the dark, and with them came three squires. It took me a moment to recognize one of them as Kieren Shieldson. I had forgotten about him.

"So you actually made it to the battle?" I said flatly.

Kieren eyed me with a dark, accusing look but he said nothing.

"I am supposed to serve at your side, my Gorm," he said stiffly, his voice barely carrying over the sounds of burning and dying. "How can I earn may place as a full battle-magus without fighting at your side?"

"Fair point," I pointed to the retreating figure of Ceterum Cinis and company. "So why don't you and your friends get us over there, already?"

Kieren hung his head, but I felt the gathering of magic and then heard the arcane words punching like blunt spikes of sound through the tortured ambiance. The fire, the Drakes, and the strangely reflective dust of the steppes flew beneath my feet. The magical windstorm yowled in my ear, and I joined its voice with my own as we soared over the heads of the racing Gythraul.

We touched down a hundred yards ahead of them, and before they could raise their crossbows, lances of fire, lightning, and will-sharpened stone bore down on the bodyguards. Red-armoured bodies hit the ground in small clouds of moondust.

One bodyguard staggered to his feet, and I snapped off a round from my M-Core that burrowed into his chest, right above his heart. He didn't bother to scream as the poison gnawed and smoked; he only only gave a grunting sigh as he slumped to the ground.

I walked toward the two Ceterums standing stunned amongst the wreckage of their bodyguards. The battle-magi flanked me on either side, slowly and quietly encircling the two.

"It didn't have to be this way," Cinis called, his voice tight and hard, so unlike its usual, easy power. "Now these lands will drown in the blood of both our peoples!"

"You're wrong," I replied, advancing with my rifle held across my chest. "It *did* have to be like this, Cinis. Thinking otherwise was just stupidity. A wasted dream."

To my surprise, Cinis unclasped his dragon helm and toss it aside to look me in the eye. "All hope is just a dream that is unashamed of its foolishness," Cinis said, his voice grown quieter and heavier. "I thought that you would have seen that with me."

"Put that shit on a fortune cookie and get on your knees." I raised the rifle, leveling the barrel at his chest. "I'd like to take you prisoner, but my Queen will be just as happy with your head on a stick."

"Like Ceterum Lacertun?" the huge Gythraul beside Cinis bellowed in voice that matched Uzran for depth and power. "Like the prisoners you barbarians butchered even as they knelt in the dirt?"

"Basically," I said without taking the barrel off Cinis. "Yeah, that works for me."

"Whoreson!" the big Gythraul roared, ripping his sword from his belt as he started taking long steps toward me. "I'll carve each of their names in your damn bones!"

"No! Bellamarus, wait!" Cinis screamed, but it was too late.

Out of the corner of my eye, I watched an arc of lightning hiss and crackle across the ground and hit Ceterum Bellamarus in the chest. The Gythraul's feet came off the ground, then he crashed down, limbs twisting and popping this way and that before he collapsed, limp and boneless. At my shoulder, I spied Kieren looking for approval of his handiwork, but I ignored him and motioned to Fian.

With a nod and a quick twist of eldritch syllables, wedges of stone burst from the ground around Cinis, pinning him between their blunt edges. He gave a winded grunt, but the defeated Ceterum didn't struggle against the unyielding prison. Instead, he watched as I advanced.

"You are going to be a little gift for Queen Meabh," I told him, stepping around the body of Bellamarus, the battle-magi moving with me on either side, like a pair of armored wings.

"It's such a damned waste," Cinis said softly, his voice shaking a little, his eyes never turning from mine. "A shameful, stupid waste."

"The only thing you wasted," I began coolly, "was my time and your breath with those peace talks."

Ceterum Cinis searched my face, and it was then I saw the tears forming at the corners of his eyes.

"What was done to you?" His voice was just above a whisper. "What sorcery changed you?"

"Nothing you—"

My answer was cut off by a surprised shout, and then I was knocked to the ground.

Scrambling in the dirt, I spun with my M-Core aimed upward, but another blast of lightning erupted, two voices screamed in unison, and it was over.

Squire Kieren Shieldson and Ceterum Bellamarus fell to the ground, bound together with static sparks snapping off their burnt bodies. Bellamarus clung to his sword with a rictus grip, the blade buried to the hilt in the gap between the Squire's gorget and his neck.

With a grunt, I climbed to my feet and looked at the two corpses, both smoking and filling the air with the smell of burnt hair and roast pork.

"If you'd done it right the first time, you wouldn't be dead." I looked into Kieren's cracked and peeling face, then raised my eyebrows when that face twitched to agonized life.

"I . . . serve . . ." he gasped, the effort splitting the cracks on his face into thin, bleeding seams.

"Heal him if you can," I said turning my eyes back to Cinis who looked on me with a kind of dawning dread. "But make it quick. I want the Queen's prize in Duanon's dungeons by daybreak."

15

STAINED

Uzran stood on a floor of packed earth and looked at the night sky, savoring the light of the stars. If he was going to die, he was glad that it would be here beneath the open sky rather than in the darkness of the Cavern of Meeting. The People of the Stone had lived and dwelt upon and within the mountains for as long as anyone could remember, and many seemed to prefer the latter, but for the Ogre captain, the stars on a clear night were hard to beat.

The Trial of the Guiltless was always held in one of the outer arenas near the base of Mount Falchrreg, with the exception of when the Grand Thaig happened to fall during the harsh winter months. Without ceremony, the Sentinels had hauled him roughly down the southernmost slope and deposited him there in the well-used arena where competitions of strength and violence were held.

"If they don't hurry this up it'll be dawn before this show gets started," Droth growled from where he hung, chained to the timbered palisade that encircled the arena of packed earth.

In a petty jab at Uzran and his companion, Master Sentinel Kugin adapted the Trial of the Guiltless slightly by having the Troll chained within the arena with Uzran. "If you are guiltless before the People and the Wyrd, surely your friend will be spared, too," he sneered as Uzran protested and the Sentinels roughly bound Droth to the thick, log walls.

Around the Ogre and Troll, voices babbled and yammered beyond the palisade, and here and there faces pressed against the gaps between the timbers to leer at the condemned. A single, masonry platform reserved for the Elders loomed over the blunt points of the wall. They looked down from there with complacent patience. The crowd from the Settling of Grudges contented themselves with smashing their faces between the splintery wood or listening to another describe what was happening.

"You in a hurry to die?" Uzran looked at the open expanse of earth he was given to die in. "Why not enjoy these last few moments?"

Droth spluttered, gave the chain shackles around his wrists a rattling tug, then leaned back gingerly against the wood wall. "Easy for you to say," he groaned, squirming a little. "I am pretty sure Kugin's goons fitted me over a splintery knot on purpose. No matter which way I twist, I've got somethin' sharp diggin' into my ass!"

"Would you like me to see if I can dig it out?" Uzran said with a long-suffering sigh.

Droth's face twisted with indignant outrage, and he fixed Uzran with a baleful glare. "It's no joke, Uzran, but don't you mind anyhow," he chided, nodding toward gate opposite where they stood. "You just need to be ready to kill whatever comes through that gate."

Uzran gave another sigh and held up his hands, a

knobby club in one and a round shield of unlacquered boards in the other.

"With these?" He grunted. "Come on, we know what this is, Droth."

Droth shifted and gave a snarl of pain as something sharp scraped against his battered back.

"Fine then," he said, his voice a touch breathless. "Why aren't you deliverin' your speech?"

Uzran shook his head. "Timing is everything." He hefted the club and shield into guard position, testing them out. "It isn't just the words, but when they are delivered that matters. I'll know when the time is right."

"Your time is about up," the Troll protested. "You can't very well deliver a speech while you're being eaten."

Uzran was about to reply when the gate shuddered. With a slow, creaking groan it swung open, hauled by ropes looped along pulleys and over the opposite wall. The gate should have opened to reveal a broad, well-worn path that wound its way up Mount Falchrreg, but instead there was a tight lattice of iron bars, not dissimilar to the door of the cell Uzran and Droth had been in earlier.

It was the door of a cage, and within the cage, something gave a hungry growl.

"Dread Morg?" Droth posited gravely.

"No." Uzran tightened his grip on the crude weapons. "Sounds too sharp. Blooded Manticore, maybe?"

"You best hope not," the Troll said, his face turning into a frightful, grinning mask. "Otherwise we're both pincushions, right quick."

"NABURAS IS YOUR DEATH!" snarled a huge and thunderous voice from within the cage, setting the bars rattling on top of each other. "I WILL DEVOUR YOU AND THE FOOLS THAT DARE CAGE NABURAS!"

Uzran and Droth shared a wide-eyed, slack-jawed expression before they spoke the same word together.

"Lamassu."

Both had only met one of the last warriors of Lamashur when he visited the Gloaming Court between the quests of justice and guardianship their kind still engaged in. The Tuatha viewed the Lamassu as inscrutable relics of a time before theirs, so the Queen's reception had been cold and brief, but neither would ever forget the creature's powerful voice, its enchanted depth and strength.

"A gift just for you," a hard, jeering voice called.

Their expressions still slack, Uzran and Droth looked up and saw Kugin standing on top of the cage, a thick rope of corded leather in his hand. It took only a moment to see that the rope led to catches around the cage facing them. With one solid tug, the catches would come free and the creature within would be released.

"I was afraid the old brute would have to be put down before you could be brought to justice," Kugin called from his perch, his feet spread wide—and for good reason. The shuddering cage doubtless made for unstable footing, and tripping could have proven fatal.

"RELEASE NABURAS, WRETCHED FOOLS!" the voice boomed again. "RELEASE NABURAS, AND FACE YOUR DAY OF RECKONING!"

Kugin's smile was putrid with malice, and he waved the rope in his hand at Uzran with obscene playfulness.

"It seems even your playmate knows what time it is." The Master Sentinel laughed and fixed Uzran with a hateful glare. "I will enjoy watching him rip you open and gnaw your bones."

Uzran made to speak, but Kugin lifted his head, the cage release taut in his hand.

"Most respected Elders," he bellowed over the growing snarls in the cage and the raucous voices of the crowd. "The Trial of the Guiltless for Uzran Thrice-Curse has begun!"

At his last word, he hauled back sharply on the braided leather, and four iron clasps popped free. Something surged from within, and the cage door tumbled across the arena floor, skidding past Uzran and thudding into the timber less than an arm's length from Droth's outstretched hand.

To call him a beast would have been fair. His body was akin to a giant lion or other great cat, with large, rolling sinews beneath a coat of tawny fur, shamefully streaked with filth. The creature stood as tall Uzran at his feline shoulders, and from those shoulders rose two blackened stumps where towering wings had once been. The stumps, flecked with weeping sores, were cruelly capped by ensorcelled iron that still smoked, filling the arena with the acrid smell of burnt hair and charred meat. Dark ringlets of hair and beard matted and tangled into a rough mane surrounding a humanoid face. Fanged teeth were bared in a wild, terrible snarl beneath slanted golden eyes. From his bronze brow, a pair of horns swept up and back like the crest of a regal helm.

On each broad foot, black claws flexed forward in lethal promise as he stalked forward, fixing Uzran with a fierce, penetrating stare. Black eyes met gold, and Naburas saw that, for all his power and fury, this Ogre stood before him unafraid, with no tremor in the hands that hefted club and shield.

"Naburas will pluck your skull from your shoulders," the Lamassu swore, his roaring replaced by a low, deadly snarl. "Then Naburas will eat your heart before destroying every last thing which crawls upon this accursed mountain!"

"I will defeat you," Uzran said simply, and then he raised

his voice, clearly addressing more than just the creature in front of him. "But this victory will not b—"

"NABURAS COMES!" the creature roared, and pounced forward, claws and fangs bared.

Uzran raised the shield, twisting under the creature as it bore down on him. Black claws raked splintered furrows in the wood but found no purchase, and the Lamassu snarled in frustration as he slid off to the left, a stinging stroke from the Ogre's club helping it along. The blow landed with a sharp *thwack on* Naburas's filthy, well-muscled flanks, but elicited only a grunt.

Uzran raised the club and shield to meet Naburas's retaliation, but it did not come immediately. Instead of twisting and launching himself again, the Lamassu allowed his run to transform into a bounding sprint toward the palisade wall. Legs coiling beneath his body and then exploding with force, Naburas leapt towards the wall, sailing through the air.

For a heartbeat, Uzran thought the enraged Lamassu was trying to escape, attempting to scramble over the wall, but when Naburas's forepaws struck the timbers, he twisted with feline agility. Almost too late the Ogre realized that the Lamassu was rebounding toward him, all four deadly paws splayed and reaching out hungrily. He hoisted the shield, bracing it with both arms to avoid being shredded by the descending claws.

Naburas's weight and momentum bore down on Uzran, and he sank to one knee. The shield was too small to provide a point of balance for the larger creature, and the Lamassu began to slide to the ground. Snarling and hissing furiously, Naburas reached over the intervening shield and drew his claws across the Ogre's back and shoulders. Before his hind legs reached the ground, they opened long gashes on Uzran's belly and thighs as well. The voices beyond the palisade rose to a roar at the sight of red.

With a bellowing shove, Uzran drove the shield into Naburas's chest, the rough rim coming up under his jaws hard enough to snap the threatening fangs together. Still roaring, feet pounding his own blood into the hard earth, the Ogre surged toward the Lamassu, bowling him over and down to the ground.

Naburas snarled and snapped, claws raking wildly, but Uzran punched out with his shield. With a dull pop, one or two ribs within the Lamassu's chest came unhinged, and he screamed in pain and rage. In a display of acrobatics unexpected considering his huge size, he twisted and leapt into the air, flying clear of the Ogre's oncoming club. Lashing out in midair, Naburas's claws strained to remove Uzran's face, but succeeded only in turning a third of the abused shield into kindling. The Lamassu landed and pranced back a few steps, wincing with each footfall but circling Uzran who had stationed himself in front of Droth.

"You are hurt," Uzran panted, pointing with the jagged shield edge to the Naburas's limping steps. "Yield, and I will show you mercy."

"Ha! It is . . . not Naburas's blood watering the earth . . . fool!" Naburas sneered, but his cutting rejoinder was disjointed from his labored breathing.

Uzran's wounds bled freely, and strength dripped away from him with each flex of his muscles. Even his phenomenal resilience had limits, and he was fast approaching them. He needed to finish this, and quickly.

Sensing his flagging strength or unwilling to spring so recklessly to the attack with his dislocated ribs, the Lamassu paced back and forth a few strides away.

With a steadying breath to beat back the greying edges

of his vision, Uzran threw himself forward, lashing out with both broken shield and club. The Lamassu slunk backwards, batting with his claws, scoring furrows on the wood as he fought off the assault. Each strike seemed a rushed and desperate attack to Naburas, but he didn't see the measuring look in Uzran's eyes. Naburas slashed out with a claw at a sweep of the jagged shield. The jutting spurs of the splinter-edged shield twisted mid stroke, and the wooden points bit into the broad pad of the Lamassu's paw. Roaring to match Naburas's scream of pain, Uzran yanked the shield and pinioned paw hard to the left, exposing the damaged ribs.

Once, twice, three times, the club came down, driving snarled curses and then thick moans from the Lamassu. His legs wobbled, his claws retreated within their sheaths, and then Naburas collapsed.

The voices behind the timber walls were a roaring congress of competing storms threatening to overflow and flatten the arena.

Glaring hatefully, Naburas watched Uzran step forward and place the bloodied edge of the shivered shield to his neck.

"Naburas will not beg," the Lamassu wheezed, teeth showing in a tight grimace of pain.

"And I will not abide this cruelty." Uzran suddenly dropped both shield and club. Gasps and curses rose from around the entire arena. Before the Lamassu grasped what was taking place, Uzran reached out and wrapped his hands around the smoldering iron on the wretched stumps. The flesh of his fingers sizzled and rose in angry welts, but he bore it with a snarling bellow as the muscles of his arms, shoulders, and back stood out in thick, knotted ropes. WIth a sharp crack and a sound like a canvas sail being torn in a high wind, the caps of enchanted iron tore free in a welter of blackened blood.

The greedy metal twisted, seeking to burn its way into Uzran's bones, but he threw it to the ground where it smoked and hissed in the bubbling blood.

A deafening roar emerged from Naburas, and, maddened beyond all conscious thought, he lunged up to bury his fangs in the closest living thing. Uzran, charred hands trailing wisps of smoke, drove a fist between the wild, golden eyes, and the Lamassu fell to the ground, poleaxed. The tortured creature's body was motionless except for the hitched rise and fall of its breathing.

Uzran raised his eyes and saw Droth's awestruck stare give way to a smile, then he turned to face the Elders.

Each sat stone-faced, looking down with hard, inscrutable eyes.

"The Trial of the Guiltless is incomplete," the spokestroll declared at last, drawing low rumbles and angry murmurs around the arena. "Uzran Thrice-Curse, you cannot be cleared until you present your conquest to the Elders. Bring us the beast's head, or you will still stand condemned."

"Here is my conquest!" Uzran roared and kicked at the cursed lumps of iron on the ground before him. "A trophy of victory if ever there was one."

The crowd's seething babble quieted by degrees, but the Elders looked on sourly.

"The beast I defeated was not this wronged creature." Uzran swept a hand to the sprawled form of Naburas. "The beast I call you to behold today is the one we have let ourselves become!"

A stunned silence enfolded the gathering as the first rays of dawn ignited the sky.

"You are the one who stands condemned for your

barbaric acts," the Speaker declared archly. "Do not think you can lecture the Elders on such matters."

Uzran looked down at his hands, the blue-grey flesh seared to ashen black and textured with clinging grains of iron and angry lines of raw, red flesh.

"I am condemned," he said slowly, fighting back a wave of dizziness as more grey invaded his vision. "I have allowed myself to be the blunt instrument in unworthy hands—an eager tool—and for that crime, I deserve the worst punishments that our people can devise. But standing now before you, I am the voice best suited to speak the truth."

"Do not dare to lecture the Elders, Thrice-Cursed," the old Troll spat venomously as whispers spread beneath in rolling waves.

"Those same Elders who sent the sons of the People of the Stone to Thrice-Cursed to die for a cruel Queen? The same Elders who would take one of the last proud warriors of fallen Lamashur and turn him into an unwilling executioner with cursed iron?" Uzran shook his head and lifted his hands to the Elders. "My hands are stained black, but the Elders' hands are far from clean."

"You are condemned for your insolence!" roared one of the Fomor elders, rising to shake his staff at Uzran. Other elders rose, fists and voices trembling with outrage. "Execution! Execution!"

The angry shouts from the crowd behind the palisade sprang up, and soon the Elders' shouts were joined by hundreds, even thousands of agitated voices.

Uzran, feeling as if his head was bound to his body by a string, staggered back a step and laughed drunkenly. Why scream "execution" when he was dying of his wounds before them.

"How dare you!" an ancient Ogre shouted in a cracking voice.

The words cut through the gathering fog behind Uzran's eyes.

"How dare I?" he laughed, leaning back until he nearly lost his balance. "How dare you? How dare all of us? How dare we accept our place beneath the feet of sorcerous schemers? This world was ours before they came, and it was by our strength as much as their magic that it was won, but we became servants rather than allies. We settled for letting others decide our fate, our traditions, and our identities for us. How dare we sell ourselves so cheaply!"

At some point the cries and clamor had fallen away, and shamed silence settled over the arena.

"For ages uncounted our people held fast with blood and blade against Darkling and Wyrm, but a sorceress came and promised us peace and prosperity. We sold ourselves like whores, and no one understands that better than me because I counted my soul so cheap that I traded it for an honor as false as the one who gave it to me. Have we truly known peace? Prosperity? We have been the bloodied fist of the Twilit Kingdom for millennia and have nothing to show for it, but we persist because it is easier to be the faithful brute than to think for ourselves. Living like that doesn't just keep us from who we should be, but like my sad example, it transforms us into those we should not be."

Uzran swept a hand toward where the Lamassu lay, and then pointed down at the enchanted iron. His eyes roved this way and that, across the Elders and the faces pressed to the walls of the palisade, and no matter where he turned, they were grey, blurred shadows. The shades of a slate-colored world grew deeper even as the sky brightened above him.

"We have let ourselves become cruel, short-sighted, and disposable. We have lived as brutes so long, we think that is who we truly are."

Slowly and softly—as though he intended to beg—Uzran sank to his knees; he saw nothing but an endless saturnine expanse, the definition of sky and earth banished.

"How dare we?"

He fell forward, nervelessly on the hard ground.

As the grey enfolded him and sank to black, Uzran thought he heard Droth calling to him from somewhere very far away.

16

———

DESTINED

I looked at the vast representation of Other-Realm, worked in miniature on a table in the Royal Palace, and plotted the advance of the Queen's army.

"I think if we make our move now, it would have to be against Lord Arawn." I pointed to the black ziggurat in the center of Cinderstone's ashen plains. "He is as disconnected from the politicking as Mother Gwiddon, but he also possesses some of the strongest defenses and the least estimable forces. It makes sense to hit him when we are closest to full strength, uncertain what we will face."

The Queen nodded, considering the map below. She looked up to eye the animated corpse at my shoulder. I had decided to use the silent dead rather than finding another squire while Kieren recovered. "And what about your menial supports?" She inclined her chin slightly at the dead. "Can our army function without the tireless laborers provided by the caulder? What will their absence mean for our supply lines and field fortifications?"

"The supply line can be sustained without them, and for the most part, field fortifications won't be necessary." I jerked a thumb back towards the mute bodies. "But I don't think we will have to do without. I believe I can secure the services of Lord Arawn's daughters, and they control the caulders."

"Do explain," the Queen commanded, her eyes glittering with conspiratorial interest.

"When I first met the three daughters of Lord Arawn, one of them, Wrenneth, came to me and intimated that she and her sisters are little more than slaves to their father," I explained. "I promised that I would never hurt her and that my only goal was the good of the kingdom. She seemed . . . moved by the sentiment."

As I spoke, I recalled Wrenneth's sudden embrace in front of the stairs. Inadvertently, that brought thoughts of Bryth to mind and a strange tightening in my chest. The Gormstone spilled blissful numbness across my breast, and I continued without pause.

"I think it wouldn't be too difficult to turn her and her sisters to our side." I crossed my arms over my chest, rolled my shoulders, and let the welcome chill spread across my whole body. "That way we can function at full capacity."

"Clever boy." The Queen beamed and gave another nod. "Very well. Make your preparations and call on Wrenneth, but one should never go into battle with only one weapon at hand. Promise her that if she convinces her sisters to join, she will be named Lady of Cinderstone in her father's place when he falls."

"Very well, but just her?" I asked. "Don't you think that betraying not just her father but her sisters as well will push her too far?"

"We think you underestimate the slave's dream of being the master." The Queen smiled like a cat grinning over a cornered mouse. "Begin by offering the slave her freedom, and she will lead the charge against her own father. Then offer to make the little wretch mistress of all she knows, and she will hand you the raw hearts of her sisters if you ask it."

"As you wish," I said perfunctorily and called to a squat shadow cowering behind the dead. "Sec, see that Lady Wrenneth attends me for a private dinner tonight. And have something official- looking drawn up to show her we are serious about the whole 'her taking over' thing."

"YesGorm, yesGorm," the shaded figure burbled, poking his wide, toad-like head between the corpse servants. "Donebynight."

The dead couldn't take notations or write memos, but for that, I had acquired a quick-penned Gremlin who was to have been executed for cowardice in the last battle if I hadn't taken him as my functionary. I didn't bother to learn his name, deciding to call him "Sec" for "secretary." He didn't seem to mind.

"You obviously aren't planning to let her stay in charge long?" I asked, my eyes trailing back to the map of Other-Realm and plotting all the conquests to come.

"No, in fact you will make certain she never touches her father's throne," the Queen intoned regally. "Once Arawn is gone and his spawn disposed of, you will search his keep and bring any sorcerous discoveries or artifacts to Us. He has the artifice for the Gormstone, We are certain of it."

Another wave of cold washed over my body, and when I spoke, my words were even and mildly curious. "I thought Lord Lughan Redfinger, your former consort, created the Gormstone?"

"He did, but not alone." The Queen paced around the map, the train of her blue dress rippling in resplendent waves behind her. "Though one of Our lovers, he was no fool, and he feared that if We possessed the ability to create more than one Gormstone, We might have turned the arti-facts on him and any others who could have rivaled Us. He kept his methods and his accomplices from Us, but we learned that Lord Arawn was his collaborator on the project. It seems control of the dead was not enough for him."

The Queen's pacing quickened, and her voice became more animated even as her eyes grew distant.

"We hoped that what We fostered through Cinis would result in Gorm Valoise being captured and the Gormstone lost, but we did not count on Lughan being present, nor on Captain Uzran carrying their broken bodies back to us. What a spiny nest of frustration and relief We felt when that oaf, still panting like some dying beast, laid their bodies before Us. He had undone Our hopes by rescuing the Gorm, but in so doing had spared Us from losing a potent weapon we couldn't replace, since Lughan was dead. Our goals were set back by a century, but now We can finally claim what We sacrificed so much to acquire—what We were destined to hold."

Her hands came together, fingers gripping each other as anxiety crept into her voice. "And then at last He will come to us," she hissed hoarsely. "He will find us when We have made this wretched realm worthy of Him."

She stopped and surveyed the expanse of Other-Realm before her then looked at me sharply, as though startled I was still there.

"We are the Twilit Kingdom and the Twilit Kingdom is Us," she said in a hungry, breathless whisper. "Every last breath, every last drop of water, every last grain of dust shall be Ours to command."

Lady Wrenneth watched me with blood-red eyes, her small, sharp teeth working behind carmine lips.

"The truth is, though our fight with the Gythraul is all but finished, much is left unaddressed in the Twilit Kingdom itself," I said, pouring dark wine into her goblet and my own.

"What do you mean?" Wrenneth asked after daintily pressing a silken napkin to her lips.

I reclined in my high-backed chair and swept my arm toward the windows of the solarium that adjoined my bedroom in the Royal Palace. Beyond the thick panes of glass, dusk was drawing to a glorious close.

"Just look anywhere out there, and you will find some abuse that has been excused for two thousand years." I rested my head against the chair back, hoping my face was fixed in a rueful frown. "Many wrongs are excused in war because victory seems so important."

"Isn't it?" Wrenneth's thin, dark brows bunched in confusion.

"It is," I assured her quickly, leaning forward. "But righting those wrongs after victory is just as important."

"But Grimple said you left her to fight legions of Gythraul." She pouted in confusion. "And the next thing I know, we move the entire army back to Duanon."

"Grimple was being dramatic," I lied, shaking my head in an imitation of weary exasperation. "Why would the Queen permit us to come back if there were any significant threat left? You were there, Wrenneth. You were a part of breaking the last great Gythraul invasion.

"I suppose you are right." Her shoulders straightened ever so slightly, and she pushed her plate away. She hadn't been hungry, picking at her food, and I had finished as quickly as was decent. I needed to keep up the show for her now so the entire dinner didn't seem like pretense from the start.

"What did you have in mind, then?" She eyed me, taking a sip of the freshly poured wine.

"Well, the things closest to your heart come to mind, obviously." I twitched and twisted my face into what I imagined an abashed confession looked like. The comfortable cold of the Gormstone made this all playacting now, and I was confident I was hitting all the right notes. "The truth is, Wrenneth, I cannot stop thinking about what you said to me months ago, back in your father's keep."

Her red eyes flared with panic and began darting to corners, as though expecting some accusing figure to emerge from one of them.

"I say so many things, my Gorm," she laughed nervously, drawing her hands into her lap. "You should not pay attention to such trivial things as my wayward musings."

Her reaction was strange to me, but some frostbitten instinct told me what to do.

"Wrenneth, please listen to me." I reached across the small table and took her fidgeting fingers in my hand. "Do you remember the promise I made to you?"

She shook her head, eyes running away from me to search the corners again, but then she stopped and slowly looked into my eyes. Incrementally, she nodded.

"I promised that I would never hurt you," I said softly, making sure the spastic little thing remembered it correctly. "And that I only wanted what was best for the Twilit Kingdom. You remember all of that?"

Again, she nodded.

"Well, Wrenneth, you are part of the Twilit Kingdom, and it is unacceptable to me that you should live as a slave to your father."

Terror flashed across her expression at the mention of

Lord Arawn, but she kept staring into my eyes and, little by little, the electric tension in her body dissipated.

"His cruel and callous ways were tolerated because of the war, but now the war is over, and it is time to make things right." I gave her fingers a gentle squeeze when they began to tremble again. "It is time to remove him from power and set someone else over Cinderstone. Someone who can rule justly."

"Lucius . . . I mean, Gorm Bollham." She fumbled for words with a wine-heavy tongue. "Are you telling me what I think you are?"

"Depends," I said with my best knowing, slightly teasing smile. "Do you think I am asking you to help me raise you up as Lady of Cinderstone and punish your father for his crimes? Because if so, the answer is yes."

"But what about my sisters?" she asked, her question sounding half-hearted and unsure.

"You were the brave enough to seek me," I said, drawing our faces even closer together. "This is what you were destined for."

Her eyes widened again, and I was afraid that she would fly into a paroxysm of panic. But she took me by surprise, as she had all those months ago. Before I knew it, her lips were pressing against mine, hungry and hard.

I nearly pulled back in surprise, but realizing I was not under attack—at least in any life threatening way—I let my mouth move to match her own. With our lips and tongues searching and entwining in carnal unison, I drew her to me, and then her small, tightly-knit body was pressed hard against me. My hands held her and tore at the her dress. One hand rose so my fingers slid around the back of her neck, my thumb at her throat, and I held her face to mine. Her cold, almost icy skin matched my own.

Like a master opening the treat tin, my frigid mind decided to throw my longing body a bone. It would not be the satisfying dominion I craved to exert over Byth, but it would do for now.

She tugged at the strings of my breeches as her mouth fell on me bruising kisses and teasing bites which kept up their relentless assault even as I crushed her to me. With a primal growl deep in my throat, I swept the the remnants of our meal aside. The dishes and goblets clattered to the floor as I lifted Wrenneth bodily into the air and laid her on the table.

Her fingers reached out and ran appreciatively across my chest, but withdrew sharply just as I pushed back the skirts of her dress.

"Wait!" she panted, her hands grabbing hold of mine. "What about Lady Bryth?"

"Who?" My face drew into a fierce, ravenous smile.

Wrenneth's face frowned into a pensive stare, and then with a wild, cutting laugh, she hooked her legs around my hips.

17

MOTIVATED

Grimple Guthook stood up to her waist in the murky water of Mistmire swamp, hands dangling below the surface.

"I have some rations in my pack if this is really an issue," Bryth called from beside a small fire on firmer ground. "There is really no need."

"I like eel," Grimple grunted softly, her amber eyes narrowed to thin slits. "There's yer need. Now quiet."

"But even if that is the case, couldn't you use Snyrl for this sort of thing?" Bryth asked, referring to the ragged Malk which the Goblin insisted be brought along.

The Malk, sitting regally on an overturned tree trunk, watched and listened to their exchange, its pale eyes reflecting nothing except vague curiosity.

"Him? He's useless at fishin'." Grimple raised her chin slightly to the large feline who gave a subtle flick of his tail in response. "Six paws all wicked keen for opening throats, but piss-poor at hooking an eel. Now, shut-up—two've slipped by already,"

Chastened, Bryth sat on the bank and watched.

Moments slid by in the dark. The Goblin underboss remained so still that, to Bryth, she appeared to have fallen asleep. But then with a splash and a short cry of triumph, the Goblin hoisted a thick, black snake, wriggling and wrapping around her arm.

Bryth's stomach retreated to her spine at the sight of the writhing creature. It reminded her of the Fiendspawn, but only for a moment. The darkness flicking off the eel's body was not sorcerous shadow, but mud, and the smell assaulting the nose was of earth, water, and swamp plants stewing together, not ripening corpses. It was not appetizing, but it was not the wrongness that leaked from the darkling's get like corruption from a sour wound.

Bryth was on edge in these swamps, especially now as the mist seemed to thicken and the light began to fade. It had been difficult enough to ally herself with the Goblin when she first levelled her treasonous questions, but now, having just taken herself, Grimple, and Grimple's pet to Mistmire, she felt all the paranoid dread of conspiracy but with none of its thrill. Still, she was more convinced than ever that she had made the right choice—that she had to act.

After the rush of agreeing to work with Grimple and some mysterious ally had faded, she had doubted herself and that choice. It was not just the fear of discovery but honest conflict with the rightness of it all. The Queen, despite her many worsening flaws, had been mother and guardian over her since she was a child. It was not for nothing that the Queen called her the 'child of Our heart', and, whatever had taken place, she still believed that at one time, the monarch had loved her. It was easy to say that she would free Luce from the Gormstone, but the reality that it might—no, that it would—put her in direct conflict with the Queen, gnawed at her.

Wasn't there some grave sin, some unforgivable wrong in turning upon the one who cared for and taught you all your life? To call it kin-strife, or even the unthinkable—kin-slaying—was not quite true. No actual blood bound them, but weren't they bound by cords nearly as strong? More than once, when battle with the Gythraul was upon them, and Grimple refused to share more information, she had nearly given up and summoned up a Path to Duanon where she would confess and beg forgiveness. She convinced herself that she would not be asking to escape punishment —she deserved it for even considering such treachery. She had only hoped that she might be absolved as the executioner's axe fell.

But Bryth had beat back her fears and guilt long enough to watch Luce devise his callous battleplans, and little by little, her guilt turned to resolve. What happened on that hilltop tore the last vestiges of self-loathing and remorse from her the instant Luce's hands reached out to tear at her clothing. Her hopes for his salvation were confirmed in that single instant of restraint he displayed before she was forced to blast him away with her magic.

The Queen had taken the man she loved, but he was not so far gone that he could not be redeemed. So she hid herself with the help of Grimple's Finger teams and waited. After the rest of the army returned to Duanon, the Goblin underboss instructed her to open a Path to Mistmire.

Ignorant of Bryth's musings, Grimple hauled her catch onto the bank and laid it out. With a quick, curved knife, she gutted and flensed the eel, and the swampy air thickened with a faint, fishy smell. Both pairs of shoulders rolling, Snyrl slid from his seat on the gnarled trunk and padded over to the growing pile of offal. Grimple paid no heed to the Malk's hooking claw or bowed, sniffing head until it bent over a long strip of pale pink meat. "Hey," she growled, giving the offending snout a sharp rap with the flat of the knife blade. "That's mine, greedy-guts."

Snyrl's hackles raised ever so slightly, and the corners of his lips curled to reveal the points of long fangs, but Grimple held his stare with a sour glare. The battle of wills lasted less than thirty seconds, but for the two belligerents —and for Bryth who watched them raptly—it seemed like a breathless struggle of long minutes before the Malk gave a soft chuff that drew his lips down and his eyes away. With a sulky hunch to his shoulders, he fetched the choicest giblets between his teeth and stalked back to his fallen perch.

"He's useful in a fight and has a nose for trouble." Grimple sniffed at the retreating creature. "But he's a willful one. Thankfully, he ain't too hard to handle if yer'll just show him who's boss every now and again."

Grimple looked up from her work, her free hand having gathered up three long fillets of meat that dangled nearly to her toes. "But I suppose that's all livin' things, eh? Just need to be reminded o' who's in charge and *why* they're in charge."

Bryth scooted over to make room for the Goblin who knelt beside her and began to drive the meat onto skewers. She had cut them from the branches of Snyrl's tree prior to wading out into the swamp.

"It seems you aren't just talking about the cat," Bryth took up one of the skewers and affixed a long hank of eel meat.

Closer now, the meat smelled stronger, but to her surprise it was not the overpowering scent of fish—though there were hints of that—but an oily, vaguely sweet smell.

Some of the Gloaming Court occasionally fancied eel, particularly in pies, but it had never looked appetizing to her, especially as it was often prepared with the eel's basted head emerging from the crust. The stare of the dull eyes, watching as its corpse was greedily consumed, always struck her as grotesque so she avoided the dish.

"What else would I be talkin' about then?" Grimple asked, with what passed for coyness in her rough voice. "Yer don't think any other creature in this wide world is in need of a lesson or two about place and position?"

"I think the subtler arts of comparison and innuendo are notably stunted in you, my dear Grimple, that's all," Bryth said with exaggerated patience. "Do you mean to imply that our Queen has need of such a reminding?"

Grimple set the first skewer in the ground at an angle over the fire. A few drops fell from the skewer, hissing on the crackling firewood.

"Not just Queen Meabh," Grimple said as she set the last skewer in place. "All yer Tuatha need to wake up. If yer don't, all of this is is going to happen again."

Bryth made to protest, but Snyrl gave a low growl, and when they glanced his way, they saw him poised in a fighting crouch on his tree. With his hackles raised, back arched, and ears pressed flat, Bryth thought he looked ready to burst into violent action or flight at the snap of a twig.

This theory proved wrong a few moments later when something cracked a few dozen feet beyond where they sat. Snyrl and the two females turned toward the sound with rapt attention.

"Were you expecting someone?" Bryth breathed, her will beginning to gather up the threads of magical power which composed the Contracts.

"Yes," Grimple said softly, her hand falling to the

bandolier that clung tightly to her sinewy frame. Her sharp-nailed fingers rested on the grip of a Daerg-retrofitted pistol from the last campaigns against the Gythraul.

"Is this them, then?" Bryth's voice deepened with the power she was focusing.

"We'll see," the Goblin said softly, sliding the pistol free.

The sidearm was a St. Etienne 8mm, but in place of the light, accurate rounds for which it was intended, its cylinders housed six Cockatrice teeth fitted with Boreal cyclone caps. One full pull of the trigger would set the double action hammer to work, and the knuckle-length tooth would fly free to bury into the flesh of an unlucky victim. Rarely fatal, the paralytic the tooth injected into the target's body was the real payload, locking down motor function in seconds. That, as Grimple was happy to explain, was what made it okay to shoot first and ask questions later.

Further commotion was heard as something moved in the dusky mist. Whoever it was made no special effort to hide their approach, and Bryth wasn't sure if that was a good thing. A soft breath of air stirred the mist, and she glimpsed a tall figure moving smoothly toward them. Fear clambered up her spine.

The figure was a Tuatha without a doubt—Lord Nadder?

Bryth shunted the power she had gathered for a curse aside in order to make room for a weave of scrying, but the sweep of the probing magic found no traces of the Fiendspawn or their repugnant spoor. Bryth relaxed an inch or two, quite certain that Lord Nadder would never confront them alone, but not until she saw Grimple's hand come off her pistol did she feel safe enough to unravel the potent curses she had been shaping.

"Took yer long enough," Grimple called to the figure

before turning back toward the fire to turn the sizzling skewers. "If yer'd been much longer, you'd've missed supper."

The figure that emerged fully from the mists to stand beside their fire was armored in the full ebon warplate of a battle-magus, including the the enclosed helm with its sharp, conical crown. Bryth herself preferred lighter mail over the encasing shell, so she rarely wore the warplate, but she could not deny it was a striking sight. The entire suit gave the impression of a creature encased in black glass, staring down through the thin portals of the eye slits with a fierce, almost pained light in its grey eyes.

Bryth looked into those eyes for a moment as they stared back at her, and after a moment of struggling recognition she voiced her disbelieving guess. "Kieren?"

The tall figure nodded once, bowing slightly, but said nothing.

"But how?" Bryth was stunned, unsure whether to address her cousin or the Goblin who had expected him. "Why?"

"Kieren's been reportin' to me ever since he was made Luce's squire," Grimple explained without looking up from the skewers. "It weren't easy to make sure the Queen chose 'im, but the boy's played 'is part well enough until now."

At the last word, the helmeted head drooped, and Kieren took a step away from them to the other side of their cookfire. As he moved, Bryth noticed that Snyrl was no longer on point but watching them with his tail occasionally swaying left and right.

"I heard from some of Grimple's team that you were hurt after the battle, but I . . . I couldn't come see you," Bryth said lamely, knowing that even if things had not gone the way they had with Luce, she still might not have visited him as he recovered. And if she had, it would have been out of courteous duty rather than familial affection. Her relationship with Kieren had never been strong, and the blame for that lay entirely on her shoulders. He adored her father's legend as the great magus and consort of the Queen, and as the bearer of that legacy, he revered her as well. Rather than allow that reverence to create a bridge to know the promising young Tuatha, she had been repelled by it, especially in the wake of the Gormstone's use on Valoise as well as the part her father played in that tragedy. She had supposed he was just another sycophant and had kept him at arm's length, as she did the rest of the Gloaming courtiers. It seemed he had fallen in with quite another crowd.

"Kieren," Bryth said looking at the figure staring silently down into the flames. "I am sorry."

"Can't-Won't speak, no-no," chirped a small voice at Bryth's ear, but before she could turn around, something whistled past and lighted on Kieren's armored shoulder. "Blade and bolt, burn-cut him fierce," pronounced a Pixie with batlike wings for arms and a shock of red hair jutting from her head in wild spikes. "Poor Kieren still much hurt-tired."

"That'd be Twilip." Grimple took skewers of eel meat from the fire. "She's what yer might call the liaison betwixt yer cousin and I."

"And friend-love of Kieren," the Pixie protested with an agitated flap of her wings.

"That too." Grimple handed a skewer of eel to Kieren and then held one out for Bryth.

"I am really not that hungry," Bryth protested, but the Pixie flapped her wings sharply again and gave a chiropteran squeak.

"Not about your hunger-gut, silly she-thing," Twilip said with impish impatience. "About Mother-Mistress magic."

Bryth raised an eyebrow at that and looked down at the Goblin, who still held the skewer up to her. "So this is all a scheme of Mother Gwiddon's, then?" she asked, eyeing the faintly hissing meat like it was something venomous.

"Do I have to draw yer a map?" Grimple groused, flapping a hand to encompass the expanse of swamp behind her, sworn domain of Mother Gwiddon. "What creature in all of Other-Realm is older than Queen Meabh and a seer to boot?" The skewer was thrust forward forcefully. "Are yer in or out, girl?" Grimple pressed.

Bryth's eyes darted to Kieren, sinister in head-to-toe black, then to Grimple, her feral, amber eyes squinting impatiently, and finally to the cooling length of seared flesh. She wordlessly accepted the skewer and took a bite. It wasn't bad. Unseasoned, it was a bit bland for her taste, but it was light, with just a hint of sweetness—not nearly as flaky or fishy-tasting as she expected. Chewiness kept it from feeling spongy or watery.

Grimple nodded and then held up her own skewer and muttered a quick incantation that thrummed with magic for the very barest of seconds. "Mother, we savor your bounty. Hear our gratitude," the Goblin said, and then her needle teeth tore at the eel vigorously.

Bryth looked over at Kieren and saw he had taken his helmet off to partake, taking turns between his own bites and those Twilip snipped off. The sight of his ravaged visage caught the bite she had taken in her throat. She could not stop herself from choking and coughing as she stared at the livid burns which ran over his throat and cheeks, continuing up to his scalp, forks of angry red on ashen, grey skin. Her vision blurred with tears as she hacked and gagged, and as his face turned toward her, she felt her heart pierced by his forlorn eyes.

For his service Kieren had paid a dear price indeed. "Hardly . . . dashing," the former Squire rasped with a dry, hoarse voice.

Bryth was too busy trying not to choke to death to reply.

"Don't you chuck that mess up," Grimple warned around a mouthful of eel. "I ain't got time to catch another one, and then you'll have to hoof it to keep up."

Bryth finally felt the offending chunk of meat slide into her belly, and she drew in a ragged breath. "Keep up?" she panted, and then endured an aftershock of coughs. Her pale face was flushed, and tears ran freely down her cheeks. She took a small sip from the waterskin hanging from her belt, its contents magically cooled with a minor enchantment. The sharp chill of the liquid soothed her inflamed throat.

"Well, wouldn't exactly be a clandestine meeting if we walked in the front door for a public audience, now would it?" Grimple admonished curtly before turning back to her eel.

"Finish snakefish-food, she-thing," Twilip chirped from Kieren's shoulder as her friend-love took another bite, making his scars writhe obscenely across his face.

Clearing her sore throat several times, Bryth obeyed, slowly and deliberately chewing the remaining bites. After each one, she drank from the waterskin. Finishing, she looked at Grimple who had already thrown her skewer into the fire, and was wiping her hands on the leg of her britches. "What now?" Bryth didn't like how raw her voice sounded.

"By the time dusk settles, you'll know," the Goblin replied evasively, taking up the knife she had used to flay the eel.

"Are you just averse to giving anything except cryptic

answers?" Bryth asked acidly. Grimple ignored her, shuffling past, knife in hand.

Without a word, the Goblin went over to the remains of the eel on the grassy bank and flicked away entrails until she found what she was looking for. The knife jabbed down and came up with a long strip of the eel's black skin hanging from the point. A few scraps of meat still clung to the glistening flesh.

"Grimple!" Bryth said sharply, but the Goblin ignored her as she brought the dangling length of skin to Snyrl. The Malk, who had been distinctly not watching Grimple's approach, relented and took the proffered treat. The Goblin underboss stroked the creature's bowed head as it snapped up the eel skin.

Her anger mounting, Bryth stepped toward the insolent Goblin, unsure of what she would do when she got there, but thoroughly put out at being ignored.

"Bryth." Kieren's coarse whisper drew Bryth's attention like a shout. "Please. Wait."

She met her cousin's grey, imploring eyes and felt her agitation melt away. "Yes," she said, mostly to herself. "It seems I have no choice." She did not have long to wait.

The last deep reds in the sky had faded to bruised purples when she felt the thrum of magic, like what had passed by her senses at Grimple's incantation, but now constant and steady. With her aetheric sense of the sorcerous, she traced a thrumming cord of power emerging from the misty swamp to where they stood. No, not just where they stood, but to them. Their bodies. Their bellies.

The eel.

Grimple had invoked some localised Contract, something known only rarely in the modern times of Other-Realm. The meat they had ingested, even Snyrl and Twilip, was an anchoring point for the magic, tying them to some kind of force that was accelerating toward them. Not knowing what was moving along this magical tether was a little frightening, but she reminded herself that the magic was tied to Grimple as well. Grimple was many things, most of them unsavory, but suicidal was not one of them.

The thrumming grew, and as it did, Bryth felt her eyes drawn out into the mists which hung over the swamp. The marshy landscape, usually abuzz with the sounds of fauna, was notably subdued. Only an occasional croak or squawk broke the oppressive stillness so at odds with the vibrating ethereal pressure she felt. The swamp held its breath with her as she waited on the bank for whatever was coming for them out of the mists. The thrum reached a pitch and intensity that actually pained her, and then a wide shape burst from the mists with incredible speed. Bryth lurched back, afraid that she was about to be run down by the zooming bulwark rapidly growing larger in her field of vision. WIth a sinking realization, she knew she could not avoid the hurtling object, and she braced herself for a fatal impact. She shut her eyes, trying to grasp a last, meaningful thought, but located nothing except paralyzing fear. But nothing happened.

She opened her eyes and stared at a vast, bronze pot, one whose hot, glowing sides she had seen before.

"Our ride's here," Grimple said cheerily, stepping up beside Bryth, Snyrl trailing along. The pot sank lower, nearly resting its cherry bottom on the grass. Careful to avoid the sides, Grimple grabbed the lip of the pot and hoisted herself in. A moment later Snyrl, in a careless display of feline agility, leapt up and over, landing gracefully next to her inside.

Bryth stepped forward and peered into the pot. From the

outside, it looked as though it could hold Grimple comfortably or maybe Snyrl, but not both of them together. She expected to see the ludicrous sight of both of them crammed in on top of each other in a tangle of limbs, but instead she saw only darkness.

"Hurry up!" Grimple's voice reverberated crankily from the depths of the pot.

Sighing deeply, Bryth followed Grimple's example, carefully staying clear of the sides and bracing herself on the lip. Gingerly, she threw both legs over the lip and slid into the darkness.

There followed an incredible sensation of falling and a muffled sense of detachment akin to entering a Path. Her heart seized, and every muscle tensed at the sensation, but then came a sense of enfolding as the air thickened into a pliant cushion. The tension slid form her body and she was overcome with the sudden soft, density of the world around her. Existence became a wall of soft, white, swirling impressions.

Bryth sank into the languorous, colorless embrace, soporifically uncaring, but soon realized that she was, indeed, sinking into icy liquid. It enveloped her, rushing up her body and filling her mouth, nose, ears, and finally her eyes, swallowing the ethereal white in dark, bubbling black.

Something huge and frighteningly strong gripped her shoulders hard enough to make her joints give little pops of protest. An undeniable pull upwards, and she was clear of the cold and darkness, dripping wet and gratefully swallowing gulps of air.

After grabbing enough air to assure herself that it wasn't going anywhere, Bryth looked up and saw that she was on the floor beside a fire pit. Blue flames licked up the sides of a bronze pot, sides glowing with heat. Above, she saw the totem and fetish-festooned pillars of Mistmire Hall, and as she watched, she realized that her view was lurching from left to right, not because of her harrowing experience within the pot, but because the entire hall swung and shook from one side to another.

Grimple, damp but grinning, waddled to her with a ratty-looking blanket in hand, swaying with the movement of the Hall. "First time's the roughest." She draped the blanket around Bryth's shoulders.

"Just rest thyself, little one," a cracked voice called from over the top of the pot.

Bryth staggered to her feet to see a huge crone plunge her long, knob-knuckled hand into the pot's boiling contents, her face stretched in a sharp, black smile.

Bryth struggled to pay attention, clinging to her stool by the fire, as Mother Gwiddon explained her scheme again. "Thou must understand it all has to do with the Gorm-stone," she said emphatically. "The Gormstone, and the fact that it lies in the breast of a human."

"Why does it matter that it is in Luce's chest?" Bryth tried her best to ignore a bucket that skittered past her for the hundredth time. The few articles not secured in the Hall jounced and rolled across the floorboards, back and forth, seemingly unnoticed by everyone except her. The only thing immune to the Hall's lurching steps was the pot in the fire pit which sat rooted in place by the stroking tongues of blue flame.

"Because thy beloved is a mortal man, born and brought up in a world empty of magic," the hag answered patiently. "As thou knows, his world is not just empty of magic but hostile to it, greedily devouring it. That hungry resonance is on him, and though she does not realize it, when Meabh controls him through the stone, she is touched by that resonance too."

"So it is weakening her? Robbing her of her power?" Bryth said, her knuckles white as she gripped her stool and tried to sway with the Hall.

"Making them fragile, more like," Mother Gwiddon said, baring her teeth in a disquieting smile. "The deeper she presses her will into the Gorm, the more brittle her connection to the magic of Other-Realm becomes. Very soon she will have tuned herself to his resonance so completely that it will take only one note—one spell— to sunder her connection to the Contracts and Fundaments."

Despite her distraction, Bryth found she could appreciate the enormity of this realization. Queen Meabh's authority had, for all the flowery pomp accumulated around it, been born of conquest and power. And that power lay in her near godlike mastery of magic which, combined with thousands of years of experience, made her nigh unassailable. True, she was neither omniscient nor omnipresent—her many mistakes and the war with the Gythraul proved that—but as far as direct confrontation went, she was nearly all-powerful. That fact assured her dominion and the fearful, faithful servitude of most of the Twilit Kingdom. Without her magic, she was simply a paranoid woman.

"And will that spell free Luce?" Bryth sought to organize her thoughts in light of the revelation.

"Without her connection to the Fundament of Animus, thy Queen loses her power over thy love." Mother Gwiddon slowly bobbed her head. "It will then only be a matter of removing the stone and shattering it before she recovers her powers."

"Recovers her power?" Bryth baulked, feeling her hopes sink as suddenly as they had risen. "I thought we were sundering her connection to the Contracts and Fundaments."

"Thy people have magic within thy very blood, which is why thou make such fine magi," the hag said with a weary sigh. "She will lose all her power for a short time, and then she will recover it by degrees. I do not know how quickly, but eventually she will recover her full strength. Until then she will be vulnerable."

"And that is when we put the bitch down," Grimple said grimly.

"That is your business," Bryth said, her face that of someone tasting something particularly sour. "I am no assassin. I only want to free Luce and then get as far away as possible from Meabh."

"And where would that be, your Ladyship?" Grimple sneered. "Thanks to Luce, there isn't going to be an inch of ground she don't control. You goin' to set sail on the Barren Waves and just not come back?"

Bryth didn't answer because she didn't have an answer. It was akin to a wall in her mind, and every time she reached the point in her imaginings that Luce was free and they were together, all thought stopped. What were they going to do? Where were they going to go? She didn't know, and that made her angry. "I don't know, and I don't care," she said hotly. "But I am going to say it again in case you didn't hear it—I am here to free Luce, not murder the Queen."

"They are . . . the . . . same thing," Kieren declared hoarsely, and the twist of his face testified to what those words cost him.

"Thy cousin has the right of it." Mother Gwiddon craned her long neck downward to look into Bryth's eyes. "Thy love will be ever at risk as long as she sits on her throne. I know she stood in the place of thy mother since thou were very young, but think thee not of her as thy mother, but as thy father's murderer."

Bryth had begun to tear up, but the last words caught her as smartly as a blow to the face. "What?" Bryth sniffed back tears as she gave the hag a sidelong glance. "My father's murderer? He was killed in Ceterum Cinis's ambush."

"And how now did Valoise fall into that ambush?" Grimple asked impatiently. "He wasn't Luce, but he was no fool, and he had the Gormstone to ensure he didn't do something stupid for you."

"But not something foolish if thy Queen wished it," Mother Gwiddon said. "The truth is that not all mysteries of the Gormstone lie with thy Queen. In her jealous desire to hold such knowledge, she ensured the Gythraul knew when and where to spring the ambush. She hoped that Gorm Valoise would be taken, and thy father forced to make another Gormstone. In that process, she hoped to discover the means by which it was made. She had not counted on thy Father joining Valoise on patrol."

"And she hadn't counted on Uzran bringing both their corpses back," Grimple snorted, arms across her chest. "So yer whinin' about killin' is just plain stupid. Yer got more reason than most to want the bitch dead."

If what they said was true, they were right, but Bryth realized she was here as part of a secret conspiracy plotting treason against the Queen. It was not hard to imagine that they might lie to win her over. Grimple and Mother Gwiddon were not new to clandestine operations, and even Kieren, her own cousin, seemed comfortable with the idea. Only hours ago she would have sworn such things were beneath him, but she now wondered at the truth of who Kieren was as she considered the motivation for his actions.

Was he driven by some kind of noble intention to save the Twilit Kingdom from an evil despot, or was it simply as pretense for an ambitious power grab?

The world was not as she once believed it to be, and it was becoming less familiar as she soldiered on. Things once certain melted like sand before lapping waves, and she was desperate to keep her feet under her. She needed something solid, and all that seemed true and immutable was that moment she and Luce shared in his tent before their first true battle together. True, it wasn't free of the Queen's artifice, but she was learning there wasn't anything in her life which was free of that. Yet she had gone to him because she wanted to, had spoken her heart, and he had responded in kind. Sealed with a kiss of promise, it was their moment, and what it foretold had been snatched from them.

Bryth felt her lips tingle with the memory of that kiss, and then she raised her gaze to meet the eye of her fellow conspirators. She determined in that moment that she would get Luce back no matter the cost. "Alright then." She took a fortifying breath. "How are we going to do this?"

"Good," Mother Gwiddon remarked, sensing her resolve. "I am glad to see thou hast found thy motivation. Now down to business. Grimple was kind enough to acquire some information with a little of my help, and that will prove key to this plan . . ."

18

AWAKENED

Uzran rose stiffly from his bed, one hand resting on the bandages across his belly. Bright morning light spilled through the window, filling the room with a warm glow as it shone off the red oak of the walls and floor. A steady, cool breeze passed through the open portal and brought with it the sound of birdsong and the spicy scent of pines in summertime. But all this was lost on Uzran, who was struggling to take a few steps.

"Back to this," he grunted, steadying his breathing, which had grown labored from his effort.

"He is awake," came a buttery, deep voice from the ground level of the alpine cabin.

"No thanks to you," Uzran hissed peevishly between clenched tusks.

He took a few more steps along the smooth boards, gripping the exposed rafters for support as he did so, but then he was forced to pause and take more deep breaths. Each time air entered his lungs, he felt his chest expand and the stitches across his back pull taut, threatening to tear. The Ogre wasn't sure which was worse—the actual pain of the stitches tugging on his flayed skin, or the bowel-melting fear that they might pop and spill his insides out his back.

"I'm willin' to bet he is out of bed again." Droth's thumping steps on the stairs heralded his arrival. He poked his grizzled face through the doorway, spoiling the ideal, rustic decor. "Cap'n, you're supposed to ask one of us to help you get about. Can't have you poppin' a stitch again."

Standing in the middle of the small room, naked except for bandages around his shredded belly and back, Uzran gave his lieutenant a baleful look before attempting another step. "Go to Hell, Droth," Uzran snarled as another step rammed a lance of pain through his ribs and down to his groin. "I have to piss."

Droth took the venom with a smile, and scuttled in to put an arm under Uzran's shoulder. "That's not a problem," he said cheerily. "I'd be happy to help you to your chamber pot, Cap'n."

Uzran gave the Troll a sour look, but let go of the rafter with one hand to grip Droth's shoulder. "You going to shake it for me when I'm done?" Uzran growled through the pain of another few steps.

Droth didn't bat an eye as he braced his Captain with gentle care. "If you ask me nice like." He grinned, showing how many of his teeth were chipped and cracked from their recent adventures. "Just because you're low doesn't mean you can't work on your manners."

"*My* manners!" Uzran spat as they finally reached the chamber pot and he relieved his strained bladder. "I will be fodder for a Gremlin corpsemonger the day I need you to advise me on my manners."

"Well that's hardly courteous," Droth began, stopping to take note of the fluid filling the earthen vessel before them.

"Would you look at that Cap'n! I think there's actually more piss than blood in there today. You're on the mend!"

"While encouraging, Naburas believes your observation proves Uzran's point," a rich voice said from the door.

Uzran managed to look over his shoulder despite the tugging at his stitches. The Lamassu sat on the stairs with his head resting on his forepaws at the threshold. He did not come into the room, as there was no place for a creature of his size, especially with an Ogre and a Troll already present.

"Yeah." Uzran finished and began the laborious process of returning to bed. "See, he's known you less than a week, and he's got you figured out."

Naburas gave a soft chuckle that rippled through his shoulders and down to the tufted tail lying on the steps just above the ground floor. With the exception of his wings, the trauma from Naburas's captivity was mostly expunged. Only a few scars and bare patches in his short, glossy coat remained. His black beard and hair were oiled and plaited, the latter held clear of his face by a green ribbon. His wings were another story, with red-stained bandages and not a single feather, but they were no longer just festering stumps behind his shoulders. They had regenerated into jointed extensions of bone. Free of the cursed iron and allowed into the sun, he had sung the spells of his people at dawn and dusk for the last few days. He told his new companions that his wings would soon be restored.

"Well, you just remember how wise Nabby is when he gives you those elixirs to drink today," Droth chided as he helped Uzran settle onto the bed. "And besides, even if I can afford to be rough as scrub, you can't. Yer the S'anlar now, and you gotta start actin' better than a grunt like me."

"I've always acted better than you." Uzran shifted on the bed, but refused to lie down yet. His limbs quivered, and droplets of sweat glistened on his brow, rolling down the contours of his face.

"So they're determined to make me S'anlar, then?" Uzran reached for the water-filled gourd that hung over his bed.

"Yep," Droth said, and a lopsided grin twisted his thin lips. "Kugin himself brought the message. I think the Elders blame him for the kerfuffle, and they'll be takin' it out on him for years to come."

Uzran almost remarked on Kugin, but the effort of uncorking the gourd dug another barb of pain into his guts. He paused, letting it subside into a low, burning ache before taking a drink then leaned heavily on his other arm.

"Even knowing that I'm like this?" he asked bitterly, still shocked at the decision made shortly after he was kept from dying on the floor of that arena.

"I doubt any of them knows how bad you were, really." Droth's smile tilted towards rueful. "We've worked hard to keep it that way. But hey, Nabby says once he gets his wings back, he'll be able to start usin' his magics to heal you. So yer useless for the moment, but by the time we are ready to do anythin', you'll be back on your feet."

"How much longer those feather-dusters got?" Uzran pointed at Naburas's bandaged, skeletal wings with the water gourd before taking another drink.

"Naburas believes it will be a few more days," the Lamassu said with a quick look over his shoulder. "Four at most, and then they will be ready to reflect the healing glory upon your wounds. It will be much longer before they are ready to bear Naburas's body in flight, but that is his concern."

"And the elixirs will help in the meantime?" Uzran's eyes pinched in suspicion. "You're sure?"

"Yes," Naburas chuckled again and rose with a creak of the wooden steps. "Which reminds Naburas to go out and collect herbs before brewing more this afternoon."

"Going out? I'll come." Uzran grunted, and before anyone could stop him, he pushed off the bed and reached for the rafters. Stabs of pain in his abdomen and back ambushed him with sudden ferocity, and he sank onto the bed, falling back to lie on the soft surface. The gourd fell from his hands and poured the last few swallows of water onto the floorboards before Droth picked it up.

"Rest, Cap'n," Droth said softly, putting one clawed hand on the Ogre's shoulder. "Rest is goin' to do you a deal more good than pushin' it to the breakin' point. You heard Nabby. Four days at most, then you are goin' to be walkin' around and stirrin' up more trouble."

Uzran fought back tears of frustration and shame, and rolled his head to look out the open window. Recovery felt as distant as that clear blue sky out there. In the mountains, the sky seemed so open and close that a person could touch it, but when you reached out your hand, it became clear that the celestial was just as immutably far as ever, mountain or no. Uzran sighed and closed his eyes, trying to think of a way to ask them to leave without seeming rude.

It was not that he had never been badly injured—far from it. His service in the Royal Guard was a log of one near-mortal injury after the other, but he had always had access to the magic of Twilit Kingdom's magi to piece him back together. Even after crippling injuries like those he sustained in the Battle of Luchath Valley or the ambush of Gorm Valoise, he had known the magic working in his body would eventually heal all ills.

Now he was not certain. Naburas said the natural magic of his people could heal Uzran, as it did his own body, but when pressed the Lamassu admitted he had never used it on one so injured. What if he could not heal Uzran, or at least not fully? What if Uzran was destined to become the crippled wreck of a once-proud warrior? How could he help his people then?

"Naburas will go now and collect the herbs." The Lamassu seemed to understand Uzran's unspoken need for privacy. "Rest well, Uzran, and fear no darkness of foe or heart."

The stairs gave a few more creaks, but the Lamassu's paws were quiet as he made for the ground floor and the woods around the cabin.

"Droth," Uzran groaned softly, still facing the window, eyes now closed. "You can go about your business."

"What business've I got besides you, Cap'n?" the Troll asked solemnly. But he turned and got up from his seat on the edge of the bed just the same. "'Suppose I could clean up downstairs a bit, and make sure we're squared away on firewood and water."

Droth made it halfway across the room when he turned smartly about, one open hand smacking his forehead. "Well flog me pink, Cap'n, I almost forgot!" He came back, fishing something out from the pocket sewn inside his tunic. "You got yourself a letter of some sort, from Lady Lighttread, I think. Kugin brought it up last night with the news about your election. Said some shifty Goblin brought it. Didn't seem like the bastard tried to open it at least."

Uzran held out his hand, taking the letter without looking at his lieutenant.

"Let me know if you want to send a reply," the Troll said, backing out of the room. "Don't suppose there's anything to write on in here. Kugin doesn't strike me as the scholarly sort, but I can scrounge something up if you need it. Oh, and I'll empty this here pot for you, Cap'n."

"Thank you, Droth." Uzran rested the letter against his chest with one folded arm. With that, the Troll descended the steps, and Uzran heard occasional scuffs of furniture being moved or the clang of a platter, but not much else.

Uzran eyed the folded parchment, and there indeed was the seal of Bryth's family—an open hand with a star set onto it—in a blob of green wax. He expected he knew what it would be—the depressed ravings of the broken-hearted, interspersed with details of military victories. Gorm Bollham, the man who had once been Luce, was on a winning streak. Were the Gythraul defeated yet? Possibly, and Uzran believed if any could accomplish it, the new Gorm could.

In his heart, besides the still embarrassing twinges of jealousy he felt about that tiny human, Uzran now understood that victory over the Gythraul would be a hollow thing. While Queen Meabh still sat in Duanon with her Gloaming Court, they only traded fear of an invader's tyranny for a familiar tyranny. That was why he had come to sound the call to arms, hoping someone would rise up and lead his people to some kind of freedom. Impossibly, hilariously, he had succeeded. Even more absurdly, his awakening people had chosen him to lead them. But instead of preparing his people for the greatest struggle they had faced since the time of heroes, he lay in bed, needing help to go fill a chamberpot.

Uzran took the letter in both hands, the folded square of parchment tiny between his huge, war-scarred fingers. He considered tearing it up or crushing it and tossing it out his window, but then he thought about Droth or Naburas finding it as they went about their business. He thought about the sad, knowing looks they would give him—the pity in their eyes as they looked on an invalid who couldn't even stand to read a letter, so great was his grief and loss.

A sigh rasped into a snarl at the thought, and he popped the wax seal and unfolded the letter. He was determined to read the damn thing in defiance of their imagined sympathy. But what he read was not ramblings punctuated by forlorn tearstains. Yes, Bryth spoke of Gorm Bollham and his victories over the Gythraul, but she was more concerned about how these events affected a conspiracy than her broken heart. Uzran rocked himself—with no few curses and gasps—more fully into the light of the window to read her small, tightly-woven script. When he did, he found himself forgetting his self-loathing and aversion to pity. Bryth was planning an assassination—an uprising, a coup —and if half of what she wrote was true, she might actually pull it off. But not without help.

"Droth!" Uzran roared, ignoring the pain driving into his belly. "Droth, get me some parchment like your life depends on it!"

19

SACRIFICED

I was up before Wrenneth, dressing myself in the dark of the bedchamber, and in the glow of low, burning braziers, I had the mute dead armor me quietly in the entertaining area beyond. This new tent was exponentially larger than the spartan thing I had when I first was on campaign. It had dedicated spaces for different activities, the space within partitioned by sheets of tent cloth. It made things like this easier, and it was also more comfortable. In passing, I wondered why I never sought such comforts before, then I strode out to view the mobilization of my army.

We had moved into Cinderstone a day ago, deploying in a wide arc across the western edge of the central plain surrounding the walled ziggurat that was CInderstone Keep. The army had grown large enough that mobilizing our forces to one location all in one effort was unfeasible and inefficient, so I staged it out over several hours, planning for our heavier and most veteran companies to spearhead the invasion.

Except it hadn't been an invasion—at least not a resisted

invasion. It was more a collection of strategic maneuverings. I expected Lord Arawn might be shocked by the sudden arrival of the Queen's Army at his doorstep, but to make no move or response did not seem like the cool-headed Lord. When the first shots rang out, I thought he was mustering some kind of defense, but reports came back that some squads had stumbled on nests of the verminous Arcghuls and were putting them down.

And still no forces marshalled out of Cinderstone Keep. I eyed the ground suspiciously, remembering Arawn's display of necromantic power, summoning the clawed hands of the dead to wipe out an encroaching mob of Arcghuls the last time I was here. But nothing stirred the drifting expanse of ash besides the wind and the movement of my forces.

I asked Lord Fian and Wrenneth if they could sense any of Lord Arawn's magic at work, perhaps waiting for us to cross a certain threshold or reach a critical mass, but they detected nothing.

So I filled the plain with my forces, spreading them out in a wide, encircling arc with companies staggered to create flexible avenues of movement and killzones. If anything short of a full armored division rode out of those gates, my forces could meet the advance and tear it to pieces. Lord Arawn—if he was in that black stone fortress—was completely trapped.

Like we had nothing but time, I called a halt to the noose-tightening advance of the army, and we made camp for the night. The dead dug out and erected everything needed with remarkable efficiency as Wrenneth and her two sisters muttered incantations over the mist-oozing black caulders.

Cinderstone Keep stood silent and still, not so much as a

sentry stirring atop the sharply crenellated walls. I began to fear that word had reached Lord Arawn somehow—that he had fled into the blasted wilds of his domain. But it didn't change what I had to do: secure the keep and install Wrenneth as Lady, gathering any and all research related to the Gormstone.

I drew plans for the storming of the Keep, broke bread with Lord Fian and Wrenneth, took Wrenneth in my bedchamber, twice, and then slept the sleep of the dead. No dreams distracted me, no nightmares plagued me, and I awakened ready to lead my forces in a glorious, if brief, battle for the Keep.

I emerged from my tent to see the Drakes being fitted with their armor in preparation for a strafing run on the curtain wall that surrounded the central ziggurat. Due to its location in the Kingdom and terrain, Cinderstone had not called on the Queen's Army for aid or protection since the very first Gythraul invasion, so the nature of its forces and defenders was unknown. Even Lord Arawn's three daughters, living secluded in the north wing of the Keep until they were sent off to serve a Paladin or Gorm, pleaded ignorance. They knew their father was always busy on some project or another, but he was cryptic about his work.

I would not cower in fear of some vague phantom, but I also wouldn't waste my forces blundering around. We would sweep in with Drake fire, hammer with banshee shells, and probe with reconnaissance teams before I sent a single company to secure the place. I had the Morgs and some older, heavier artillery from Valoise's tenure, but I would hold off on using those until I knew there was something worthy of that kind of punishment in the Keep. Overwhelming force didn't mean I had to level the place. After all, it would be a lot easier to search for Lughan and Arawn's research if I didn't have to shift tons of rubble.

Lord Fian came to where I stood watching the Drakes, his shifty eyes dancing from the Drakes, to me, and finally to the silent Keep. "Does it not strike you as strange, my Gorm?" Fian licked his lips nervously. "Could it be that Lord Arawn has retreated? Or perhaps, seeing the futility, has surrendered himself to the inevitable?"

"Doesn't matter." I waved the objection away like buzzing insect. "It won't change my battle plan. Is everything ready?"

"Oh, yes," the battle-magus answered as he stared at the Keep. "It is a rather imposing structure isn't it."

"Only for people scared of black, pointy things," I grunted. "I will make a sweep of our disposition personally using the Bogle. Within the hour I want Cinderstone Keep scoured with hell's brush."

"Yes, of course, my Gorm," Fian remarked. "Did you want me to find a Bogle for you first, then?"

"No, of course not." I gave him a bemused frown. "I have Sleepyhead and the hagseye."

"Oh yes." Fian smiled unctuously. "How could I forget the wormy-looking creature with the butterfly wings? My apologies. I will go and make sure things are in motion"

I watched him leave, my mind still gnawing on his strange question.

How could Fian forget about Sleepyhead? I realized it was because the Bogle, who had once loved to ride on my shoulders and hang around like a pet, now spent his every minute hiding from me unless I specifically called for him. At first I hadn't noticed, but when a few of the company commanders asked, I had taken time to summon him with the hagseye.

"Scared of Gorm," he confessed. "Master changed."

I couldn't argue, though by then I couldn't remember exactly how I had changed. Regardless, I impressed on him the need to be available to do my bidding even if he preferred to stay out of sight. The pathetic little thing was shaking, but replied in the affirmative. Since then I had not had much reason to use him, but I occasionally peeked in on him using the hagseye to make sure he was in the general vicinity.

Now I fitted the eye and called to him. "Bogle," I said curtly as my senses swam. They cleared, and I saw ashen ground and the side of a tent getting closer with each little jump of my perspective. The advancing hops stopped, and I heard a small, burbling voice reply.

"Master?"

"I want an aerial perspective of our positions, now," I commanded. Sleepyhead hopped into the air, and I heard the soft hum of six pairs of butterfly wings beating furiously to keep him aloft. But he didn't rise more than a few inches above the ground.

"Hungry, Master," he whined, and I watched an arm extend and point with a raccoon's claw at the tent flap before us.

"Now," I said, firmly but without irritation. Sometimes he needed consistent direction.

"Yes, Master," he moaned and began to climb. "Look for what?"

"I am not sure, but keep your eyes sharp and your ear listening to the other Wee Folk. I can't believe Arawn is just going to roll over. He's got a plan and I want to know what it is."

Cinderstone Keep was open to us. The Drakes and

mortars thoroughly scoured and beat upon the walls and the Keep, but nothing and no one emerged to challenge us. Even when I sent squads into the unbarred halls, nothing stopped us. The place was not only open, it was abandoned. Its legions of dead thralls were absent except for a few corpses found inanimate and moldering in the ziggurat's lower levels. The deepest dungeons hadn't been searched, but Wrenneth told us that it would take some effort as they were guarded with many locks and enchantments. The keys and counterspells most likely lay within Lord Arawn's personal chambers.

Those chambers and the deepest parts of the keep were most likely to hold evidence of the ousted Lord's work on the Gormstone. I was concerned that he might have run away with such prized information and artifacts, but I had hoped our sudden appearance would have kept him from taking everything. Even if he took the bulk of it, there would be some pieces the Queen could use, or some hint as to where he had gone. But first I had to search those areas, and to do that, I had to indulge Wrenneth in her little ceremony.

Lord Arawn's personal chambers claimed the two entire upper tiers of the ziggurat, just above the dining hall where I first met the mysterious Tuatha. Access was gained via an enchanted doorway—a massive, arched double door of black marble veined with seams of garnet. It would only open to the one proclaimed Lord or Lady of Cinderstone Keep, and that happened by a ritual sacrifice and magical incantation before that very door.

So there I stood with a sacrificial blade in my hand, naked from the waist up with eldritch symbols being drawn on my chest in the silvery pink blood of a Hobb. Wrenneth, also bare-chested, finished the last sweep of gory markings and stepped back. She held the wide bowl full of the blood from a member of Echo company who had volunteered to be a sacrifice. Her own sigils—spidery runes meshed together but sharp on the edges—she had traced before sketching mine. They kept their shape despite their less-than-articulate nature, and after a moment, they rang with a mournful sound, resonating with the stones.

Five more soldiers knelt in line next to the body of their companion. They were naked except for the warpaint that every member of Echo company wore, each one staring straight ahead, faces grim and focused.

"They have to be willing," Wrenneth explained before I sent out the call for volunteers. "The magic is very specific. If any of them are compelled, it will not work."

It had been a momentary irritation in truth, because with our victories and the vengeance I had allowed my soldiers to inflict on the Gythraul, there were more than enough volunteers. In the end, I had chosen six from Echo company, knowing that the fanatical credo they embraced would ensure that none of them would have second thoughts.

True to form, the first Hobb, his face patterned in whorls of black and red, looked me straight in my face as I lifted the blade to his throat. "For you, my Gorm," he said in a hushed but earnest voice. "For the Twilit Kingdom." His blood spilled into Wrenneth's bowl and onto the floor where the thirsty, porous stones drank deep.

Once the symbols were sketched on the both of us, the other five soldiers were offered up in similar fashion. Though none of them gave dramatic pronouncements like the first, all met my eyes steadily, conveying that they did this for me, because they trusted when their commander told them their lives would serve the Kingdom. It was better that they didn't know the specifics. Having second thoughts at this point would be frustrating.

The last offering of blood taken, Wrenneth dipped her finger into the cooling mixture and drew it out, muttering an incantation. The stones continued to hum their tuneless song of mounting power, and suddenly the blood dripping from Wrenneth's finger transformed into a thick, viscous cord. With a single gesture she flicked the scarlet rope onto the stone of the floor where it curled into a perfect circle. The dark stones evaporated into a hole full of empty darkness. Wrenneth's incantation increased in speed and volume, each incremental increase accompanied by the flick of another bloody strand to the floor. Each one wrapped around the hole set there, making it wider, until the sixth time, when Wrenneth threw her head back, body arching, and poured out the entire bowl into the gaping abyss.

A subaudible snap, like ears popping, but a thousand times more potent, made my sense of balance shiver. My feet splayed wide, and beneath them the stones shuddered. I looked up as a grinding of stone on stone followed the tremor. The double doors parted few inches. The way was open.

"Finally," I grunted, stepping forward to yank the doors open, but came up short as pale, sharp-nailed fingers crept over the edges from the opposite side.

"Quite," came a soft, dark voice. "I do abhor ceremonies." The door swung open, and there stood Lord Arawn, Master of Cinderstone Keep, his face set in a razor-sharp smile.

20

RUSHED

Uzran didn't realize so many of his people could be battle-ready so quickly. Nearly two hundred warriors had stepped forth from among the clans represented at the Grand Thaig and the surrounding areas. They gathered in the shallow vale beneath Arzgund's Skull.

At any one point in time, the People of the Stone who dwelt on Mount Falchrreg or the stretch of low peaks known as the Linden Spine saw only a third of the native males in residence. With the Grand Thaig in full swing, the numbers had risen to about half for this exceptional event, but most of them were relatively young. Typically, the older the males were . . . the longer they spent abroad, if they returned at all. The vast majority were elsewhere working as laborers, mercenaries, and in other occupations where their size and strength were considered assets. The females, consequently, were often tasked with defending hearth and home from intrusion by the occasional mountain monster and, of course, raiders from rival clans. That translated into an abundance of arms in fairly good condition—either those of the scarred males or the tools of protection of the doughty females.

They were archaic by the standards of the most recent Daerg inventions—fireseed blunderbusses and thornboar cannons along with a wide assortment of hand weapons and polearms—but they were well maintained, and their wielders were well-versed in their use.

"The Sentinel's place is on the mountains," Kugin had told Uzran in the morning as the call to arms echoed across cliffs and vales. "We are sworn to protect our homes and keep order, not go charging into wars in foreign lands."

Uzran knew the Master Sentinel had come to argue and fight with him. In the time since the Trial of the Guiltless, the Elders had acquiesced to every one of Uzran's requests, and later, his commands as S'anlar. But they took out their frustrations at their humiliation on Kugin at every opportunity. It was even whispered that once they tired of punishing the Ogre with impossible tasks, they were going to exile him. It was unfair and only legal in the most technical and tortured sense of the word, but none doubted that the Elders could do it.

Despite the vitriol Kugin nursed in his heart toward Uzran, the newly chosen S'anlar could not find it in himself to return the animosity. "We all do as we must," Uzran said from the litter that bore him on the backs of four stout volunteers. "I only ask that you make all preparations to defend our homes from the eventual reprisals by the Queen and those clans that remain loyal to her."

"And if some among the Sentinels fall among that number?" Kugin asked, a wary threat lurking in his narrowed eyes.

"Then tell them what I already announced in the Cave of Meeting yesterday," Uzran said wearily. "Any soul who cannot stand with us should return to their clan if they will have them. If not, make the journey to Duanon where they will no doubt be welcomed as loyal servants."

"Or taken as spies and tortured for information," Kugin spat sharply.

"Why torture a voice willing to speak?" Uzran shook his head. "No, if they fear such treatment from their 'lawful' Queen, then perhaps they should reconsider their loyalty."

"This is madness," Kugin muttered, almost whining in an uncharacteristically pitiful voice. "You have somehow bewitched everyone to follow you into death and ruin. First you stain our People with your continued existence, and now you lead us to destruction."

To the surprise of everyone present, including himself, Uzran swung his legs over the side of the litter and stood to meet Kugin eye to eye. The Master Sentinel stared with his mouth gaping as Uzran reached out and took him by the straps of his leather breastplate. With staggering force, Uzran pulled Kugin forward, and their heads collided with a dull but thunderous impact. Kugin's vision swam, and his hearing muffled. When his senses cleared, he was looking into Uzran's eyes staring shark-eyed back into his soul.

"You are Master of the Sentinels, and next in line to be head of your clan," Uzran growled deep in his huge chest. "Reach down, take hold of your stones, and decide where you stand before I choose for you. You shame yourself doing otherwise."

Uzran released Kugin with a flick of his wrists that sent him stumbling backward. Uzran did not move, his black eyes staring as the Master Sentinel turned and began to shuffle away.

"I . . . I will see to the defenses," Kugin said over his shoulder, unable to bring himself to look at Uzran. "The

Sentinels will be ready no matter what you bring down on our heads."

"Good," Uzran said stiffly, watching stony-faced as the other Ogre retreated toward the Skull.

Once Kugin was out of sight, Uzran collapsed back onto his litter, rolling to one edge to vomit violently.

"It will not happen," Naburas told Uzran as they sat with Droth looking down on the vale at the campfires burning. Five hundred and twelve. That was the number of warriors who had stepped forward. They were archaically equipped, and their numbers were dwarfed by the gathered might of the Twilit Kingdom's forces, but Uzran hoped that the physicality and stubbornness of his people would be enough to make a difference in the battle to come.

"Even if Naburas were to shed healing glory upon you for another two or three days, you would not be ready for battle," the Lamassu said gravely, his golden eyes reflecting the firelight with strange intensity. "Your wounds are too deep to heal that quickly. Naburas is no Tuatha magus."

"But the one opening the Path for us is," Droth said eagerly, stirring their campfire. "Couldn't he use some of his magic to see you on the mend?"

"The magus is inexperienced," Uzran said morosely as he looked into the fire. "And he will need to keep his strength to open the Path that will bring you to Cinderstone, and then again to bring you back. We can't risk his faltering for my sake." They all sat silently for a long moment.

"So the idea is," Droth began, rehashing the morrow's plan for the third time, "I am goin' to romp over there with this ragtag bunch and try to convince as many of our folk— and whoever else is listenin' in the midst of a damn siege— to join up with us against the Queen. Now smack in the middle of this lunacy, Nabby is going to fly over and pick up Lucius in the hopes that he is no longer under the control of the Gormstone and won't try and kill our new friend."

"Essentially," Uzran grunted, not looking up from the fire. "Though you may hold off on your proselytizing before Naburas can secure Luce. It is more likely to succeed if you have him with you and in a fit state to speak on our behalf. In the meantime, securing some better arms and equipment could go a long way."

"And you're sure your feather dusters are up to snuff?" Droth turned to the Lamassu.

Naburas stretched his snow white wings out behind him, the last bald patches having filled in during the morning as he basked in the dawn's light. "Naburas will take to the skies and rescue your friend tomorrow," he said with absolute surety. "You need not fear."

"You do realize that you'll probably be flyin' into the middle of a serious fight?" Droth pointed out cautiously. "Luce never was much of a behind-the-front sort of commander."

"Naburas is a son of Lost Lamashur, the last scion of House Humbaboth," the Lamassu said simply. "It shall be done." Facing Uzran and Droth in turn, Naburas's eyes gave a wordless challenge to accompany his declaration. The Ogre and Troll met his eyes and then both shrugged.

"Seems confident, at least," Droth said. "And it's not like we've got much in the way of other choices. Last I checked,Trolls can't fly. No matter how fast we flap our arms."

Uzran nodded and lay back on his litter, trying not to wince at every pain and ache. At dusk, Naburas had mended some of the internal injuries he had suffered, while his dextrous claws changed the bandages. During the Trial of the Guiltless, the Lamassu's claws had been working for an entirely different aim, cutting serious gashes in the Ogre's flesh and tearing at vital tissue deep inside his body. It had been a testament to his own tenacious hardiness and Naburas's elixirs that he had lived at all.

He looked at his black-stained hands in the firelight, seeing the places where flecks of metal still glittered in the flesh and along the lines of his bones. "This is just the beginning," he said softly, but both his companions looked at him. "The opening skirmish to a war that will either save or destroy our world. I can't stand with you now, but I will take the field before all is decided." Droth and Naburas sat in mute witness to the quiet, fervent promise.

"Save Lucius, and rally who you can. This is just the beginning."

21

INTERRUPTED

Bryth stalked along the corridor, every nerve trembling as she followed Grimple Guthook and her team through the silent, stone passages.

Bryth had lived in the Royal Palace of Duanon since she was an infant, but she had never paid heed to the network of passageways which honeycombed the massive compound. As a Tuatha moving through the ensorcelled halls, she had always benefited from the magic which quickly and subtly bent space around her to allow her to reach wherever she wished. Intellectually she knew that the numerous servants, functionaries, and guards who were not Tuatha had to make their way along more pedestrian routes, but she had never considered how extensive such passageways were.

There were some passages barely large enough for her to fit through at a crouch and others wide enough for a small wagon to slide down. Some were little more than shortcuts from one set of rooms to the next, while others were extended tunnels, winding and branching like river channels between the walls or under the flagstones of the Palace. Some places bore fresh scuffs from boots and the occasional cast-off item—a crumb of food or dropped bit of laundry—but others had a patina of dust over the floors that suggested centuries of disuse. A good many were lit by candles or small windows where the light streamed in softly, or they had sconces haloed with greasy, black stains where a torch had rested. But just as many were as dark as abandoned mine shafts. Weaving across the sprawling citadel between floors and connecting the various keeps and manorial wings, the passages formed webs within webs that no one creature could ever remember or understand entirely.

And that is why Grimple had obtained a map.

It was nothing like the glorious, illuminated maps Bryth had studied in the grand library they passed under nearly an hour ago. Nor was it like the spartan but neatly detailed military maps that sat in the Gorm's study or the Royal Guard's arming halls, through which they had slunk, hardly daring to breathe, half an hour ago.

The map was actually not one map but several bound together with thick, black thread. The patchwork creation had been composed by various hands and on different materials, but despite its ramshackle appearance, it had not steered them wrong on their winding trek. Bryth saw over Grimple's shoulder that there were notes at different junctures of the map, and these seemed to correspond with instances during which Grimple made them pause and wait in silence.

"Schedules," Bryth mouthed. "Routines and patrols."

They wound their way through these veins of the Palace, one Tuatha battle magus and six Goblins. Thus far their passage was unnoticed, but the sounds of the Palace denizens teased them with the perpetual threat of discovery. Bryth winced as they slid past a narrow door set into the wall of the corridor, a portal so tight she would have had to shuffle sideways to avoid striking the doorposts. She could hear the buzzing speech of a Gremlin occasionally interrupted by the clipped, gruff voice of a Boggun. One of the speakers had only to poke his head into the corridor and see them, and everything would be for naught.

Feeling her heart pounding within her chest, Bryth followed Grimple until they reached a fork that was two twists and thirty yards past the anorexic door. Grimple crouched at the junction, glaring at the map she held. Her handpicked Hardnails spread themselves out along the corridor. They had come armed to the teeth, three of them and Grimple toting M-Cores and bandoliers heavy with drake balls. The other two Goblins sported what Bryth realized were Frost Pops with most of the barrel cut away, and what remained was nearly a foot of vented compensators. Regardless of armament, they swiveled their attention up and down the passageway, pointed noses sniffing softly at the air and blade-like ears twitching at every barely-perceived sound.

"Is there a problem?" Bryth whispered, sliding between the Goblin commandos and sinking down next to Grimple. "Are we lost?"

Grimple let go of one side of the map to press a finger to her lips, and then continued glaring at the map.

The passage to the right was lit by widely spaced candles dripping wax in little islands of light that stretched away for dozens of yards. The left-hand passage was a black cavity— an expanse of dust-caked floor swallowed by a bottomless dark throat. Bryth considered offering to summon some magical light, but dismissed the thought out of hand when she remembered Grimple's grave warning.

"No magic, yer hear me," she had said, one finger held

up towards Bryth's face. "None, not even the gatherin's of a spell to itch yer ass."

Bryth accepted it, trusting that it was to avoid the many wards and sentry enchantments the Queen and her courtiers had constructed about the Palace. When they crept through the absolute dark of a neglected passage and she had to be tethered to one of the Hardnails to avoid wandering down a side tunnel, she had not worked even a minor charm of light or nightsight. Now she settled onto her haunches and waited for Grimple.

Grimple tugged her nose a few times and then crouched low to sniff near the left-hand fork. Tiny plumes of dust curled away as the Goblin's nose swept this way and that like a divining rod. Grimple pulled back, her face scrunched up in consideration, then she laid a single claw into the dust. It sank through hundreds of years of accumulated dirt until it came to stone with a subaudible click.

A slow, crafty smile crept across the underboss's face as she ran her finger through the dust, outlining a rectangular furrow in the grime just wide enough for Bryth to wriggle through. The frame carved in the detritus of ages, Grimple then ran her hand along the seams worked into the floor, then her fingers flexed downward. With a soft click the grime fell back in a miniature avalanche and a hatch in the stone rose, opening into a lightless space beneath.

Grimple nodded in self-congratulation, motioned to Bryth, and pointed toward a positively reptilian Goblin with layers of overlapping scars. The Hardnail still had the tether from earlier coiled to his belt. Bryth fought back a groan as she moved to take the tether and loop it around her wrist. Grimple took point, and they slid into the dark, Bryth positioned behind her warder and in front of a metal-studded Goblin who brought up the rearguard.

The underpassage was incredibly tight, forcing the Goblins to creep along on hands and knees while Bryth wormed her way on her belly. She was thankful she had decided to keep with her tradition of wearing lighter mail instead of the battle magus's traditional warplate. In that, she would have been forced to strip down to her gambeson and leave the collection of magically wrought armor sitting in the dark.

The air seemed cool, if stale, when she first followed the Goblins into the tunnel, but as she dragged and squirmed her body along, the air warmed, and within moments she was panting in the heat. That, combined with the total darkness and soft, shuffling sounds of their party's progress, compounded her discomfort and claustrophobia until she was afraid she might scream. But she held her nerve, even as the passage climbed upward at an increasingly sharp slant. Up and up it curved until she was in a wider space, and with ginger slowness born of sightlessness, she rose first to her knees then to her feet.

It was still pitch black, but she could stand and follow the tether's tugs, which were directing her to move almost vertically. Her outstretched hands came to rest against a rough, rounded span of metal, her fingers closed around it, and the tether tugged upward still. One hand followed the leather cord and felt another hard, pitted cylinder, and another a short space above that. A ladder.

She quickened her pace to avoid having the tether go taut—yanking the Goblin off the ladder or stretching her arm up past the range of usefulness. Fighting not to think about how easily she could misjudge a rung and plummet, Bryth moved hand over hand up the ladder, careful not to let any slack in the tether become tangled during her ascent.

It was hard to judge how high they climbed, but once

they were at least a few dozen feet into the air, Bryth felt a change in the tether's subtle tugs. Her warder's movement levelled off. Two rungs later, she felt strong, spidery fingers gripping her arm. She bit back a cry of surprise and allowed herself to be led off the ladder onto a broad ledge and then into another corridor low enough she would need to go through on hands and knees. When she first crawled into it, she clipped the top of her head on the upper lip of the portal and scuttled in, scowling in irritation. Somewhere ahead of and behind her, two voices gave the softest susurration of laughter. Choosing to ignore them, she crept along and tried not to rub her smarting skull, just to deny the Goblins their fun.

By degrees the darkness lessened, giving way to a soft underlight. Faint hints of blue and green suffused the growing illumination, defining the shapes of the hunched figures of the Goblins in front of her. She saw that the glow was coming from narrow slots—vents in the stone—which ran in parallel lines along the lower corners of the square passage.

She stole a glance down at the vents as she passed and realized with a sickening lurch in her stomach where they were. Suspended nearly thirty feet in the air, they crept along a hidden gallery over Queen Meabh's audience chamber. Below, she caught glimpses of a single figure on his knees before the Queen's white throne, gripped on either side by a Royal Guard. Another stolen glance and she realized the kneeling figure was Lord Nadder, his burnished skin unmistakable.

The chamber had been emptied of the Courtiers that should have been thronging and buzzing at this time of day.

Bryth joined the Goblin ahead of her in a wide, circular chamber at the center of the ceiling, handing her tether to the scarred Goblin. The Queen's voice carried up to her from a wide hole in the floor ". . . you really think that We would not find out about that vermin's corpse?" Meabh's tone was witheringly cold. "Have you spent so much time in the shadows that you really believed anything could be hidden from Our sight?"

Lord Nadder's voice was a pained and tremulous thing, not at all like his usual, brash drawl. "Have mercy, my Queen! I am a victim in this as well as you. I did not know about the Goblin's body—"

"And that is precisely why you bid the Fiendspawn devour it, then?" said the Queen acidly. "This is not court, Lord Nadder, and you will not worm your way out of this."

"My Queen, please," Nadder whined, his voice climbing higher and becoming jagged. "I did not know about it until very recently! The corpse was ripe with corruption by the time I learned of it, and I thoughtlessly sought to dispose of the offensive smell!"

"Silence!" Meabh snapped.

Bryth was drawn from eavesdropping on the drama below when she saw the Goblins sliding together into a tight huddle. Not for the first time since they had set out, the Tuatha felt the unfamiliar and unwelcome sensation of being ill-fitted and clumsy as she tried to wedge herself among the Hardnails.

"One shot," Grimple mouthed more than spoke, the barest trace of air escaping her lungs. "Do or die time." She pointed at the two Goblins armed with Frost Pops and intimated something to them in rapid hand signals that Bryth could not follow, much less understand. She gave instructions to the rest of the Goblins in the same manner. Without a word or sign, they went to work, noiselessly slinking to their positions.

Then Grimple was cheek to cheek with Bryth, her lips hissing softly into the Tuatha's gently tapered ears, "Fiendspawn down there?"

Bryth closed her eyes and let her magical sense stretch out, taking near-painful care to ground out any ripples of nascent magic that might be drawn to her unfurling mind.

At first, all she felt was a muffling spell the Queen placed over the chamber to prevent eavesdropping from without. Other than that enchantment, she sensed nothing as she rolled across the ceiling and then slid down the walls toward the floor. It wasn't until she came to the ground around and behind the throne that she drew her senses back with a hissing breath. She had brushed against the aura of the foul creatures, but even a momentary touch left her feeling soiled and nauseous. She didn't think the Darkling had noticed, and even if it had, the contact was too brief to give it any real sense of what had been alerted to its invisible presence.

"The throne and behind it," she whispered to Grimple. "At least a few, maybe more." She felt Grimple nod.

"Frost Pops will hit guards, rest of us strafe area for Fiendspawn," the underboss explained, whispering. "You get Queen, fast." Grimple retreated toward the opening in the floor, motioning to the two Frost Pop-armed goblins to join her.

Bryth felt faint realizing she was past the point of no return. She would pronounce the incantation that shattered her surrogate mother's connection to magic so that these Goblins could kill her. She would do this, or she would die. There it was, baldly staring her in the face.

A flush of uncertainty washed over her as the Goblins opened fire.

The two Royal Guards, a spiral-horned Fomor and a

towering Sylvankin, twisted into pieces as giant slivers of Jotun bone struck them with incredible force at short range. Ragged flesh pumped blood from within their armored shells, and they flew apart around the terrified Lord Nadder who had no time to scream before he was impaled from multiple directions by spears of bloody ice.

Before the Queen could look upward, the shadow cast by her throne began to seethe and stretch. A black iron sphere dropped by Grimple plummeted into the swallowing darkness, and for half a second, the grenade seemed to simply have vanished impotently. Then the darkness bulged outward in all directions and burst into a torrent of luminous green fire. The shadows and then the Queen upon her throne were swallowed by the rolling flames.

Not satisfied, the Goblins with the M-Cores shouldered past their comrades, dropping more dark spheres before they opened up a hail of hissing quills. The torrent of firepower pouring down with such suddenness and precision was breathtaking, but so was the noise of the rifles unloading bursts of fire in the echoing stone chamber. Grimple screamed at Bryth, her mouth working in exaggerated enunciation, but Bryth couldn't hear or decipher a single word. Ignoring the Goblin, she looked down and searched for the figure of the Queen.

The flames flickered and winked out, and in the clearing smoke, three coiled forms sprawled out around the charred throne. But before that flame-licked throne—on her feet and glaring imperiously upward—stood Queen Meabh.

Bryth frantically marshalled the power of the incantation, a simple vexing curse, made more potent by a new understanding of the Contracts shared by Mother Gwiddon. All it would take was a single syllable, and Meabh's magic would come undone. She knew this to her very soul.

Whether because of a brittleness sensed in the aetherics or some sixth sense, it didn't matter. This would be the final stroke.

But the incantation did not pass her lips before Meabh swiped her hand and spat a curse that made the very air screech with its power.

Bryth's focus snapped as the floor beneath her feet disappeared, and she plummeted downward amid a hail of broken stone.

22

TRAPPED

I judged the distance from where I stood back to my M-Core—about three strides. I never got a chance to take even one.

"Hold that thought, lover," Wrenneth whispered in my ear, tickling my throat with a blade produced from the folds of her blood-stained skirt.

I looked into Wrenneth's eyes, and in place of the customary fearful, downcast gaze, there was a defiant, almost flirtatious stare. The shock of the betrayal vanished in the face of a black rage that drove me forward, one hand coming up and becoming a strangling claw while the other lifted my own sacrificial blade. It was only the feeling of the tip of Wrenneth's dagger digging next to my Adam's apple that caused me to draw back. Wrenneth's blade withdrew. Blood—my blood—glistened along its edge, and I felt burning pain at my throat. That had been close.

"My, this awkward." Lord Arawn had a pensive frown of concern stamped on his features. "Perhaps we should make certain this remains a private conference for all concerned." With a wave of his hand, stony doors ground to life and the room sealed from every direction except that which led into Lord Arawn's private chambers.

The army had been sent to secure the ziggurat and surrounding area while we performed the ritual. Now, even if I cried out, there was no way for anyone to know what was going on. At least not before it was too late. My mind went to the hagseye, still dangling from it leather thong below my throat, but before I could make a move toward it, Wrenneth guessed my thoughts.

"No need to have the Bogle peeking in." She yanked the stone away with a snap. "Now, why don't you put the knife down and listen to Daddy."

"Why don't you go first?" I hissed. Then I saw movement out of the corner of my eyes as magic stirred the air. Lord Arawn finished his spell and the bodies of the sacrificial victims rose smoothly to their feet. Without a sound, heads hanging limply forward on their ruined necks, they formed a tight phalanx before him.

"Let him keep the toy, daughter," Lord Arawn called from behind his wall of corpses. "It will be of no avail to him at this point."

Wrenneth winked at me, and stepped back toward her father. "He is dangerous, father." She averted her eyes to look back over her shoulder. "Are you certain—"

The second her eyes were off me I pounced, my chest blooming with delicious lances of ice in every vein. Moving faster than my conscious mind could appreciate, I slapped her blade aside, sending it clattering to the ground. Her head snapped around in time to meet my eyes as I rammed my knife into her abdomen, the blade angled to slide under her ribs and into the vitals. Her face didn't register anything at first, but I twisted the blade free and drove it home four more times in quick succession. With each one her body quivered, and something like a smile formed on her lips.

Sure she was done, and with my weapon's hilt spilling blood across my white-knuckled fist, I swatted her aside with a vicious backfist. Her body followed her smashed face, lurching hard to the left. I whirled to face Lord Arawn and his animated dead, my red blade upraised.

I didn't know exactly what to expect when I looked at Lord Arawn's face, but certainly not a teary-eyed smile. "That was beautiful." He dabbed at his eyes with the sleeve of his embroidered coat of midnight blue. "Absolutely marvelous."

I stepped forward, crouching a little on light feet and shifting my weight between front and back foot. Five corpses stood in my way, but they were slow and clumsy. If I was quick and clever, I could outmaneuver them and get at their puppetmaster. A knife in his throat would cut their strings, sure enough.

"Don't you understand?" Lord Arawn sniffed, holding out a hand toward me. "This is the first time I have ever seen my handiwork in action. I knew it worked, but look at you. Simply marvelous."

The words cut through my clouds of murderous brainstorming. "Wait, what?" I kept the knife up in front of me as I eyed the line of corpses.

"You, dear boy, you! And that work of art sitting in your breast!" He stepped forward to the back of the nearest corpse. "When we first met you, even with a blade at your throat, you would have been crippled with concern and morality over attacking my daughter. Now, only a few months after receiving the Gormstone, you brutally and efficiently dispatched her without pause. I can see it in your eyes—you don't feel a single shred of remorse."

Lord Arawn drew himself up, nodding approvingly. "Absolutely marvelous. I readied these contingencies in preparation for our dear Queen's betrayal—poor predictable thing that she is— and while not everything is perfectly ready, I appreciate the chance to finally see the Gormstone's power."

Cold crawled through my belly and into my legs. I tensed for a zig-zagging spring at the marvelling Lord, when something moved to the threshold behind Arawn. Its movements were smooth and unhurried, but hinted at a frantic energy being held tightly in check. The dark shape loomed as large as an Ogre, filling the doorway to the Lord's chambers, and six emerald green points winked into view.

Lord Arawn broke free of his reverie and followed my eyes to the doorway. "Oh yes." He made a beckoning wave toward the door. "Come in now, don't be coy."

The stone doors opened completely, pushed by long, claw-tipped legs sheathed in hairy chitin. What emerged was an arachnophobe's nightmare worked out in nine feet of monster. The emerald points were the creature's eyes, strung over its wickedly curved mandibles like a string of festering green sores. Beneath its twitching jaws, a thick, cylindrical body armed with four clawed limbs stretched from its segmented shoulders and brushed against the floor. The whole was supported by two set of legs, thickset on splayed, clawed feet. Falling around its shoulders, fleshy tendrils that were strangely familiar in shape formed a kind of mantle.

"Last time you were in Cinderstone you encountered some Arcghuls," Lord Arawn said nonchalantly, and I realized that what I had assumed were drooping ears on the scavengers composed the mantle on this monstrosity. "Those were mere worker drones, not like this glorious warrior, a prince of their kind. And you were a firsthand witness to the violence the Archguls are capable of when properly motivated."

The warrior Arcghul stood impassively, a few strands of venomous, yellow spittle dripping from its furled fangs. The knife in my hand was as long as one of those hungry spurs, but what really worried me was the half ton of arachnoid they were attached to. Out of the corner of my eye I saw my M-Core, an asset that could be a great equalizer in this fight, but the phalanx of dead was directly between me and the rifle.

"So you raised a psycho ant farm," I spat, buying time. "Do you really think that is going to keep my army from bringing this place down on top of your head?"

Lord Arawn gave me a sardonic smile, the last of his misty-eyed softness sliding away from his flat, red eyes. "I think you misunderstand exactly how deep you've led your army into my web," he said, and a ripple of magic set the hair on the back of my neck on end. "That incantation in which my late daughter led you wasn't simple mummery. It is going to transform my little experiment into the single most potent army in Other-Realm."

I heard the echoes of screams and rifle fire from beyond the stone doors, and felt tremorous vibrations through the flagstones. My army was under attack, ambushed, and I was trapped in here with the dead and a mega-spider.

Subconsciously drawing deep on the chilly power driving through me, I sprang for my rifle. The Gormstone propelled my limbs with preternatural speed, and after two quick steps I actually took to the air, leaping up and over the clumsy reach of an animated Boggun. I came down in a bouncing roll, and an enormous shadow fell over me. I tumbled to the side on pure instinct.

In the space where I had just been, the Arcghul soldier drove a single spiked forelimb into the floor. The stone buckled with a crack, and the arachnoid loomed between me and my carbine. With one of its four legs, it kicked back and sent the weapon skittering toward Lord Arawn and the open doorway. It was as fast as I was, probably stronger, and it had more stabby bits than I did. I was screwed.

"Come now, Lucius." Lord Arawn chided gently. "Don't be boorish. Your part in this drama is over. Surrender, and I can free you from that burden in your chest."

"You want the Gormstone?" I asked, backing away from the arachnoid who made no move to follow me except with its six staring eyes. "Didn't you just say you made it? Make another."

"Do you really think I would go to all this trouble if I could do that?" Lord Arawn sulked. "No, Redfinger and I worked together, and the success was a happy combination of factors and expertise. Without a compatible partner, duplicating that success is just not possible, and finding a partner that is both capable and trustworthy has been tiresome. But I still have plans for the one you possess."

"What happens to me if you take it?" I prowled toward the other side of the room, somewhat disheartened when the Arcghul soldier didn't adjust its position as it watched me. Probably meant the thing was confident it could be on me in one jump.

"Oh, you will die. There is no avoiding that." Lord Arawn gave me a rueful smile.

Outside the chamber I heard banshee shells detonating.

"But I think at this point it is for the best, don't you?" the Lord of Cinderstone asked with irritating sincerity. "At this rate, there will be nothing left of you beyond your martial abilities by year's end, not even those helpful emotions which feed your violent aptitudes. The recipient I have in mind has little in the way of personality to lose, and controlling her will not just give me a general, but an ever-growing army as well. After all, without more direct control the Arcghuls are an inexact tool at best."

I paused as I realized what he was talking about. Worker drones, soldiers. I was willing to bet my left nut he was going to use the Gormstone to control an Arcghul queen. The psycho ant farm jab was more accurate than I thought.

"But this is all time-sensitive and rather taxing," Lord Arawn said without conveying an ounce of effort or strain. "If you won't submit to a quick and painless death, I'm afraid I'll have to resort to more barbaric methods."

The Arcghul soldier took a single step in my direction.

"You know I can't surrender, even if I want to," I growled truthfully in the back of my throat. "I may be dead, but so are you." My grip tightened on the knife in my hand, and a savage laugh tore from my mouth. "You didn't just lock my army out, asshole. You locked yourself in!"

With a wild scream, I feinted toward my M-Core and the Arcghul, but then twisted into a mad rush at Lord Arawn, puncturing the phalanx of dead with a shoulder charge.

The sacrificial blade glinted greedily as I raised it for a disemboweling thrust.

23

PURGED

Bryth and the Goblins' fall was broken by a blast of sorcerous wind that arrested their momentum and pitched them into a roll across the floor. The reflexively-cast spell saved them from a violent landing, buried under hunks of stone, but they sprawled, stunned and breathless. And the Queen was coming.

Descending from her throne with slow, measured steps, Meabh refused to walk around the grotesque ice sculpture that had been two Royal Guards and the kneeling Lord Nadder. With a single-syllable curse, the rimed corpses flew apart in jagged shards, and still she advanced on the staggered bunch of assassins.

Bryth remembered that she was supposed to use a special spell, but the impact of the fall had robbed her of the exact sequence of the Contractual loophole. She wanted to scream in frustration at her mind's sluggishness, but her body struggled to steady her breathing.

"How dare you?" Queen Meabh snarled, a primal sound of outrage enhanced by the magic resonating in her voice.

"You ungrateful vermin! You treacherous, scumborn, little . . ."

The Queen paused in her tirade when her burning blue eyes rested on Bryth's recumbent form on the floor of the audience chamber. "You, Bryth?" she said, her voice almost a sob. "You are part of this conspiracy, too?"

Bryth couldn't reply to the question and that pained stare, even if she could draw enough air into her winded body.

"We see," the Queen said slowly, an ugly, paranoid dawn breaking over her features in a rush of furtive glances. "Lord Nadder, and now you. The entire Gloaming Court has become a nest of traitors. We have been too trusting, too lenient. Well, that stops now!"

One of the Goblins with a Frost Pop rolled away from the lot of them on the floor and snapped off a shot at the Queen as she stalked toward them.

Impossibly, the terrifically propelled munition struck the Queen's shoulder and flew apart in a spray of icy crystals, leaving the fabric of Queen's dress a little tousled. The second shot never came, as the Queen hissed another curse, and the Goblin burst into flames. The Hardnail managed a single, high shriek before the conflagration poured into his mouth and nose.

"Very well then." Meabh didn't spare the flame-wreathed wretch another glance. "We suppose it is high time We purged the Court of its malcontents and schemers. We were patient and understanding before, hoping that as many as could be saved would be there to witness His coming, but it seems those were the hopes of a mother, not a queen."

A queer, almost frightened light came into the Queen's eyes, and though she did not pause in her advance, her steps grew even slower. "Perhaps that is why He tarries." The fury in her eyes dimmed and she seemed to look past Bryth and the Goblins before her. "Does He watch me even now and wonder if I have been made unworthy of Him?"

"Shut up, bitch!" the Goblin with the assortment of piercings snarled, hurling dark balls first from one hand, then the other.

Distracted, the Queen did not see iron orbs until they struck the ground in front of her and detonated in quick succession. Emerald flames engulfed the Queen, shrouding her in a holocaust veil, and heat like the breath of a blast furnace struck Bryth's face.

Bryth found the will to hope that the fiery explosion would stop the Queen, but then the deathless monarch strode out of the blaze. Her eyes burned with their old intensity, more than a match for a crude grenade.

"Bryth!" Grimple gasped from her knees. "Now!"

Bryth stared at her bemusedly, the fog from the fall clearing with agonizing slowness.

"The days of mothering and mercy are over!" Meabh declared as the last of the flames fell away from her pristine form. "We have tried to gently shepherd this world, but that was a mistake."

With a flick of her wrist and one word, the Queen drove the piercings of the Goblin grenadier blasting through the opposite side of his skull. The Goblin collapsed, and bloody piercings flew against the far wall, tinkling softly as they struck the stone.

Bryth drew a trembling breath, tentatively drawing in the threads of magic as the incantation finally took shape in her mind.

A bellow of pain and hate erupted from the scarred Goblin who had been Bryth's guide, and he was on his feet,

M-Core crackling shot after shot into the oncoming sorceress. Some of the quills zipped by like misguided hornets breaking the sound barrier, but many more struck home. The rounds that collided with the Queen imploded into blobs of viscous grey that smoked in the air, but ultimately slid harmlessly from her body and garments to sputter and bubble on the floor.

"We will bend this realm and all its peoples to Our will," Meabh announced. "And We will do so even if it must be done over the broken bodies of those We loved." Queen Meabh leveled an accusing finger at Bryth. "Even if your body is the first, daughter of Our heart."

The scarred Goblin's carbine clicked on empty, and he threw it aside with a string of ranting, incomprehensible curses. Not satisfied, he gave a deranged laugh, tearing the pins from the remaining grenades on his bandolier, and threw himself bodily at the Queen. His wild leap carried him onto her, his arms wrapping about her in an insane parody of a hug.

Meabh didn't resist the suicidal embrace. Her eyes never left Bryth as the drake fire enveloped her and the madly cackling Goblin. The explosion shook the flagstones with its force.

This time, the rush of superheated air actually burnt Bryth's face and eyes, and she was forced to look away. Bryth, through sheer will, kept her grip on the incantation even as she twisted away from the searing wind, eyes watering and skin blistering.

The glow of the flames began to dim and a pounding emanated from the audience chamber doors. It seemed the muffling spell could not keep the noise of that last detonation from those on guard beyond the chamber.

"Come," the Queen called in a triumphant, ecstatic voice. "Come and witness the new order of things."

Bryth blinked back tears as the tall double doors swung inward, and a bulwark of Royal Guards stampede in, weapons drawn. A gaggle of courtiers milled about behind them.

"Behold these fools," Meabh sang out, melodic in her fervour, "these assassins who would dare to raise their hands against your Queen."

With another throat-tearing curse, the two remaining Goblins who knelt next to Grimple pitched forward, vomiting blood in torrents from nose and mouth. Grimple shrieked in rage, yanking a wickedly curved blade from her belt as the Queen strode past her toward Bryth. The enraged underboss leapt over the enervated bodies of the last of her team, but was caught by the throat, midleap, in the strong grip of the monarch. Grimple's blade plunged over and over, but it found no purchase in the Queen, ever glancing left or right.

Muscles in the Queen's forearm corded beneath her tawny skin, and then Grimple was gagging, gasping for air. The curved blade clattered to the floor as the Goblin fought to wriggle her fingers between the crushing grip and her throat.

Bryth felt the magical energies reach their apex, and she struggled to her knees to deliver the sealing syllables.

"See what becomes of those who confuse Our kindness with weakness," Meabh said, and, still holding Grimple aloft, she planted her sandaled foot into Bryth's chest. Bryth was driven to the floor beneath the Queen's heel.

"Let this serve as an example to all of you!" The Queen cried, her voice a shriek. "We are the Twilit Kingdom and the Twilit Kingdom is Us!"

Bryth loosed the incantation's full force toward Queen Meabh, the sound of the final magic tearing from her throat with incredible power, splitting her lips in seven places. A sorcerous blow struck the monarch like a titanic hammer to the chest. Grimple fell from her grasp as Meabh was thrown through the air.

The Queen struck the floor and rolled towards her throne, tumbling in an ungainly tangle of fabric and limbs until she came to rest among the last sticky remains of Lord Nadder and the Royal Guards.

Spitting out blood that filled her mouth, Bryth got to her knees and crawled toward Grimple as the rest of the chamber's occupants stared in mute horror.

Fragments of bone and smears of chilled offal covered Meabh's arms as she struggled upward. Still on hands and knees, she glared across the room, catching Bryth's eye. The Queen's eyes swam with tears, and her entire face was drawn and white as milk. In that frozen second, Bryth and Meabh stared at each other, both understanding what had taken place and both trying to come to come to grips with what it meant.

Queen Meabh was quicker, and with one blood-stained hand, she leveled a condemning finger at Bryth and shrieked, "Kill her! KILL HER NOW!"

24

SMASHED

When Droth led the first ranks of his people's ad-hoc army—already called Uzran's Throng—onto the plains of Cinderstone, they stepped from the rough beauty of alpine slopes onto a hellish waste caught in the grip of total war.

The forces of the Twilit Kingdom spread across the wide plain, its many companies caught between great chasms in the earth, from which poured a living tide of Arcghuls. Small arms blasted away at point blank range while mortar shells shrieked as they flew by at wild, desperate angles. Some of the beast companies, the Morgs and the Sylvanocerous skirmishers, had an easier time of things, the former clearing out swaths of the scavengers, and the latter breaking free to race about the plain. But everywhere else endured a constant, brutal struggle. The spindly forms of the Arcghuls seethed over the dead and wounded. Some fastened themselves, tick-like, on downed soldiers, but most rushed on to claim fresher victims.

By itself that would have been enough, but the companies were beset from within as well. The animated corpses flailed and struck out at the living they once served, forcing soldiers to alternate between felling waves of Arcghuls or putting down the treacherous dead. Overhead, two slightly-built Tuatha in flowing silk gowns engaged in a running battle with three Drakes and a half dozen battle magi. At a glance Droth couldn't tell who had the upper hand.

"What's the word, Droth?" Jalla, a sturdy Fomorian female chosen to act as a field sergeant for Droth, asked. "Do we stake out a position and wait, or move to engage?"

The Troll lieutenant looked across the plain, his claws twitched in irritation.

The bloody drama was more desperate and chaotic than any of them expected, and he was gripped by a sudden upwelling of doubt. He had never commanded so many directly in a battle, and those he had commanded were Royal Guards, seasoned and oathsworn. They knew what they were about, and only needed to be pointed in a direction. If they died, they died doing what they had sworn to do. This was different.

All of Droth's soldiers were veterans of mercenary operations or of defending their homes, but this was violence on an entirely different scale. Looking back, the Troll could see that realization dawning in the eyes of the warriors emerging from the Path behind him. They saw the weapons used, the number of combatants, and they heard the roar of the bloody conflict like a wave crashing over them. Was this what any of them had stepped up for? Droth doubted it.

Yet the Troll didn't see one of them look back to the Path. While the cynic in him thought it was because they were busy trying not to piss themselves, his heart hoped it because of something else. Then their gazes shifted, a few at a time at first, and then in mass, until they were all looking to where he stood.

No, not to where he stood, but to him. They were looking at him.

Droth felt his own nethers clench, and thought he would rather be caught in the midst of one of those roiling cracks than standing before the Throng.

"Droth?" Jalla stepped forward slowly, a hint of concern in her voice. "What is the plan?"

Droth looked at her, noting how the jeweled, bronze disk fixed between the horns on her forehead seemed so out of place on her plain, honest face. The Troll knew his mind was floundering and becoming lost in trivialities, but nonetheless he wondered at the garishness of the eyecap concealing the Fomor's third eye.

"Droth!" Jalla hissed, her face tightening with fear.

"Patience, young one," Naburas said with soft, absolute authority as he padded toward them with the black-armored battle magus in tow. "Your commander shall speak to you when he is ready. He merely considers how best to deploy his forces."

The Lamassu's steady tone and unhurried approach broke the spell of panic that paralyzed Droth, and with much clearing of his throat, he began to issue orders.

"I want a firin' line along the flank over there." The Troll pointed with a claw he was thankful to find wasn't trembling. "Take half our number to do it, and then see Tuulk and Ragund get to me so we can put some blunt arms on that line. Once in position you can put the Arcghuls down, at least the ones that come too close. Go easy on the ammunition."

Jalla nodded and cocked an eyebrow. "What about the royalists?" she asked, and Droth found it frightening how quickly the line had been drawn between those serving the Queen and those not.

"Fire only if fired upon," Droth instructed. "But unless we provoke them, I don't see that happening. They've got enough trouble. I'm hoping they don't even notice us."

Jalla gave a doubtful frown and nod before she spun around, voice booming out. "Alright you flimsy-spined dregs, sort yourselves into your squads already! There's work to be done, and you won't get it done gawking like some Hobb at the Queen's bath!" Shouts and deprecations followed, but with gathering momentum, the Throng took on a semblance of order and mobilized.

"Where is the human?" Naburas looked from the battle-field to the battle magi.

"One moment, please," rasped a voice from inside the tall, enclosed helm, every word sounding pained.

"You sure you've got enough juice to get us back?" Droth cast a concerned look at the Tuatha. "You sound pretty rough."

The magus nodded, though in confirmation of the Troll's assessment or in answer to his question, Droth didn't know.

Just then a dark streak cut toward the three of them. A tiny, feminine shape with flapping bat wings and a crown of red hair came to flutter in place before the Tuatha.

"Spoke-shouted with Bogle, say-whine that human in keep," the Pixie reported. "Found-Spied balcony near where Bogle think-feel human is."

"Show Naburas the way," the Lamassu ordered, a hungry timbre rising in his voice.

"Coming with," the battle-magus said, his hoarse voice hardened with adamance. "Must remove stone quickly."

After a long look between the Troll and Lamassu,

Naburas nodded and crouched down. "Quickly then," Naburas said, beckoning with a toss of his horns.

The Tuatha paused only a second before lighting on the Lamassu's broad back. Tentatively, he slid his fingers through the braided plaits of mane for support, happy to find Naburas showed no discomfort.

"Do not lose your seat," Naburas instructed, his limbs coiling like giant springs beneath him. "If you fall, Naburas may not be quick enough to catch you."

"Follow-find me!" the Pixie chirped, shooting up into the air. The Lamassu leapt upward and beat his broad, snowy wings. The wind from each powerful stroke kicked up clouds from the ashy ground, forcing Droth to raise a hand to spare his eyes.

"Hurry back!" Droth shouted after them. "I don't fancy my chances winning many hearts in this shitstorm!"

Droth jogged to catch up with the last ranks of the Throng deploying across the barren plain. By the time he shouldered his way to the fore, the front line had come to life with the snaps, pops, and booms of sporadic fire.

He worked his way toward where Jalla stood centering the line, shouting to bring the fusillade of varied armaments into cohesion.

"Hold your fire until we can advance together, damn you!" she howled. To her credit, the salvo slackened and eventually ceased.

"Advance?" Droth shouted over the din of the battle sprawling out before them. "I never gave the command to advance!"

Jalla's face clouded with sudden doubt in the face of Droth's outrage, but she leveled her blunderbuss's fluted barrel downwind toward the battle. "That company is about to be overrun," she shouted. "I thought if we saved them, they might be grateful, sir!"

Droth followed her outstretched firearm and saw, indeed, an entire company of foot soldiers hemmed in on all sides by surging waves of Arcghuls. Rising at the their center, a few hulking figures in Royal Guard armor laid into shuffling animates threatening to pounce on the backs of the infantry. Step by bloody step, their position was contracting, imploding by degrees.

"Well, what are we waitin' for then?" Droth roared with a maniacal laugh. "Sound the advance!"

A hard-edged smile split Jalla's face, and she lifted a horn hanging around her neck and blew one long blast, followed by three short blasts. All along the firing line and sweeping out toward the flanking wings came short blasts of confirmation.

With a steady march, the Throng advanced, three firm strides taken between each salvo driven into the bare backs of the Arcghul swarm. Some of the weapons borne by the warriors were not ready to fire every third stride, as fireseeds were packed by ramrods or salamander flake cartridges were fitted into smoking loading breeches, but discipline was maintained. No weapon fired until it joined its brothers and sisters. The steady beat of the marching People of the Stone formed the rhythm to their warsong, every third measure punctuated by a roar of fire.

At the center of the line, Droth marched with his djinn gun thundering to life in time with his warriors, and the worries of command washed away as the old battle glee came over him. Lips peeled back from his teeth in a savage grin, Droth raised his voice in a familiar war song.

"Cut 'em back! Cut 'em back! Cut 'em back!
Snicker-Snack

Lay 'em low! Lay 'em low! Lay 'em low!
Hew-n-Hack
Blood on dirt, so lovely red
Corpses mashin' at our tread
Leaky brain, smashed head
Perfume wasted on the dead!
Cut 'em back! Cut 'em back! Cut 'em back!
Snicker-Snack
Lay 'em low! Lay 'em low! Lay 'em low!
Hew-n-Hack
Notch on me hilt, freshly scratched
Nab one more, guts snatched
Banner o' hides, newly patched
Split some skulls like eggs a'hatched!
Cut 'em back! Cut 'em back! Cut 'em back!
Snicker-Snack
Lay 'em low! Lay 'em low! Lay 'em low!
Hew-n-Hack!"

By the second round of the gory tune, the entire Throng had the gist of it, and they sang lustily as they felled Arcghuls in droves. Here and there a soldier of that arachnoid ilk emerged from the distracted horde and made to plunge into the oncoming People of the Stone, but all fell, scorched and pierced, short of their quarry. Too late the mobs of scavengers turned and saw their coming doom, pressed between the Throng and the beleaguered Twilit soldiers.

Both sides scythed down those smashed between them, and Jalla's horn sounded again. With commendable precision, the Throng split into two pincers to sweep around the flagging company and harry the remaining Arcghuls back down into the chasm from which they came. The yards-wide crack in the earth was clogged with dead, and at last, no more of the mandibled heads peeked hungry eyes over its edge. At least one small corner of the battlefield was cleared.

The infantry company did not open fire on the newcomers, but neither did they cheer or welcome them. The soldiers at the fore eyed the Throng warily while those deeper within the formation put down the last of the animated corpses.

"Where's your captain?" Droth hollered over the mounded corpses between the Throng and the company.

"Dead," a powerful voice boomed, and the ranks parted to reveal a Fomor shouldering a blood-spattered banner with one hand and gory mace in the other. "I am in command at the moment."

"Hurrahn?" Droth called to the banner-bearing Fomor. "Hurrahn is that you?"

"I thank you for saving us, but I have to ask—what's going on, Droth?" Hurrahn eyed the line of Ogres, Trolls, and Fomors with a weary bemusement in his good eye. "This doesn't look like your standard company."

A few of the Throng chuckled at that, but it only served to set the Twilit company's teeth on edge.

"Hurrahn, old friend." Droth measured his words slowly and carefully, realizing that their insurrection could fall apart right here. "So you know how we've been fightin' this war since we barely knew our asses from a hole in the ground?"

"Yes?" Hurrahn's eye ranged up and down the line of ragtag fighters.

"And you've noticed how things've seemed to get worse with each passin' year," Droth said, making it a statement instead of a question. "I mean the schemin', the human wranglin', and all the warrin' is bad enough, but then the

Queen starts rammin' magic stones into humans, consortin' with darklin's, and now look at where we are. You're wagin' war without cause on a recognized Lord of Far-Hold."

Hurrahn rocked back a little at that and then looked out across the plain before turning a hard glare back to Droth.

"It seems, for a loyal vassal, Lord Arawn was certainly well prepared to wage war on his liege."

"Lord Arawn's a slimy bastard," Droth said dismissively, fighting to keep ahead of Hurrahn's insinuations. "But he's not the one who broke faith first. The Queen did. It's always her, and you've seen it gettin' worse and worse as the years pass. This has got to stop."

Hurrahn considered this, looking at the ranks of the Throng, his gaze hardened again. "So you take up arms to fight your sworn liege?" A snarl curled on his lips. "Our own people marching against their brothers and sisters?"

"Last I checked, all we've done is save your ass," Droth growled, fighting to bring his temper under control even though he felt its fire stoked by his fear and insecurities. "These weapons aren't meant for any purpose other than defendin' the folk of Other-Realm, be they of the Stone or otherwise. Can you say the same about what the Queen is askin' you to do with yours?"

Hurrahn frowned within his helmet and looked at the gore-smeared banner in his grip, then at the bodies of his soldiers which lay cooling on the dusty ground. Some had throats, guts, or groins opened by the mandibles of the Arcghuls seeking tender flesh. Others lay twisted with bloated faces the color of a deep bruise, victims of the venom from fangs that could find no tenderness to gnaw. The Arcghuls were still coming, even though looking out to the other companies still engaged, Hurrahn could see the scavengers forming miniature hills with their dead.

"We've been killers since we were younglin's Hurrahn, but that don't mean we've forgotten what life is worth," the Troll said to the Fomor he had served with for over a century. "The Queen's forgotten though, and little by little, she's made the Kingdom forget. She's been a slow poison, but it's to the point you can't close your eyes to the harm she's done—the harm we've let her do."

"By rights, I should kill you where you stand for such words, Lieutenant," the Fomor said, and the title came out as a bitter hiss. "A Royal Guard speaking treason like that."

In a burst of inspired desperation, the Troll threw down his djinn gun and then the axe on his belt as well. Next, off came his helmet and Droth set it brusquely atop his weapons. Finally he took the dagger from his boot and threw it point first into the ground. Hands spread wide, he trudged forward a few steps.

"You really think that is what's right, then go ahead, Hurrahn," Droth shouted, bending his head forward to offer a clear target. "Have your lads put some quills in my skull, or man up and pulp it yourself with that old skull-cracker you haul around. Come on now, I won't even flinch, I promise."

Hurrahn's hand visibly tightened on the grip of his mace until his whole fist shook, but he stood stock still.

"It's what your Queen wants isn't it?" Droth roared, head still bent. "Drown the Kingdom in blood. War until the only thing left standing is her throne on ruins and piles of dead. Assassinate and besiege, sucking will and hope from any who don't beg for their life. Is that what you became a Royal Guard to defend? That maniacal dream of hers?"

Hurrahn's eyes darted rapidly between his soldiers, the Throng, and Droth's bent head.

"Hurry up already!" Droth bellowed again, making some on both sides jump. "We should be helpin' save our brothers and sisters, but instead we're waitin' for you to make another sacrifice to your Queen. If you are goin' to kill me, get it over with!"

Hurrahn's grip on the mace steadied, and with a long, low sigh, he stepped toward Droth.

25

FRACTURED

The sheer audacity of my charge caught Lord Arawn off guard. With his tottering shield of corpses scattered across the ground and his super spider scrambling to check its misdirected pursuit, I was sure that, in that instant, there was nothing he could do to stop the blade coming for him. Perhaps he kept some kind of blade-turning enchantments on all the time, but not knowing that, I gave my best shot at gutting the bastard right there.

Abruptly, something cruelly seized my chest, cleaving through the frosty shield of numbing cold, and I felt a surge of pure agony.

I screamed, finding that my knees had gone watery with my blade only inches from plunging into flesh. Collapsing, I looked up to the ceiling, struggling to breathe through the relentless waves of pain racing through my body. I wanted to keep screaming, but drawing in the air to do so was impossible. I gaped like a fish out of water as pain swallowed me up, dancing along my every nerve with ruthless precision. In that mind-erasing reality of torturous life, I longed for the icy, numbing venom of the Gormstone to take it all away.

Silhouetted in the light of the overhanging chandelier, Lord Arawn peered over me, his eyes shimmering with infernal, crimson light. "Fascinating," he purred, squatting down to examine me more closely, a hand held out as if to feel the heat radiating off a fire.

I knew I should snatch at that hand and use it to drag him onto the point of the blade, but I was consumed with pain—it was all I could do to hold onto the knife. Even that action sent up flares of burning cruelty from every muscle fiber.

"Do you realize what this means?" Lord Arawn's wickedly gleeful smile was a rictus of sharp, white shadows within the silhouette of his face as bright spots burst across my vision.

Talking was beyond my cognitive capacity, but I snarled and spit at him before falling back on my face and chest, seizing in fresh paroxysms of agony.

"The Gormstone has been unmoored," Arawn said, not even noticing my pathetic act of defiance. "Something or someone has severed your connection to Queen Meabh. All that pain is your soul catching up on what it has missed since you became the Gorm. How fascinating that your body translates it into physical pain."

I heard every word, and though I understood them singly, they didn't connect with one another in any meaningful way. Still, the pain subsided a little, but its place filled with something I realized with a dreamlike certainty was even worse. At first it was just flashes—an image or a scent —but with each throb of my heart, they expanded and became fractured scenes from the last few months.

"Ah, here they come," Lord Arawn cooed, his hand still

held over me, his burning eyes hooded. "All those delicious emotions, the grips and barbs of conscience and guilt taking hold from all that you've done in their absence."

I heard him, and this time, free of the worst of the pain, I understood what he said. A sledgehammer of psychic power smashed my senses and I remembered . . . my callousness, my calculated cruelty, my lies, and yes, I remembered my terrible lust for dominance and pleasure. I remembered attempting to rape Bryth, and I remembered all the other terrible things I had done. Though the Gormstone had made them easy, I knew deep in the dregs of my soul that I hadn't fought hard enough to keep myself from doing them. Maybe the magic would have won out, but step by step, inch by inch, I had surrendered, until I welcomed the cold that made horror so easy and commonplace.

Guilt was too small a word, too meager a concept, to explain what I felt in that moment. Every breath was a burden which I felt not only unable but unworthy to bear. In the face of my absolute shame and corruption, I couldn't hide from what I was or what I had done. In that crushing moment, I saw only one thing of worth that I could do—end it all.

"I am sorry," I heard myself say as I brought the sacrificial knife up to claim its last victim.

But the pain robbed me of my strength, and when Lord Arawn's fingers closed around my wrist, I gave only a soft mewl as he shook the blade from my grip.

"Now, now," he chided, kicking the weapon away to clatter across the stones. "Time for that soon enough, but to remove the Stone properly, I need to be exact, so I am afraid you must hold very still."

A hiss of magic passed his lips, and I became a prisoner in my body. I felt and saw everything through tear-blurred eyes, but no matter how my mind ranted and roared at my body to respond, I lay still and stiff as stone.

"That's better," Lord Arawn said softly, and with another whisper of sorcery, he raised a hand shrouded in black fire. "Now this will probably be utter agony, but the good news is it will all be over soon, and with any luck you'll get your wish in the process."

Not even the thinnest of screams escaped my locked jaws as I watched the ebon flames descending on my chest.

Then, from within Arawn's chambers came the sound of glass shattering and metal shrieking in short, tortured protest. The Emperor of all Lions roared.

26

CHASED

Naburas flew at the huge arachnid as he rushed into the room, and his armored rider sprang free, tumbling across the bloody stones.

Kieren Shieldson rolled to his feet and advanced on Lord Arawn, one hand tugging his sword free while the other gathered tendrils of dark mist, and eldritch sounds snapped from the newly-appointed battle magus's lips.

Five corpses moved towards him in a drunken charge, arms stretching outward. Kieren's blade licked out like a tongue of steel, taking the lead corpse's arms off at the elbow. The mists which had condensed into a disk of coiled storm clouds about his hand punched outward. A ripping crackle and a thunderous boom resounded, and the disarmed dead flew backwards, chased by smoking contrails and the smell of ozone. The thunderstruck corpse became a missile, toppling three of its ilk. The one left standing had its legs cut from beneath it before Kieren's blade cleaved its head from its shoulders, and it collapsed.

Lord Arawn rose, his right hand raised and covered in sorcerous sable fire. "How rude," he said, and with a flick of his wrist, sent three darts of burning darkness at the advancing magus.

Two winked out with a static snap on Kieren's stormy shield, but the young Tuatha staggered as the last dart found its way around his defenses, striking his left hip. Kieren felt the impact and heard the grinding click that told him his armor had been penetrated, but no pain issued from the hissing wound, and that filled him with dread, even as he forced himself to move forward. Lucius lay on the floor, unmoving, and though some rational part of Kieren's mind told him that the human was dead, he refused to listen.

Whatever happened to his hip had turned his stride to a lurch, but when the Lord of Cinderstone sent a fresh volley of the black darts hurtling toward him, Kieren's shield doused each one. Its opaque surface was thinning though, and after another salvo—maybe two—he would be taking those curses in the chest and face.

"Get out of my house!" Lord Arawn snarled, lunging forward with his burning hand outstretched toward Kieren's throat.

Ducking the immolated claw, the battle magus delivered a ferocious uppercut to Arawn's chin with the magical shield. Another peal of thunder echoed, and the Lord of Cinderstone flew backward, turning head over heels as he went.

Kieren straightened with a cry of victory, ready to chase his foe, but it turned to a shout of dismay as his left leg buckled. The leg sprawled behind him at an awkward angle as he sank to the ground, keeping his right leg bent beneath him. Sick anticipation in his stomach, Kieren looked down and stifled a moan. His hip and the upper portion of his thigh were a twisted snarl of tortured metal and ruptured flesh, and unwholesomely curdled blood seeped down his thigh and knee.

The battle magus fought to raise himself on his good leg, but hard fingers dug at his armor and hauled him backward. The dead—three battered and blood-smeared corpses—had stumbled and crawled to lay nerveless hands on Kieren. Unsteady already, the Tuatha managed a defiant howl before he was dragged backward, his storm shield vanishing in an electrified pop. The warplate took the brunt of the impact, even as it sparked on the hard stone, but two of the corpses had an arm each, and the third wrapped itself across his waist and good leg.

Kieren stared frantically into the slack faces of a war painted Boggun and Hobb, fighting to free his sword arm. Their gripping, twisting fingers were useless against his armor, but their grip and weight held him to the floor all the same. Over and over Kieren threw himself against their grip, certain that if he drew on magic to remove them, he would endanger his ability to open a Path back to Mount Falchrreg.

Lord Arawn hove into view, his dark hair scorched and falling away in clumps around his blistered face, his pale sharp features now a bloom of inflamed flesh split by jagged bloody fissures. Looming over Kieren, his face split into a sickening smile, the teeth obscenely white against the ruined red mask. "I will savor every scream I wring from you," he promised, stretching out his burning, black hand.

A snarl from the depths of a primordial nightmare filled the chamber, and Naburas descended on Lord Arawn like a golden-shrouded spectre of death. Arawn's face became a visage of utter bewilderment despite its ruined topography, as the Lamassu bore down on him. Restrained by huge paws encompassing each shoulder, the Tuatha seemed a recalcitrant child being laid to bed, then Naburas's head descended and the Lord of Cinderstone gave only a pained squeak before a distinctly wet snap.

The corpses clutching Kieren went limp, and with a sob of relief, he crawled free of their weight.

"Lucius," Kieren grunted, as he struggled to his feet, left leg hanging uselessly. "Lucius?"

Naburas turned from Arawn's corpse and spat something ragged and dripping onto the floor where it landed with a heavy thunk.

"A curse of holding," the Lamassu growled, golden eyes frighteningly bright. "Naburas can smell the hex upon him."

Kieren limped toward the human, tugging a gauntlet off, and sank to lay a hand on his chest. The mortal's chest rose and fell slightly, but the breath was steady. The battle magus's fingers tingled as they felt the spell locked in place over the man, but Kieren was too uncertain of his remaining magical fortitude to spend what strength he had to free Lucius.

"Mount Falchrreg. Now," Kieren gasped as the rush of battle subsided and he became aware of the pain radiating from his hip. He rose unsteadily and looked about the room for something with which to lash the recumbent Lucius to Naburas's back. He would face his own struggle to stay mounted with his injuries.

Kieren claimed the rope suspending the chandelier, and with a hurried sawing from his sword, the chandelier crashed down in a tangle of candles and mangled bronzework. The room darkened as most of the candles were put out by the violence of the fall or tumbled into the ichor oozing from the remains of the Arcghul soldier.

As he gathered the rope, Kieren spotted a twinkling glint amidst the blood and was rewarded with recovering the hagseye from the carnage. Slipping the simple but singular stone inside his cuirass, Kieren went back to coiling the rope and trying not to think about dead weight which seemed to hang from his hip.

Working together, Kieren and Naburas secured Lucius and made for the balcony beyond the former Lord of Cinderstone's chambers.

Hurrahn, with both banner and Wee Folk communicators, was frantically signaling a retreat from the plains around Cinderstone Keep when Droth watched the Arcghul swarm explode into a mad frenzy of violence.

Tearing at each other, tearing at the Twilit Army, tearing at the dead—the scavengers lost what coordination they possessed in their efforts, and more and more of them spilled out of the cracks in the earth.

"What in all the Wyrm-burned hells?" the Troll breathed, his arms automatically motioning the Throng to fall back.

Like an ant-hill desperate to divest itself of all its inhabitants, the Arcghuls no longer came in waves, but in a steady stream. The remaining companies that would not or could not heed Hurrahn's call for retreat should have been buried in seconds, but the insane actions of the frenzied Arcghuls bought them precious time. Some used it to clear great swathes of the wretches as they grappled and mauled each other, while others simply ran.

Standing on a low rise looking over the battlefield, Droth saw the fighting disintegrate into three distinct sectors. The bulk of the Twilit Army closest to their position followed Hurrahn's lead, falling back in relatively good order toward Droth. Ten ragged companies in total made their slow withdrawal from Cinderstone Keep and the Arcghuls. Another seven companies stood closest to the

Keep and they fought on, butchering the Arcghuls in droves. On the far edge of the battlefield, Droth saw four or five companies' worth of soldiers break away and race across the plains. He hoped some would peel back toward his position, but all seemed determined to flee the hellscape around the Keep by the most expedient means possible.

Looking out over the battle, fear griped Droth as he saw the Drakes and thought about Naburas. Now hale and free of the cursed iron, the Lamassu was a deadly warrior, but the Drakes—bastard offshoots that they were—were monsters of a different caliber. Thankfully, the Wyrmbloods harried the flying sorceresses, two of Lord Arawn's treacherous daughters. If they had not, they could have wreaked a terrible toll on the Throng and any companies that he bamboozled with Hurrahn's help.

The Troll knew it would be a delicate situation once they got everyone back to Mount Falchrreg. Most of the companies assumed they were still part of the Twilit Army when they retreated, but that was a problem to be sorted out later. For now, he needed to get everyone to the fallback point and keep them alive until that magus showed up.

"Where are you, damn it?" Droth snarled. He gave a hoot of joy when he spotted Naburas's white wings powering the Lamassu toward him.

It was hard to tell from here, but something seemed tied to the Lamassu's back, and the magus slumped forward, barely keeping his seat. Watching them, Droth raised a cheer, but the sound died in his chest as he spotted two forms in singed silks racing after Naburas. Behind them, cumbersome compared to the darting, magically-propelled sisters came the Drakes, all three dripping flame from their gaping jaws.

With a cry Droth drew the attention of as many infantry

as he could and marshaled them along the hill. "See those two bitches chasin' the white wings? As soon as the white wings fly overhead, I want you to fill the sky with fire. You got that?"

The squad shared uncertain glances, but all gave an affirmative before the Troll could repeat the question. Spreading out smartly, they arrayed themselves across the hills, rifles pointed skyward.

"Now to get Nabby's attention," Droth grunted, hoisting the djinn gun and pointing it straight up.

The skein of storm djinn hide gave sharp pops just audible over the sound of the crackling bolts lancing into the sky. The reverse-action lightning flared over and over again into the grey, puckered belly of the clouds. Droth didn't dare stop until he saw the white-winged form cut a sharp turn from its arcing path toward the fallback location and choose a trajectory that would take them right over the hill. The Troll didn't hide his smile when he saw the pursuing Tuatha adjust their flight paths as well.

"You'll empty a clip into 'em and then get the hell off this hill," Droth roared as he leaned forward in anxious anticipation. Naburas was about to pass over them.

The witching sisters redoubled their efforts, and the lead sorceress closed enough to send out a hissing lance of scarlet lightning. Droth's heart caught in his throat, and he couldn't even scream out a warning before the deadly arc was upon the Lamassu. As it struck, the magus reared back, one hand outstretched. The electrified curse coursed across his armored arm, up his shoulder, then the Tuatha threw back his head in a scream that echoed over the din of the battlefield. Forks of sorcerous lightning launched from his eyes and mouth into the sky.

Naburas flew past, no worse for wear, and the waiting M-

Cores opened up in storm of ripping quills. Exchanging quantity for precision, the entire squad blew their clips for a few seconds of fully automatic fury. A vast number of the shots missed, whistling away harmlessly, but it took only a few striking home to draw the sister's attention. Their enchantments guarded them from the worst of the impacting quills and the hissing venom, but they felt the sting all the same, arresting their pursuit to visit retribution on those foolhardy enough to defy them.

Droth screamed for the squad to run as bolts of lightning and blasts of fire swept the hill. A Hobb and two Gremlin soldiers were reduced to charred, crumbling corpses with the first salvo, and Droth knew, even as he spun around from his sprint to open fire, that a second concentrated attack would wipe the rest out.

But the second never came.

The enraged sisters may have forgotten the order of this game of chase, but the Drakes had not, and they descended on the pair in fire and snapping jaws.

Droth turned and ran again, thankful to see that up ahead, the mists of the Path to Falchrreg were already rising.

Behind him the snarls of Drakes rose over the din of the desperate battle as they fought over the choicest morsels of their shrieking prey.

27

SURVIVED

"Yer should have forgot about me," Grimple spat hoarsely, her voice rougher than usual in spite of Bryth's healing magics repairing the livid bruises around the goblin's neck.

"Don't speak. It will slow the healing," Bryth chided softly.

"Fuck your healing," the underboss shrieked, her voice cracking as a fit of coughing drove her back onto the cloak Bryth had laid out for her.

"Just rest," Bryth instructed, but the Goblin's amber eyes cut daggers at her through their tears.

"Can my lads rest?" she gasped after the coughing subsided. "Can they catch their breath, while yer damned magic stitches their pieces back together?"

Bryth tried to hold Grimple's cutting stare, but couldn't bring herself to do it. She hadn't been this tired since the battle on the steppes that nearly killed her. The amount of magic she expended to get her and Grimple back into the tunnels safely had been recklessly excessive, but as Tuatha launched spells and Royal Guards hurled weapons, it had seemed the only choice. Thankfully the conservative Royal Guards still did not adopt the Daerg firearms when in the Palace, or else she and the Goblin may never have reached the passageways.

From there it had been a mad rush to a room with a window from which they could launch. The confusion and ignorance of the pursuers regarding the passageways of the Palace bought them enough time to fly clear of the city before Rothwrenns and vengeful Tuatha sallied forth in frantic patrols.

Her strength flagging, but knowing they couldn't hide so close to Duanon, Bryth had opened a Path to Mistmire, taking Grimple on her back. Arriving hours later, Bryth collapsed, with not enough strength to set up even the most rudimentary camp. She slept until woken by night's chill, one arm over Grimple's laboring chest. Checking her charge, she had lit a fire and laid out her cloak.

Grimple awoke shortly after Bryth managed to spear two fat frogs and set their skewered hind legs to cook over the fire. When the Goblin could finally speak, she asked what had happened, and Bryth slowly and deliberately explained.

Now Bryth wondered if she should have waited until they were at Mother Gwiddon's to divulge anything.

"So after all of that, Meabh survived." Grimple laid her head back and stared up at the stars peeking between the rolling clouds. "Five of my finest, years of preparation, and all of it amounted to nothin'! Nothin' because you couldn't kill Mommy! Coward!" The last word cut at Bryth and stuck.

In the silence that followed, Bryth wondered if cowardice was the answer. Had she not launched a bolt of searing fire to consume the Queen because she still saw Meabh as a surrogate mother? She couldn't pin down for certain what she felt in that moment, when Meabh had screamed for her death, but she knew what she thought when her eyes strayed to Grimple. The words had cut through the cries of the guards and courtiers and even through the Queen's condemning shrieks.

"We don't do suicide missions." Bryth whispered the thought aloud.

Grimple sat up on her elbows, breath wheezing through her damaged throat. "What?" she panted, her eyes narrowed dangerously.

"That is what Luce said, before the Gormstone," Bryth said, her voice soft but growing stronger with each word. "We don't do suicide missions."

Grimple glared at the Tuatha as she took the skewered frog legs from over the fire.

"I told you that I was in this to save Luce." Bryth knelt down beside the glaring underboss. "I won't save him only to betray what he stood for. In truth, it might have been easier to kill the Queen and then die myself instead of trying to start all over with Luce, but I believe in what he said. We don't do suicide missions because life is the harder choice, but it is always the better choice."

Grimple stared at her and took the stick of seared meat. "Well, it's a life you won't have for long," she said grimly, taking a bite.

The two waited in the dark for Mother Gwiddon's pot to arrive, but it never came, and before long, they fell into exhausted sleep by the campfire. The beasts of Mistmire, warned off by their mistress, stayed well away from the slumbering pair, but after dawn lightened the skies by several shades, a black shape slunk out of the mist.

Long and many-limbed, it was an alien ghost in an

inverted twilight, black on the white of the mist. Soundlessly, it strolled around their senseless forms, bending its head to sniff and twitch a whisker or two. Its perusal completed, it hopped lightly over the embers of the campfire and sauntered over to a tree pitched on its side on the marshy ground. Claws as sharp as sin's whispering tongue dug into the festering bark, and it nimbly scaled its way to a crook of gnarled branches where it settled in, watching the entire scene with regal disinterest.

Bryth stirred and tossed in her sleep, then awoke with a start. Her eyes searched, trying to understand the grey and shadows around her, instinctively looking for the absent bronze pot glinting in the dark. Her roving gaze fell upon the black spectre watching her from the tree.

"Snyrl?" She groggily rubbed sleep from her eyes with one hand.

A soft splash emanated from the misty swamp, and Bryth's head snapped around fast, her neck popping in protest. A figure loomed out of the mists, giant and gaunt in a long, ragged shroud of black. Long limbs moved with precision, and it picked its way toward them.

"Grimple," Bryth hissed, wondering if she had the strength to launch a single spell to drive off this horror from the swamps. The Goblin awoke all at once—one arm propped her up while the other produced her venomous pistol.

A laugh like mud bubbling up from a bog spilled from the looming figure, and the mist parted enough for them to see the black smile spreading beneath a long, hooked nose.

"Oh, hold! Don't shoot a poor mother out for a stroll," Mother Gwiddon chuckled and came to them with her arms tucked against her body, and her immense hands were held with palms open to them in surrender.

"We failed," Grimple said without preamble and slumped back onto the cloak, the pistol resting across her belly.

Quiet as a wraith, Snyrl slid from his perch and crouched next to his mistress. The Goblin's empty hand trembled for a moment then slowly reached out to stroke the sleek black fur. Grimple's eyes were pinched shut, but Bryth saw thin stream of tears flowing along the seams of the Goblin's eyes. The Tuatha decided to look away before her own vision fell victim to a tide she couldn't stem.

"*We* didn't fail. I did." Bryth took a steadying breath. "I had a chance to kill Meabh, and I didn't."

Mother Gwiddon squatted by the fire, and as her upraised hands reached for warmth, the cinders flared to life in shades of blue. "Why did thou not kill her?" the hag asked softly in her brittle voice.

"I had to save Grimple," Bryth said without defensiveness or shame. "We don't do suicide missions."

Gwiddon nodded slowly, watching the fire through her outstretched hands.

"Thy code seems wise," she said, flexing her large, knuckled claws in slow stretches. "Though I think failure is too strong a word to give to thy endeavors. Thy beloved seems much improved for thy efforts."

Bryth was on her feet in an instant and moving eagerly toward the hag. "You've seen Luce?" she pressed, her heart thundering in her chest. "Is he safe? Is he well? Has he said anything?"

Mother Gwiddon smiled again and turned to look at Bryth with a glinting eye. "Yes, yes, uncertain, and no." The hag gave a short, burbling laugh and then winked.

"What?" Bryth said, and then grasped the joke. She supposed her exhaustion and excitement worked against her. "Oh. How are you uncertain if he is well if he is both safe and you have seen him?"

"He swooned once freed from a hex of the late Lord Arawan," Gwiddon replied, scratching at the folds of her tatty raiment. "'Twas just as well for what I was to do next, but once the Gormstone was freed and his wounds knit with magic, he still did not wake."

"Yer removed the Gormstone?" Grimple interjected. "Where is it?"

"Gone," Gwiddon shrugged, settling back to warming her hands over the fire. "Seems thy Queen worked certain rituals over the thing which would devour the artifact should an unfamiliar hand remove it."

"But Luce still does not wake," Bryth said crestfallen, her eyes threatening to surrender to a watery onslaught.

"Give it time, little one," Mother Gwiddon said softly, sparing a hand to pat Bryth gently on the back. "His spirit is strong, and this was a trial the likes of which thou can hardly imagine. I trust he will join us in time, but in that time, ye both have much work to do."

"What is the point?" Grimple growled, her eyes cutting to Bryth, who ignored her glare. "The Queen still lives and will be coming for us with her army."

"Be still, child," Mother Gwiddon said with gentle reproach. She tapped the side of her long nose with one sharp finger. "Mother Gwiddon brings thee more good news."

Both watched the hag intently, and even Snyrl raised his head and stared at Gwiddon with rapt attention. "My little darlin's bring me news that if Meabh's powers are returnin', it's very slowly." She grinned with cruel delight. "So for the moment, she is crippled and is using the Fiendspawn to terrorize the Court out of fear that they will betray her.

Meanwhile her army lost its general and nearly a third defected to a rebellious Ogre at Mount Falchrreg. Those that returned from the slaughter at Cinderstone Keep will need to be divided between stopping the marauding Gythraul already bound for Thistlebough, and putting down this pesky rebellion."

Something like hope gleamed in Bryth's and Grimple's eyes as they shared a glance.

"So fret not, little ones," the hag crooned. "Thy 'failure' may yet bear some delicious fruit."

Mother Gwiddon sat by the fire—her fire—in her hall, and looked at the light reflecting off the stone—her stone.

It seemed so small in her claws—a tiny piece of something much more vast and important than the ambitions of a paranoid Queen or her simpering lover. Yet she supposed that, like all of the living things creeping about this wretched land, even the smallest pieces were needed for the whole to function. How often it galled her when she stood under the eaves of her great, unholy edifice, and her eyes were ever drawn to that bare patch, that inescapable, inexcusable flaw. She would curse her useless creations, curse the interlopers that infested the world—her world—and she would curse herself that she slept even as He crept under her nose.

And yes, she cursed Him.

She cursed Him for the killing of her favorite sons. She cursed Him for the binding of her chosen daughters. She cursed Him for taking away the means to restore herself after her deathless sleep. She cursed Him for the laugh thrown her way as she awoke too late to stop the terrible feedback which blasted Him and the stone—her stone—into a thousand pieces across the realm.

Yes, for that mocking laugh especially, she cursed Him.

It had taken her so very long to find all the pieces, ferreting them out as centuries became millenia, forced to kowtow to His addled ilk even as she plotted the glorious terrors she and her children would work. But even after thousands of years of searching, thousands of years in this atrophied state, she still could not find that single piece which would complete the stone and set things right.

Then the Queen's whore, that Redfinger, had come to court with his trinket, and she saw through his disfiguring artifice. It was the stone—her stone!

Only an effort of will as powerful as she was old managed to keep her from snatching it away along with Redfinger's head, but such an action would have spoiled her plans. Whatever the Queen's whore and his weaselly friend had done would take time and skill to undo, and for all the petty posturing and fretful scheming, Meabh was not to be trifled with. So she waited, orchestrated events, whispered in ears, and watched as one by one the fools danced to a tune whose notes only she could hear.

And now at last it, was hers!

It would still take time and all her skill to restore it, but it would be like the batting of an eye in the scope of her long, long life. And soon, a new order would come to the realm.

Yes. *Her* realm.

ACKNOWLEDGEMENTS

This second book is no less an effort of dedication and perseverance by many people, than the first, and so I gladly acknowledge my heartfelt thanks to those without whom this book would never have gotten off the ground. My editors Elliot and Lisa, your dogged determination to hack and hew at my tangled phrasing is due a congressional medal, but until you are recognized I suppose you will have to settle for my dearest thanks. The inestimable, insuppressible Ms. Knorr, my publisher who's vision for my work and ability, such as they are, is a light in stormy seas and God willing I hope to repay your trust and generosity with more than just thanks one day.

Besides these masterful professionals, I extend my thanks to my family who have loved and tolerated me beyond all mortal endurance. Each of you, from my exuberant nephew who will hopefully not read this book for some time to my gracious father-in-law who plans to never read them, are part of this story because without your laughing and love I could not bear this world, much less find the beauty in it that you show me every day.

Finally, perpetually, my darling bride: thank you for all the thousand, thousand ways you have born up under this dreamer's journey, and may you be blessed with reaping the many fruits of your labor. A mhuirnín Is ceol mo chroí thú.

Aaron D. Schneider

Oct 21, 2018

ABOUT THE AUTHOR

By age six or seven, Aaron was writing stories about a dark, reptilian avenger who brought final, painful justice to the guilty––with unsettling illustrations to boot. His beloved parents realized that budding sociopathy would simply not do, and so introduced him to tales of great and good heroes.

Aaron has now managed to cram no few hair-raising experiences into his life and it is these that drive his captured glimpses of something epic. Pull up a chair, grab a beer, light a pipe, or whatever your pre-literary consumption ritual may be and give them a look. It is been said they are truly monstrous, but as any true hero knows, monsters often guard treasure.

Be the first to learn about new releases, see covers fresh off the designer's desk, talk with Aaron and other fans of his work.

Join Aaron's Newsletter by visiting www.aarondschneider.com or search for his private Facebook group called The War Council.

PUBLISHER'S NOTE

The completion of a novel marks the end of a long-suffering spell of creative angst and birth-pains. It also marks the beginning of a whole host of new activities designed to get the book in front of readers who will love it, a challenging task in today's crowded marketplace and digital ecosystem. At least I don't have to lay awake at night wondering if the book is any good. Aaron, you've done it again. It's time for me to do my part, and I pray for the wisdom and savvy to do your wonderful talent justice.

Dear reader, unless you're an author, you have no idea how much reviews are needed, for many reasons. Positive reviews tell Amazon's complicated algorithm to show the book to more readers, but more than that, they buoy up the artist whose blood, sweat and tears produced this work. They are to the author what a spark is to a fire, or fresh-fallen rain is to a seedling.

I beseech you to leave yours.

I'll catch you at the end of book 3, War-Sworn, which will be out before we kiss 2018 goodbye.

A.L. Knorr
Oct 21, 2018